THE DISAPPEARED

ROGER SCRUTON

BLOOMSBURY READER

LONDON · NEW DELHI · NEW YORK · SYDNEY

This electronic edition published in 2015 by Bloomsbury Reader

Bloomsbury Reader is a division of Bloomsbury Publishing Plc,

50 Bedford Square, London WC1B 3DP

First published in Great Britain in 2015 by Bloomsbury Reader

ISBN: 9781448215218

THE DISAPPEARED

BLOOMSBURY READER

Discover books by Roger Scruton published by
Bloomsbury Reader at
www.bloomsbury.com/RogerScruton

Francesca
Gentle Regrets
Modern Philosophy
Sexual Desire
Xanthippic Dialogues

Share your reviews and comments with us via
info@bloomsburyreader.com.

Contents

Chapter 1

You pause on the landing, and shake your head free of men. The key to the flat is in your pocket, pressed against the thumbed paperback copy of *The Wind in the Willows*. You didn't intend to break your rules on the first night in Whinmoore. You drank that glass of wine out of politeness, and also because Justin Fellowes wanted you to stay and talk. He told you that tomorrow will be a heavy day's work. All the files have to be brought out for examination, and an office has been cleared for you to work on them. He said that he's hoping for an early start, maybe eight o'clock. Still, it was good to linger. Justin is the kind of man you like – soft-spoken, idealistic, handsome in his way, with clear blue eyes and a nice smile, but with a hint of sadness. He must be in his early thirties, and naturally you wonder whether he is married. Not that it is relevant. Since Mick did that unforgiveable thing you are not going to let a man into your life, not without unbreakable guarantees. It has been six months now since Mick left, smashing up the flat while you were working late at the office, and throwing your papers into the downstairs bin, including the file for the Ponthurst case, which was your personal assignment. Someone had poured kitchen waste on top of it, and all the pages were stained with tea. That was Mick's present for your twenty-sixth birthday, the final proof of his transformation from the poetic student who sang beneath your college window to the angry layabout who drove you at last into that disastrous affair with Finn.

It was a decision of the CEO, Justin had said, to hire a flat. It might be necessary to bring confidential papers home, and hotels aren't secure. Besides, the job could last into the summer, depending on what discrepancies you find. The CEO, he said, had asked for you especially. He had looked up Milbank and Co.'s junior partners on the web, and picked out Laura Markham: first in history from Cambridge, ACCA qualifications in three years, and the Law society a year later – all this together with a reputation for taking complete responsibility for every case you deal with. You knew from the way he talked, with just that little edge of excitement in his voice, that it was Justin himself who had looked you up, who had seen the picture on the website and thought how after all he wouldn't mind being shut up in an office for a month if he could be shut up with you. 'All that knowledge and looking so young,' he said; 'not a day over eighteen.' But you weren't going to think about it, or to wonder what he meant by asking 'Will you be OK?' as he dropped you at the door of the block. You smiled and said 'of course', getting out quickly on to the pavement.

You wonder whether Justin has noticed that your briefcase is fatter than when you arrived in this Yorkshire city from the London train. The Ponthurst case is always in your mind: it was your triumph and no doubt the reason for the contract. It taught you that the crucial file might not be in the archive, that it could be lying out somewhere, as though current, as though it had no connection to the time when the discrepancies arose. You don't know whether it was Justin's desk on which you found it; probably not, for it was in an obscure corner of the office, which looked as if no one had worked there for many months. There was no computer, no telephone, no in-tray, only a textbook of accountancy that someone must have left there before moving on, and which you lifted up out of curiosity. Underneath you found a file of correspondence from last summer. Its absence won't be noticed. Justin locked the office for the night, and you will be back there first thing.

You hold the key ready in your hand as you climb the communal stairs. It is good to have a flat of your own, but annoying that it is in this unfriendly modern block, with its uncarpeted stairwell of concrete, and its views from metal-framed windows across car parks and warehouses. The flat is warm and tidy, and the agent made a special point of opening all the cupboards to show you how clean it is and well provided. But there had been something insinuating in his manner, and you were glad when he left, peering back around the door before shutting it. He had greasy hair with dark pouchy eyes under an overhanging brow, and he spoke with an accent. You assumed he was Polish since he called himself Janusz. You shrug off the thought of him. Now, after a meal in town, a run-through of the job, and a pleasant drink with Justin, you don't care so much about the surroundings either. It's just great to have a place of your own.

You open the door into the foyer. It is dark, you reach for the switch beside the door, and nothing happens. Then you remember. That switch governs the stair-light. The foyer is lit from the passageway. It seems a strange arrangement now, obliging you to grope your way in through a pool of darkness. You reach the passageway and find the switch in the wall. A dim light smears an unframed acrylic of rose-petals between two plain white doors: one to the bedroom, and one to the lounge. You choose the bedroom, which is lit through the window by a yellow glow from the car park. You stand for a moment in the doorway, assessing the layout: double bed facing the window; wardrobe against the inside wall; chest of drawers opposite; and to each side of the bed a door: the door where you stand, and the door to the bathroom. There are two bedside tables with reading lights, and a heavy bedcover of some green silky material topped by a pile of cushions. You go back to the passageway, still carrying the briefcase. Opposite you is the door to the kitchen. You have seen tea bags, sugar and UHT milk in the cupboard there, and for a moment you wonder whether to make a cup of tea. But no: long-lasting milk tastes of loneliness. Tomorrow you must do some shopping, make the place a home. Tonight you will look at the file, read a bit of *The Wind in the Willows*, take comfort from Rat, Mole and Toad, and then sleep with the thought of them.

You go to the lounge, open the briefcase, and take out the file. There is an overhead light, a concoction of bare bulbs on flower-stalks, which you switch on from the door and then immediately off again. The glow from the car park guides you to the standard lamp, which you turn on from the foot-switch on the floor. You lay the file on the table beneath the window. The correspondence dates from last July, and concerns a deal with a Russian company, Lesprom, for a consignment of timber. Most of the stuff is pre-contractual, settling the price per cubic metre of seasoned pine-wood and the time and place of delivery. You will have to work out whether the prices and quantities tally with the company accounts. But you notice a curious detail. There is a slip of unheaded paper, inserted between two official letters in comic English from Lesprom. The slip says 'complete off-shore until delivery. MS advise. Reference Squirrel'. There is no signature, only a phone number, beginning with a foreign country code. Justin will know who MS is, and you make a mental note to enquire in the morning.

It is then that you know there is another person in the room.

Chapter 2

When he took the job in St Catherine's Academy, Whin-moore, Stephen Haycraft had assumed that he would be teaching there for a couple of years at most. St Catherine's had started life in the nineteenth century, as an independent Roman Catholic secondary school, accepting boys from the age of eleven and preparing its best scholars for the priesthood. Now it was fully integrated into the State system, took girls as well as boys, and did its best to educate its four hundred pupils to the level required for university entrance. Its pleasant situation on the edge of town, with playing fields overlooking farmland and the distant Yorkshire moors, made it an attractive place to work, and its pupils were largely well adjusted, recruited from a suburb of sturdy Edwardian houses round about.

There was one subversive factor, however, and this was explained to Stephen on his first day by the head of science, a weary man on the verge of retirement called Jim Roberts. Within the catchment area of St Catherine's were two twenty-storey concrete blocks surrounded by warehouses, which belonged to the local Council. Two hundred families had been housed in these blocks, and between them they provided sixty of the

school's pupils. Some of these pupils had honest parents struggling to achieve the best for them. But there would always be
troublemakers from Angel Towers, and it was as well for Stephen
to be aware of this. Jim reinforced the warning by jabbing Stephen in the chest with a long nicotine-stained finger and fixing
him with dark eyes that lurked under bushy brows as though on
the verge of pouncing. Stephen had the impression that Jim's life
had not been an easy one, and that Angel Towers was a major
cause of this.

Stephen was thirty years old and new to teaching. His ambition on leaving Oxford with a second-class degree in English had
been to become the foreign correspondent for a prestigious London paper, preferably the *Guardian*, whose opinions he largely
shared, and in the long run to establish himself as a writer of
informed political commentaries. But five years of fighting for
the tiny bits of disputed territory on the edge of the middle
pages, while watching with dismay as one by one the newspapers
crumbled before the onslaught of the Internet, convinced him
that he must look elsewhere for a trade. He had spent two years
behind the counter of a bank, a year in an advertising agency
drafting slogans for addictive drinks, and a year setting up a wine
import business with a friend who first provided the money, and
then ran off with it, leaving him with a warehouse of Romanian
Cabernet Sauvignon that had never been paid for.

His mother, who directed a headhunting agency, bailed him
out, and it was as a result of this fiasco that Stephen joined Teach
First, with every intention of at last becoming a useful member of
society. There was no reason to remain in London. His last girlfriend had left him for an environmental campaigner in Devon,
and his mother had indicated that she would like to work from
home and could use his room as an office. When St Catherine's

Academy, which was part of the Teach First network, advertised for an assistant English teacher, Stephen travelled to Yorkshire for the interview. His heart sank when he was offered the job, and it went on sinking as he walked around Whinmoore in search of a place to live. But he knew that a sinking heart is a sign of maturity, and that it was up to him to make the most of a life that had so far done nothing much to justify itself.

Accommodation was hard to find in Whinmoore. After a couple of days he took a year's lease on a furnished flat near the school. The four-storey building was home to eight addresses sharing a plate-glass door at street level and a central concrete stairway. Most of the residents were temporary – accountants called in by local manufacturers, supermarket buyers visiting a nearby meat-packaging firm, a husband and wife team of born-again evangelists, once a folk duo with a gig at the local pub. The building had a provisional air, like the commandeered headquarters of a retreating army. The staircase was bare and dirty, lit by rarely used fittings outside the doors to the individual flats. The view from one side was of a car park, bordered by windowless warehouses of corrugated steel and dominated by gantries of safety lighting, which shone through the night with a bleak yellow glare. The other side faced the road, and across from it, behind a few streets of Edwardian terraces, rose the two stark concrete towers of the Angel estate. It was a fitting reminder to Stephen that it was time to grow up. He moved in with his suitcase of books, his laptop, his manuscripts and a few changes of clothes. And he began to teach.

His contract was for a year of probation, after which he could be promoted to become a permanent member of staff. His duties were to prepare pupils throughout the school for the GCSE exam in English, and to cater to the sixth-formers who were studying English at A level, for which the set texts were *Wuthering Heights*, *The Great Gatsby*, and *The Tempest*, three of his favourite books. And his main task was to persuade his pupils that such books have a value of their own, quite distinct from that of any films that might be made from them.

At first he believed he could easily do this. He read aloud to his small sixth-form class, pausing to draw attention to particular words and phrases, emphasizing points of character and plot, drawing comparisons with other works of literature of which they had never heard but towards which he hoped to arouse their curiosity. Sometimes he walked up and down, declaiming whole paragraphs without raising his eyes from the text. He wrote model essays and explained how they were put together: from the premises laid out at the beginning, he explained, you advance to a conclusion declared at the end. He designed a map of English literature, and handed out copies to guide their extra-curricular studies. And for a while he explained away their illiterate, staccato essays and dumfounded looks as the effect of his predecessor's teaching – an effect that he was bound to remedy in time.

During the first term, therefore, Stephen worked hard at his classes, often spending the evenings in preparation, and keeping separate files on all his pupils. He attended to their spoken English, went out of his way to correct 'sort of', 'kind of' and 'like'. He gave extra time to the refugees from Iraq and Afghanistan, whom the Council had housed in the Angel Towers estate, to the indignation of many locals on the waiting list for social housing. He attended the meetings of the Parent-Teachers Association hoping to know their parents, who never turned up. He took charge of the third form football team, and discussed with the assistant head, Mrs Lilian Gormley, the possibility of starting a drama club and maybe putting on a play by Terence Rattigan. Mrs Gormley, a nervous and harassed-looking woman in her forties, greeted the suggestion with alarm, and told him to raise the matter with the Activities Committee, which he never did.

During lunch-breaks he often read the Koran with two Iraqi teenagers, Farid Kassab and his brother Hazim, who had taken him under their wing. The Kassab family were Shi'ites from Basra, who had escaped to Britain following the British capture of that city. Mr Kassab would send little notes via his sons; in them he explained to Stephen that Islam is an open door through which the troubled soul can pass to a state of serenity and freedom. Farid relayed this message too, and his gentleness of manner and elaborate respect touched Stephen's heart. Mr Kassab's notes were written in careful English, always headed with the *fatiha*, so that after a while Stephen learned to recognize the words in their written form – *bismillahi il-raHman il-raHim*, in the name of Allah, the compassionate, the merciful. The notes came with cakes and halwa, and once with the *Mathwani* of Rumi, in an English translation, dedicated to Mr Stephen Haycraft from Abdul Kassab with the greatest respect.

But Stephen could not reconcile the soothing faith of the Kassab children with the closed and often threatening attitude of the Sunnites from Afghanistan, who would be taken out of school illegally for weeks at a time, who entered the classroom behind blank retreating stares, and whose parents were more or less unknowable. After a while he concluded that the two faiths differed from each other as much as Mediterranean Catholicism differed from the forbidding Calvinism of old Scotland.

The opportunity to encounter Islam and to study its sacred text was, however, a source of joy to Stephen, and all would have been well for him, had he been attending St Catherine's in order to learn, rather than to teach. For here was a book that he needed to know, and here were those who could teach him to read it. But there was the constant battle on behalf of those other books – the books that had shaped the soul of Stephen Haycraft, and which he must now defend in their shrinking redoubt against the advancing army of screens, gadgets, computer games and apps.

It was three months before Stephen finally surrendered, acknowledging to himself that in the unequal battle between literature and Facebook his puny efforts amounted to nothing. The important point, he now realised, was not to attempt to plant in their minds the knowledge against which their lives inoculated them, but to show them how to fake it. Standardised essays, summaries of plots, a few apt quotations: it was all that he had the right to expect, and to insist on more was an act of gratuitous cruelty.

There was one pupil, however, who enabled him to believe in the possibility of education, and for her sake he kept a little corner of himself free from cynicism. Sharon Williams was a frail neglected-looking girl, who spoke very little, and sat in the lecture theatre a space apart. The eldest of the Williams family, she lived with her three brothers and their mother on the Angel estate. Jim Roberts had explicitly warned him of the Williams brothers, who regularly disrupted classes in the lower school and who would one day be described by their mother, as they began their first sentence for armed robbery, as 'lovable rogues'. But Sharon was different: shy, attentive, looking up suddenly from her work with a shocked expression as though she had alighted on some truth that moved her. The Williams children shared their surname with their mother, but the boys were stocky, with dark hair and fleshy faces, whereas Sharon was delicate, with blond hair and fine features spoiled only by a slight scar across the corner of her mouth, which became visible on the rare occasions when she smiled. Almost certainly, Stephen thought, she did not share a father with the boys.

It was after Christmas that Sharon became a problem for Stephen. He had spent the holidays at his mother's house in North London, looking up old friends, reading, and making occasional stabs at a down-and-out novel. Returning to the flat in Whinmoore, he observed the sparsely furnished interior, with his few books and possessions serving only to emphasize its unoccupied appearance. He felt a pang of futility and loneliness. The life into which he had fallen was not the life he had planned. On the desk, however, was the essay that Sharon had shyly pressed on him in the last week of the autumn term, saying 'please, sir, I done an essay,' speaking without grammar as they all did, since grammar marked you out as a freak.

He had read it that evening with astonishment. It was a slow, patient account of the love between Catherine and Heathcliff, of the mistake that Catherine made in despising the uncouth man who truly loved her and whom she truly loved. It described the moors, the isolation of the characters, and the absurdity of class distinctions in a place where wind and weather set the tempo and the goal of all events. One phrase in particular struck him: 'Heathcliff,' Sharon wrote, 'was a shrine, in which Catherine had placed the joys of childhood, hoping they would not spoil; one day she would return to them, and it would be too late, for the shrine was her tomb.' How could a child from Angel Towers write a sentence like that, with phrases from books and a semi-colon in the heart of it? In what corner of a council flat, with the TV blaring and flickering, her half-brothers fighting and swearing, and no doubt a mother resentful of her presence, had Sharon gathered those thoughts? And of course it flattered him that she had come with them to Stephen, hoping – no, knowing – that he would be moved. He picked the essay up and read it for the fourth time. Whatever happens, he said to himself, I will rescue this child.

There was no sixth-form English class on the first day of term. He looked out for her in the corridor. He peered into the lecture theatre at lunchtime, since she sometimes hid there. He walked for a while in the garden that had been laid out behind the Gothic heart of the school, where he had once seen her sitting on a bench, but which was now bleak, frozen and deserted. He left school late: there had been trouble with an Afghan father, who had arrived shaking with rage during the morning break, demanding to see his daughter. Eventually the man had made himself understood: his daughter was not to attend lessons in health education – the imam had personally forbidden it, and moreover the imam had explained what it meant. The man had refused to leave until he had his tearful daughter in tow. There had been a solemn confabulation in the staff-room after school, but it ended without agreement. Health education was on the national curriculum, and condoms were a part of it.

A girl was waiting for him in the lane that led to his flat. In the January dusk he could not make out her features, but the tenderness he felt, at the sight of a pale hand on the strap of a satchel, was proof that it was Sharon.

As he came up beside her he spoke her name. 'Fancy it being you.'

He regretted the words. They seemed to suggest he was hoping for someone else and that he was talking down to her, as someone who could be easily discarded.

'Had to see you, sir, din' I?'

She did not look at him, but fitted her pace to his in a way that sent a slight thrill through his body.

'You mean about the essay? I looked for you, to give it back. It's brilliant. I've got it here.'

'Oh, sir. You really like it?'

He had stopped to take the essay from his briefcase. She had turned to face him, with an astonished expression that showed the scar to her mouth.

'I looked for you at school,' he said, 'but I couldn't find you.'

'I wanna there, wan I? Shouldna tell you that though.'

'Here,' he said. 'I've written a few comments at the end. There's some beautiful writing in it. And why weren't you at school?'

She looked at him with wide unblinking eyes. The astonished expression faded, giving way to an anxious tremor of the lips. Quite suddenly she took the essay and pushed it into her satchel, turning away and beginning to walk in the direction of his flat.

'This where you live, innit, sir?'

'Yes.'

'I know cause I watched you. Once I went past an' you was in the winder.'

'So why weren't you at school today, Sharon?'

'Mum stopped me, dinna she? Here.'

She stood, lowered her satchel and reached into it. They were outside the block of flats. It would be natural to invite her in. She straightened and held a sheaf of papers out to him.

'I done another one. Thanks for saying what you said.'

He took the essay and she was gone, running across the road and down an alley between two grey stone Edwardian houses, towards the Angel Towers.

He sat in the scuffed moquette armchair. This was the worst moment of the day, shut in by the flat that refused to welcome him, facing the void of the evening with no companion save the advert-riddled kitsch of 'Smooth Classics' on Classic FM. He resolved to buy a car, drive out in the evenings, maybe stay over-night on the moors. He envisaged an old-fashioned inn beside a millstream, with a stone bridge over the water and a copse of battered, wind-swept pines. He looked down at the essay. And as he read his hands began to tremble.

The Tempest, in Sharon's view, is a play about love and fear. Miranda is as much bound in chains of enchantment as Caliban, and how is she to know that the spells are good?

'Chains of enchantment,' Stephen said aloud.

Sharon described another Miranda, whose island is on the fifteenth floor of a council tenement in Yorkshire. 'Here the spells are not so good. But there is no undoing them. Nor do you know who cast them. Was it the woman, this Sycorax who claims to be your mother? Was it the Caliban who comes and goes on secret missions, or the boys whom he kicks and cuffs for their greater good? You have your corner, however, and there you can conjure brighter and more beautiful visions. You invent for your-self a Ferdinand, some washed up, barely rescued creature who is as lost and as spellbound as you.'

With growing astonishment Stephen followed the thread of Sharon's imagination, followed it into her fear-ridden corner as though he were Prospero, hovering at the window of that high-rise flat to say 'poor worm, thou art infected'. By the end there could be no doubt about it, and she pressed the point home with simple, all too eloquent words:

'So when you walk and work in front of me, piling up words like Ferdinand stacking logs, I want to take the book from your hands, to say "let's sit together somewhere", and to free you from your chains, because I love you.'

He dropped the essay into his lap and let out a long whistle of amazement. It was, he knew, a catastrophe. He should hand in his notice at once, go far from Whinmoore, take up some other profession, forget that Sharon existed or that she could ever be rescued from the malign enchantment of the Angel Towers. But those things would not happen. She had spread the enchantment over him and he was chained by it.

'Christ,' he said aloud, 'maybe she's not reached sixteen. Not just professional misconduct but a crime.'

When, looking at the record, he discovered that Sharon had turned sixteen in October he breathed a sigh of relief, as though he had narrowly avoided the trouble to which he was now careering irreversibly. He put her essay in an envelope, and with it a note inviting her to come to his apartment after school. He sealed the envelope and placed it in his briefcase.

Chapter 3

Y ou know he has come through the door behind you, that he is moving towards you and will soon put his hands on your face. Why can't you turn to look at him? Your body is no longer your own. Nothing like this has happened before: even the time when, as a child, you lost your feet in the river Wye on that summer holiday in Monmouth, and the water closed over your head as though to swallow you forever. At last you find your voice.

'Don't touch me or I'll scream.'

There is someone standing in the car park, looking up at the window of the flat. He is thin, dark, maybe Indian. With sudden resolve you wave to him, raising your arm high above your head, and pushing yourself up from the desk. But your arm is gripped from behind and a cloth is pressed over your mouth and nostrils, filling your lungs with a hospital smell. You struggle, but to no avail. A numbness seizes you, your limbs fold and dissolve, and your eyes grow dim. Soon there is no sensation. You hear a voice saying 'Done. That's it.' Then all is dark.

Chapter 4

Justin Fellowes joined the firm of Copley Solutions PLC immediately after completing a Masters course in environmental
management at a Northern university. He was committed to
'sustainability' as a cause, a policy and a way of life. And his
good fortune in finding a secure place in the most successful
green energy company in Yorkshire convinced him that he was
fully launched on his path through life. His job was to explore the
sites on the edge of the moors where wind turbines could be
installed, to find out who owned the land, and to begin the negotiations that would turn unprofitable acres of poor grazing into
a lucrative source of clean energy. Copley Solutions received a
large subsidy from the government to offset the capital cost of
the turbines, and the profits from the sale of electricity were
divided between Copley and the farmer. It filled Justin with con-
tentment, that he was making profit for his firm, and a share of
it for himself, in ways that helped the planet. For seven years he
had been happy in his job, living a bachelor life, indulging his
taste for Heavy Metal, and playing bass guitar in a Rock band
which had acquired a certain following in the Northern city
where he lived and worked. From time to time he nurtured the

ambition of forming a Heavy Metal group of his own, and playing to the local metallurgists, as he called them, who formed a small but devoted sect.

Then he met Muhibbah Shahin and everything changed. Muhibbah was 20, eleven years his junior, and worked in a boutique in the city centre. She was from a migrant Afghan family, which had come to Britain eight years before from Yemen, to which country they had fled from the conflict in Afghanistan. Unlike her parents she had adopted the British way of life, running away from home aged 19 to avoid the marriage that had been arranged with a distant cousin in Waziristan, and sharing a flat in a run-down part of the city with two university students, both of them girls. After she took up her place behind the counter in Amanda's Fashion Boutique she was spotted by a member of the Afghan community; her father appeared the next day with two accomplices, and seized her. Muhibbah screamed, spat, scratched, gripped, kicked and clung to whatever she could, and soon members of the public – including Justin, who was passing by – intervened. Someone called the police. The three men were arrested, and Justin volunteered to take Muhibbah to her home. She raised her perfect almond eyes in her perfect oval face, swept back her perfect black hair with perfect smooth fingers from her perfect olive features and looked at him. She did not smile. She did not speak. But she gave a condescending nod in his direction, and he received it as a command.

He called each day at the flat that she shared in order to walk with her to work; he came to the boutique at the end of each afternoon ready to take her home. He went with her to the police station to give evidence against her family. The police were reluctant to act. Ever since the MacPherson Report, which issued a general accusation of 'institutional racism' against the British

18

police, they had been confidentially advised to steer clear of all involvement with the immigrant communities. Nevertheless, by dint of persistence, Justin secured a restraining order, a promise of protection and a safe number for Muhibbah to call. He kept watch over her, took her flowers and presents, encouraged her to read and write in English, and tried to pronounce her name in the way she liked, with the full-throated H of the Arabs, though she was not exactly an Arab and her parents often spoke Pashto at home. Muhibbah, she explained, looking at him curiously, comes from Hubb, the verb for love, and he practised the sound again and again until she rewarded him with a smile.

'So what does Muhibba mean?' he asked.

'It means love, or the thing loving, or the thing loved, depending how you take it.'

'And how do *you* take it?'

'I don't,' she said coldly. 'It's other people give you your name. Usually so as to trap you into doing things their way. I do things *my* way.'

Doing things her way marked Muhibbah out as a singular person who belonged to no category that Justin had previously encountered. It was not long before he recognised that she was no ordinary intimidated refugee, but an intelligent, wilful and ambitious girl, who would use whatever opportunities came her way for her own advantage. To win her he must be useful to her, and he studied how it might be done.

At first Muhibbah would not invite him into her retreat. She lived in a long street of terraced Victorian houses with abbreviated front gardens, most of which had been paved over as carports. When he rang the bell for the upstairs flat there would be a drumming of feet on the carpeted staircase before she opened the door with a quick pull on the latch. She did not greet him but began walking immediately, her bust tightly pressed into a turtle-necked jumper, her narrow waist contained by a flimsy skirt over loose Indian trousers. The colours she chose were dark shades of blue and grey and her black hair was drawn back and pulled through a wooden ring at the nape of her neck. It was as though an injunction had been granted against her body, and only the face was allowed.

When they had turned the corner towards the city Muhibbah would engage him in conversation. She had no small talk, and she held her face away from him, as though studying the sky as they walked. Always she spoke correctly and grammatically, without the Yorkshire accent that had been the lingua franca at St Catherine's Academy, where she had gone to school. She was eager to learn new words, and would practice them as soon as she picked them up. She wanted to know about universities and what you learn in them; about his career and how he got into it; about his kind of music and whether it was hard to play; about how you save money and whether it is wise to invest it. She did not say much about herself, although what she said was intriguing. She was an atheist, a free thinker, a modern person. She counted her escape from family, religion and the 'stink of the *mzrab*' as a necessary first step to becoming herself. He asked what the word meant.

'It's Arabic,' she said. 'Means stream of dirty things.'

'Gutter?'

'Maybe. Gutter. That's a good word.'

She laughed suddenly, as she sometimes did at the sound of unfamiliar words. In those moments she seemed to him like a child, delighting in discoveries. But she kept her laughter to herself, and showed no desire to share it with him: she was laughing at him, not with him.

It was a warm evening in October, two months after their first meeting, when she invited him in. There was something she wanted to show him, about which she needed his advice. A strange trepidation seized him as they entered. In the past, invited home by a girl, he would not hesitate to seize the advantage. With Muhibbah this was inconceivable. He must put on a mask of reserve, and forbid his eyes to stray to anything that might be part of her privacy or proof of her sex. She opened the door to the upstairs flat with a key that she took from her trouser pocket, and went in without a word of invitation, as though into a place of work. They were in a large sitting room with a bow-fronted window overlooking the street. Three doors led from it and she pointed to them one after the other.

'That's Millie,' she said, 'and that's Angela. And through there is the kitchen, the bathroom and me.'

He nodded and looked down at his hands, afraid that they might reach out to touch her, without permission from his soul. It was the first time that he pictured himself in those terms, as a creature with a soul. And he wondered at Muhibbah, that she had placed this antique concept in his thoughts.

'Sit down. I'll make some tea and bring you the things I want to show you.'

She went quickly into the kitchen, closing the door behind her. Justin sat in a loose-covered armchair in the window. He tried to fix his eyes on the street, but they strayed over the room, looking for traces of Muhibbah. He saw a television in one corner, and a sofa lined up for watching it. There was a glass-topped coffee table between the two, bearing a thumbed issue of *Rolling Stone*. Above a blocked Victorian fireplace there hung a reproduction of Picasso's *Les Saltimbanques* in a frame of brushed steel. A CD player and a telephone stood on a bookcase beside the kitchen door. There were no books in the bookcase, just a few magazines lying flat and two shelves of CDs.

The space had an institutional air. He assumed that the girls kept to their rooms, and that communal life was minimal. There was no sign that anyone worked in this room: it was neat, clean, transitional. And that was true too of Muhibbah: such was his thought as she came through the door with a folder of papers in one hand and two earthenware mugs in the other. She placed the mugs on the coffee table and came across with the folder.

'Please look at these while I make the tea.'

The folder contained brochures for courses: one in accountancy, another in law, a third in secretarial skills and information technology. They were aimed at adults with a few school certificates, who were hoping to better themselves in whatever way they could. Muhibbah came through the door with a teapot and he raised his eyes to her with a feeling of tenderness. She met his glance for a moment and then looked away.

'It is mint,' she said. '*Na'na*'. I hope you like it.'

'So, Muhibbah. You wanted my advice.'

She poured the tea, and brought one of the mugs to him where he sat. She drank from the other on the sofa. The taste of mint was innocent and clean.

'You see,' she said, 'there's no future for me in the boutique. I need a career, a status; I need to be known, part of things, protected. An accountant, for instance. In a respectable job, like you.'

'And living alone?'

She huddled up, and a shiver went down her spine.

'Yes. Why not? I can look after myself.'

He studied her for a moment, and saw that she was blushing.

'You don't have to look at me like that,' she said. 'I thought you were my friend.'

'That's why I am looking at you,' he said, with sudden boldness. 'More than a friend, if you allow it.'

She flung back her hair and turned her face to him. She looked through him for a full five seconds, before dropping her eyes and saying 'I don't allow it'.

'Then I'm sorry for the suggestion,' he said, falteringly.

'Look, Justin. You've been good to me. Very good. One day I'll repay you. But you have to help me now.'

'I understand,' he said, downcast.

'You see,' she went on, 'I need a qualification and a career, and I need them soon. Tell me which of those courses I should apply for.'

He looked again at the brochures, with their cheerful promise of success. Gowned graduates clutched their rolled certificates, and in the neat interiors of modern buildings smart young people smiled above their desks. He envisaged Muhibbah among them, the target of covetous glances, alone and unprotected. And he felt a stab of jealousy. The feeling was new to Justin, who had moved easily from girlfriend to girlfriend, avoiding commitment, and rarely distressed when things drew to a close. Never before had it seemed imperative to take a woman under his wing, to protect her now and forever. Muhibbah's jewel-like physical perfection would not in itself have given rise to such a feeling. But displayed behind unbreachable defences her beauty spelled his doom.

Muhibbah told him that she had been taken away from St Catherine's Academy aged 16, but had been able to acquire A level maths and English through a correspondence course. She was good with numbers and could write clear English. Because

23

of her childhood in Yemen and her roots in Afghanistan she knew Arabic, which was useful, and a bit of Pashto, which wasn't. And she was willing to work. Eventually they settled on the accountancy course. This promised to put students within reach of the Association of Accountancy Technicians' qualification after three years of part-time study.

'And how will you afford it?' he asked.

'I will work part-time. And maybe you can help me.'

'In what way?'

'Your firm. It sounds really interesting. And perhaps I could work there too.'

The idea had already occurred to him. His standing in the office was high; the CEO, a Dutch entrepreneur who seldom visited, had absolute trust in him, and as a rule Justin's suggestions were approved. Hadn't he recently acquired 50 acres of moorland for the business, and wasn't he working on a scheme for energy-saving houses, built from wooden sheeting, which promised to bring in profits long after the wind farms had given way to the next innovation? Surely he could make the case for an assistant, a student in accounting who would cover that side of his deals. He promised to look into it, and she smiled.

'Meanwhile,' he added, 'we must fill out some forms.'

'I can do that,' she said. 'But you must give me a reference.'

And in the box that asked for a reference she wrote down 'Justin Fellowes, Copley Solutions PLC', followed by the address of the firm.

'You see,' she said, 'I looked you up. I even walked past your office, to check it out.'

And she laughed her clear, crisp self-centred laugh.

Next morning Justin sent an e-mail to the CEO, asking permission to hire a part-time assistant. Permission was granted, and within a few weeks Muhibbah had enrolled for her accountancy course. Jobs in that city were hard enough to find, and Copley Solutions PLC received nine applicants, all of them better qualified than Muhibbah, including one who had already passed the first set of accountancy exams. Still, Justin finessed the interviews, wrote painstaking memoranda about each candidate with a view to explaining why he or she was too old, too experienced, too advanced in the profession to provide the kind of undemanding and flexible assistant he was looking for, and finally, after two days of carefully faked indecision, in which he communicated to everyone in the office his doubts whether Muhibbah Shahin should get the job, or whether Julian Hepworth, the only other candidate with just two A levels and no accountancy experience, would be a safer bet, he wrote a formal letter of acceptance to Muhibbah. He greeted with relief the e-mail that came next day from Julian Hepworth, withdrawing from the race. And he spent a pleased half hour in Muhibbah's flat, dictating from his place in the window, the formal letter of acceptance that he could open with a show of impatience in a day or two's time and pass to his secretary to answer.

Muhibbah came in for three days a week, and she accompanied him on his trips to the moors. He showed her the contracts with suppliers and contractors, and saw that she understood them at once. It became obvious to his colleagues that the decision to employ her had been the right one. And for six months he had the joy of working beside her, knowing that she needed him, believing that she had incorporated him into her plans, though without knowing where those plans were taking him.

He no longer escorted her in the mornings. If they worked late and were alone together, then they would walk back to her place, and often he was invited in for a cup of mint tea. He gave her a mobile telephone and explained how to use it, and she laughed at him for assuming that she did not already know.

'For us immigrants it is the *iftaH ya samsam* – it opens all the doors.'

'So you have one already?'

'I couldn't afford the subscription, and anyway, when it rang it was them. So after a while I threw it away.'

But she took the phone and thanked him, and promised she would not chatter on it uselessly. Besides, to whom could she chatter?

Some evenings she left early, having made plain to him that he should not accompany her. One day in the spring, walking alone from work to his flat in the city centre, he caught sight of her in an alleyway between two office blocks. She was with a man, whose dark hair and olive complexion matched her own. He was young, talking to her volubly and quietly. His features were small, regular and severe, and he tilted his head towards her as he spoke, raising his hand as though to adjust a necktie, though his neck was bare. The expression on her face was one of alarm. And something about the raised hand and tilted head of her companion filled Justin with apprehension. Thinking that Muhibbah might catch sight of him he entered a pub. He knew then, as he sat at an empty table with a glass of whisky in a trembling hand, that he loved her and that nothing would be right for him if she didn't return his love.

Until that moment Justin had been pleased with his routine. Entering his flat in a modern block in the city centre his eyes would sweep the room with a pleased recognition of his independence. He saw his college books neatly stacked in a bookcase, supplemented by the cult novels and modern poetry that friends recommended. He saw the computer at which he sat in his spare moments, sending and receiving e-mails, downloading videos, and driving away all thought of loneliness. He saw the bass guitar and amplifier, and the acoustic guitar on which he practised, reminding him of the clubs where he had met in the past with his fellow metallurgists. They reminded him too of the girls these instruments had hooked, and especially of the flaxen-haired Caitlin, who had shared his passion for ecology and who would have married him had he agreed to move with her to the country and take up organic farming.

Everything in the flat, from the white lambs-wool carpet on the floor to the flush metal lights in the ceiling, from the framed prints of birds by Fuertes on one wall to the stills from *Blade Runner* on the other, had symbolised the self-completeness of his bachelor life. And when, after two more whiskies and a troubled walk around the city centre, he once again climbed the three stories and turned the key in the lock, he saw at once that it would never be the same, that loneliness had crept in behind his back and taken up residence, exactly there, in the place from which he had excluded it.

After this moment everything changed. He found more and more work for Muhibbah, in order to keep her beside him in the office after the others had left. He several times invited her to dine with him in a restaurant. But when she at last accepted Muhibbah sat in silence opposite him, hardly eating and leaving the glass of wine that he poured for her untouched. An avant-garde theatre company from London brought *The Tempest* to the new City Theatre, and she agreed to accompany him to a performance. But half way through she started in her seat and whispered that she must leave. They crept to the aisle like guilty lovers, and in the foyer she told him only that there was a girl there, a neighbour from Angel Towers, and she didn't want this girl to see her, least of all to see her with a man.

Eventually it became clear to him that he could have no part of Muhibbah, save what he contrived for her at work. He put her in charge of his project for carbon-neutral houses: she was to find a suitable site, obtain outline permission from the planners, negotiate for supplies of timber and building materials, and assist the architect, a friend of Justin's from university days, to draw up believable plans. It was a huge project and Muhibbah addressed it with sharp intelligence, composing letters in crisp grammatical English, and laughing when he read them back to her.

At lunchtime she did not leave for the downstairs sandwich bar, as was the custom at Copley Solutions. Instead she hid away in the room next to Justin's office, kept for the reception of visitors and containing a table, two armchairs and a couch. Justin stayed at his desk, playing CDs of R.E.M. and AC/DC, which he thought to be appropriate office fodder, neither seriously demanding nor entirely banal. His aim was to drown the intimate small sounds of Muhibbah's privacy, and also to make it known that he was there, protecting her. For he was touched that she felt safe in his territory and always, when she returned, she gave him a grateful smile.

After the lunch break she would engage him in conversation about the books she was reading and about the meaning of difficult words. She was like an inquisitive child, except for her habit of pursuing each topic to the very edge of his desire for her. Reaching that point, when words of love gathered behind his lips in readiness to rush at her, she would veer away like an antelope at the scent of a leopard. There would be a moment of silence, and then they would both go back to their work.

28

Once she did not reappear as usual on the dot of two. After knocking quietly he entered the room to find her asleep on the couch, her head fallen into one of the corners, her legs bent at the knee. One hand trailed on the floor, beside the paperback edition of Yeats that he had given her two weeks before. Her face, whose waking eyes were always on guard against unwanted looks, lay before him undefended. Her dark lashes sat quiet under pale eyelids, her sand-coloured lips touched each other softly the length of her mouth, and her delicate nose breathed above them, rhythmical like a sleeping animal. His eyes roamed across her face, brushing every part of it until he could see his love reflected in her features.

A strange feeling came over him. It was as though he stood outside the present moment, powerless to alter it but summoned to absorb its truth. He recalled the sensation that occurs when the train in which you are travelling stops for no reason at an unvisited spot: you see grass gently stirring in a breeze beyond the window, and hear the faint rustles that come to you by no design and which will continue unheard when the train moves on. He had arrived at such a pause in his journey, his thoughts and sensations magnetised by the untouchable life before him. To wake her would be to lose her. Yet in her remoteness, asleep in her being like an unopened flower, she was more fully his than in any of her waking moments. No echo from Justin's world of easy-going attachments had reached the heart within that sleeping form. But no other man had looked on Muhibbah as he now looked on her, with a desire that was not accepted yet also not refused. She was waiting behind her beauty for the spark that would set her alight and that spark would come from Justin, he was sure of it.

He withdrew, gently closing the door. And for a long moment he sat at his desk, overcome with astonishment and awe – astonishment at himself, for being so lost in her, and awe at her, for refusing to be lost in anyone. When she entered a short while later Muhibbah looked at him curiously, as though she had sensed his vigil above her sleeping form and wondered whether to allow it. Then she smiled, sat at her desk, and asked him to explain the meaning of *Easter 1914*. Who were the people mentioned at the end, what are harriers, how do you ride to them and why was a terrible beauty born at Easter 1914? And no, you *don't* have to explain what Easter is, it is *'eid al-fasH*.

While she was with him in the office, working on shared tasks, and especially when they were alone there and conversing in that way about the many things she wished to know, he could almost believe that she might love him. But in other contexts she was cold, enigmatic, and sometimes – looking across to where she worked with pert concentration in the corner assigned to her – he felt a stab of fear: fear for her, fear for himself, fear for a situation that had deprived him of his independence for no clear reward.

And then there was the young man. Once or twice Justin caught sight of him, lingering at the end of the working day in the street below the offices of Copley Solutions. Almost certainly he was one of her relatives: a brother perhaps, or a cousin, appointed to keep watch on her. His close-cropped black hair, narrow eyes and unsmiling mouth gave him a look of soldierly determination, as though he were under orders. He did not linger in the street, nor did there seem to be any communication between him and Muhibbah. But often she arrived for work in a state of tension, her features clamped together as though in an effort to withdraw from some insult, her lips tight, straight and unsmiling like those of the young man, who must surely have accosted her.

It was at the end of a hot, dusty day in July, when they were alone together in the office, that matters came to a head. Muhibbah was putting files away in the box-room that served as their archive, and Justin was tinkering with the design for one of the carbon-neutral houses. He had seen the young man pass in the street an hour before, at five-thirty, when the staff normally left. The sound of traffic in the warm afternoon amplified the small quiet movements of the office. From time to time Justin glanced at Muhibbah. Her hands moved among files and papers with small quick movements, leaping from one poised stillness to another as lizards do. Light from the afternoon sun entered by one of the windows, casting the shadow of a disused brick kiln across Justin's desk and playing on the smooth, closed lines of Muhibbah's face. He wondered what she was thinking, wondered whether she thought at all when she was not taunting him with questions. For Muhibbah moved through the world with a kind of unhesitating need to make a path for herself. She seemed propelled by an instinct that dispensed with motives, avoided intimacy, and proceeded to its goal with a feline awareness of threats, and a virginal quickness in escaping them.

He reflected on his years since graduation, and on the habit, so effortlessly acquired, of avoiding commitment to the women he had briefly loved. And never, he said to himself ruefully, had there been anything like this. He looked through the window for a while, at the old kiln, and the little Victorian alleys that hemmed it in, with their brick walls along tiny shadow-filled gardens. The lace curtains in the white sash windows were motionless as sleeping eyelids; the slate roofs shimmered in the heat. The scene was haunting, enigmatic, like a remembered dream.

He got up and left the office for the bathroom. For a long moment he stared at his face in the mirror. Lines were forming around his eyes and mouth. The brown hair was receding from his forehead, and his blue eyes were losing some of the brightness that Caitlin had remarked on. He wondered where she was now, and what life would have been, had they married. He wondered too whether he would have found the words and the gestures to win the heart of Muhibbah, if he had not wasted so much love.

Re-entering the office he knew at once that something was wrong. Muhibbah's chair had swung round away from her desk, though that in itself was not unusual. She always sprang to her feet, and sometimes watched with a secret smile as the chair spun round in search of her. The pencils on the drawings had been scattered, but then she never gathered them up until the end of the day, and always one by one with a gentle reach of her fingers that he recalled with a pang of helpless desire. Her thin grey sleeveless coat of cotton was still hanging on the back of the door, and the accountancy textbook she had been reading was where she had left it on the edge of her desk. But something was wrong, and as he called out her name he felt a sinking in his stomach. Even as he took in the fact that she did not answer he noticed that the computer had vanished from her desk. He called out again. Silence.

Then he noticed that papers had been swept from one of the tables into a corner. There were scuff marks on the floor and an old filing cabinet had left its position and been pushed up against the wall. He started forward.

'Muhibbah!' he cried.

On the floor were two hairpins and a torn piece of the ribbon that she had tied in her hair that day.

Chapter 5

You are surfacing now. The dark swirls are clearing. Points of light glimmer in the blue-grey vapour. There is a distant rumbling noise, and the world is shaking round about. You remember voices, a hot hand on your face, shouts in the distance. Your head hurts, and thirst burns in your throat. Images advance quickly like warrior hordes, throwing up dust clouds in their wake: a bus in flames, your mother screaming when you fell from the tree, your father unconscious at his desk, a spilled glass of whisky saturating his papers. You are fighting these images, refusing them permission to take root. Your eyes are glued shut; if you could open them the images would flee like ghosts before the dawn. But each effort of the eyelids makes the headache worse. For a moment you struggle, and then you sink back.

Now you are fully awake. You are lying on a bed that rocks beneath you. Above, maybe six feet away, is a white ceiling. There is a white wall to the right, and a white wall to the left, separated from your bed by a space of a few feet. You are in a box and the whole box is rocking and trembling. You need air, water. You need out. You open your mouth, but no sound comes. You swing to the edge of the bed. In the wall facing you is a door, and you rush at it, turning the handle. It flies back and you stumble into darkness, barking your shin on something hard. There is a sink and a toilet, and you make use of them both, throwing water on your face and drinking in gulps. The water tastes of rust and chlorine.

Memories assemble like children called out of hiding. A man, with Asian looks, standing in the car park under the window. He turns as you wave. The cloth pressed across your face. Justin Fellowes asking if you'll be OK as you jump from the car. You are panicking now. The room is shaking, and there is a distant rumbling, as of an engine. You are suffocating in a box that rocks and trembles. Suddenly it is clear: you are in a ship. You are being taken away from everything you know, locked in an airless cabin from which you will emerge into places where your past, your present, your achievements and identity will have no meaning, the bartered slave of people for whom you are nothing but female meat.

You search the walls for a place of escape. There is a small round porthole at one end of the berth and a door in the wall beside the other. The door is locked, the latch of the porthole screwed fast and painted over with thick white paint. On a hook beside the door your jacket is hanging, and you take it down. In one pocket is a handkerchief, in the other *The Wind in the Willows*. The mobile phone, the wallet and the keys have gone. Your shoes are on the floor beneath the jacket, and you stare at them. They are expensive Goodwear shoes in faun-coloured leather, and you spent half a morning choosing them in Edward Green. You are crying now, tears of frustration and fear. You rattle the handle of the door. You cry out, wordless cries of panic. And then you throw yourself face downwards and sobbing on the berth.

When you look up, your last sob dry and dying in your mouth, it is to see a man standing in the doorway. He is short, Asian, with dark eyes under matted eyelids and a growth of bluish beard around his cheeks. You start up and away from him and try to meet his stare from the end of the bed. He does not smile but stares as though assessing a piece of merchandise. Which is what you now are.

'Where am I? What is this about?'

Your words are pointless. He mutters something in a language that sounds like Arabic. And then he turns away, shutting and locking the door.

Two minutes later he is back, accompanied now by a taller man, this one clean-shaven, with prominent cheek-bones, a mop of stringy black hair, and one dark eye that looks to the side of you, while the other tries to bore a hole in your skull. You recoil against the wall.

'Keep away from me,' you say.

He turns to his companion and makes a brief guttural sound that may be a word. The small man comes quickly forward and takes hold of your ankles. You scream and lean forward, beating as hard as you can on his head, until your arms are seized by the taller man and your head is pushed back against the wall.

Then you imagine your mother. She is observing this scene from her place, there in the armchair where she sat when you came in during the school holidays to your little desk in the corner, with its cast iron frame and lid of pitted elm wood. Her look of resignation. Her guilty eyes. Always apologising that there was no father in the house. And now especially, now that you need him. Why did he have to die? 'I am so sorry,' she says. 'So sorry it has come to this.' You are spitting now, but the tall man averts his face. How horrible his skin appears, with its gritty streak of incipient beard. His smell is heavy, waxy, waterless, like engine oil. They have pulled you down flat on the bed, and a voice is screaming in you, not your voice, but the voice of your mother, of your mother's mother, of all the women whose flesh has been forcibly prised apart by men.

The tall man has one hand over your mouth, the other around your wrist. You push your head upwards and catch the palm of his hand between your teeth. The taste of his blood in your mouth fills you with disgust. He shouts in pain and anger. Then the palm of his hand comes down between your eyes and you fall back, stunned and helpless. You groan in pain as they undress you. The tall man has wrapped his injured hand in a handkerchief and is unbuttoning your shirt. His companion has removed your knickers and is gripping your ankles, ready to force them apart. Your tears mean nothing to them, they are the way this meat behaves, like the bloody drops on a side of beef. When the tall man releases your wrist you cover your face with both hands.

He pulls your hands away. You understand now. It's your face he wants. He has your arms pinned down, his weight on your stomach. You gather your strength, and with a push of the legs you have thrown the small one from the bed, freeing your ankles. But the tall one has unbuttoned himself, you feel the slime of his sex on your neck and cheek. Your stomach turns, and as the grip is fastened again on your ankles you vomit: a stream of sour liquid spilling over your neck and shirt. The tall man jumps away and runs to wash himself. You are coughing, gasping. The vomit sticks in your mouth, choking you. And the little man stares at your opened legs, his face distorted in a grin. Never before have you hated like this. Both these men must die. The tall one is standing above you, looking down in disgust. Without a sign he swings on his heels and goes out. The small man follows him like a dog.

Chapter 6

When the first President Bush ordered the liberation of Kuwait, he halted troops at the Iraqi border, abandoning the city of Basra, which had risen against the tyrant Saddam Hussein, to its fate. The revenge was terrible. In 2003, following the defeat of Saddam, revenge began again. This time the victims were members of Saddam's Ba'ath Party, or of the militia, the Fedayin, through which he had terrorised the people. The forty-year-old Abdul Kassab, an English teacher at al-Mutamaizin High School, believed that it was his duty as a citizen and a Muslim to stay at his post, to teach the ways of enlightenment, and to work for reconciliation and forgiveness among the children of the warring factions. He experienced the shooting, torture and kidnap of friends and neighbours, and he saw the front part of his house smashed at the instigation of a local mullah, leader of a separatist movement among the Shi'ites who had branded Abdul as a traitor.

For Abdul, like the majority of Basrans, was a Shi'ite. But he believed that the Holy Koran was sent to open the path to illumination. It was a gift to all mankind, intended not to divide them but to unite them in the love of their Lord. From his teenage years he had dreamed of an urban oasis devoted to the life of the mind, where a team of devout and civilised scholars would study the works of philosophy, poetry and mysticism from all the great traditions, Muslim, Christian and Jewish, and teach their discoveries to the young in a spirit of reconciliation. They would form a society comparable to the Brethren of Purity, the *ikhwan as-Safa,* who had flourished in Basra ten centuries before. Like the Brethren they would devote themselves to the life of the mind, not surrendering to a specious clarity, but wrapping the deepest truths in the mystical language that turns prose to poetry and poetry to prayer.

Abdul imparted this vision to a small group of friends. Following the Battle of Basra in 2003, in which the British forces took control of the city, the friends met twice a month under Abdul's direction. They read the works of Ibn Sina, the writings of the Brethren, and the poetry of the Persian Sufis. They read popular scientific works in English, some obtained through a Lieutenant-Colonel in the British Army for whom Abdul worked as an interpreter in the evenings. For a while Abdul believed that he might be able to realise his dream. With the extra money earned from his work as an interpreter he envisaged establishing a private school in one of the older parts of town. He had already earmarked a derelict building by one of the canals. With the help of Colonel Matthews he could perhaps call on funds from a country anxious to appear as the liberator rather than, as it once had been, the imperial master of Iraq.

In Abdul's school the practical and the spiritual would be combined. The pupils would be educated in a spirit of enlightened forgiveness, and scholars would discover the language with which to bring young people back, despite all the horrible temptations that had flooded in – he did not deny it – with the Western freedoms previously reserved for Saddam and his cronies, to the true life of the mind. He looked forward to the day when his sons, Farid and Hazim, would study the Holy Koran, the Christian Gospels, the works of Plato and the poetry of Ferdowsi and Shakespeare, side by side with Sunnites, Christians – and yes, if any still remained in Basra, Jews too – in a school whose atmosphere, curriculum and calendar would be settled by Abdul and his brotherhood.

Of course, it was not to be. In the *Mathwani* Rumi tells us that true Sufism means sudden joy not only in the face of disappointment but in the very *fact* of it. A beautiful precept, but not one that Abdul could live up to when called out one evening by one of his brotherhood and warned that he was about to be shot as a collaborator. In the five available minutes he roused his sick wife Jamila and their sons, bustled them down the alleyway behind the house to the Shatt al-Arab, where the little ferryboats were tied to a jetty, paid the exorbitant fee that the ferryman demanded, and set off downstream towards the Royal Marines' base below the city. As the flames from their house lit the night sky above the Abu Al Khasib suburb the family wept and clung to each other, knowing that only a thin thread reached in their direction from the future, and that they must grasp that thread or die.

And by a miracle they grasped it. Thanks to his official pass Abdul was allowed to usher his family into the presence of Lieutenant-Colonel Matthews. And because the Colonel had been touched in a previously unacknowledged part of his being by Abdul's gentle nature, he used his influence to send the family to England, where they were granted asylum and given temporary housing in a Northern city.

By the time all this had been accomplished Jamila had succumbed to heart disease and Abdul was a widower, living with his two boys on the fifth floor of Block B, Angel Towers, and working as an usher in a city-centre car park. He had not lost his faith in the betterment of mankind, and he communicated it to his two sons, who lived for their father and trusted his vision. The fifteen-year-old Farid was beginning to take an interest in the Sufi poets and the three would often sit together in the evenings, preferring to read aloud in Arabic or English, rather than to watch television, whose content Abdul by and large deplored.

Apart from his father there were two people whom Farid came to adore. On the eighth floor of Block A lived the members of an Afghan family, whom Abdul regarded with the deepest suspicion, forbidding his boys to have anything to do with them. For the motherless Farid, however, experiencing the first yearnings of puberty and caught in the web of poetry that his father spun each evening, the sight of Muhibbah Shahin was a shock that he felt in the very core of his being.

It was not the perfect beauty of her features only that impressed him; nor was it her way of carrying herself, aloof and untainted, like a visiting angel among the fallen hosts. Muhibbah Shahin was the image of purity – the lost and cherished purity extolled ten centuries ago by the Brethren, and available now only in these fleeting visions, miraculously incarnate in human form.

Of course it was impossible to speak to her. And it was absurd for a fifteen-year-old boy to linger in the foyer of Block A in order to raise his eyes to the passing form of a girl four years his senior, only to lower them instantly with a blush that set his whole body aflame. But that was what he did each morning before school and each evening on his return. And in his bedroom at

40

home, shutting his ears to the thump of disco music from the flat next door, he would compose poems in Arabic and English, in which this girl shone a lamp in the surrounding darkness, turning her mystical beauty on her humble adorer, and permitting him to enter into the bower of her love, there to lie beside her on a bank of flowers. He lifted the intoxicating images from Hafiz and Khayyam, and cast them over her like confetti. And he felt that his poems went a small way towards uniting him with this girl who was, in ways that he could not quite define, to be his redeemer.

He discovered her name when one of her brothers called out to her. He learned from the sixth-formers that she had been at St Catherine's Academy but that her parents had taken her away. He learned from one of the Iraqi Sunnites who attended the Whinmoore mosque that her family had arranged for her to marry someone in Waziristan. And when she disappeared from the Angel Towers he learned from the same source that she had run away from home, that she had shamed the Afghan community and that she would have to be killed.

For a month he lived in confusion, oscillating between the delightful vision of himself coming to her rescue, fighting her captors, sustaining wounds to the healing of which she devoted the life of freedom that he had won for her, and the desolating vision of Muhibbah Shahin bound, gagged, dragged to a secret place, there to be humiliated, violated and stabbed. He was called back to the terrible early years in Basra, the cries and screams, the daily emergencies, from which they had miraculously escaped, but which were always there in his memories and nightmares, calling out to him that he could not ignore them for long.

Then, wandering sadly in the city centre one day, he caught sight of her behind the counter in Amanda's Fashion Boutique,

41

and his heart was put at rest. She was safe, free, protected by this secure and easy-going society where after all nothing really bad could happen, and he could go back in peace to his unending dream of her. After this discovery he would take every opportunity to pass by the Boutique, and although he did not enter it – for it was an ostentatiously feminine shop, where a young Muslim boy could not be seen without shame – he took comfort to see that she looked askance at her customers with the same cold unconcern that had characterised her way of entering and leaving the Angel Towers. She was protected by English society, but also not a part of it – removed in a heavenly sphere of her own, and one that only he could approach, through the poetry that he devoted to her name.

Then one day he passed the shop and saw that she was no longer there. For weeks he returned, hoping to catch a glimpse of her. But she was gone, and only the dream of her remained.

It was thanks to the other person whom he adored that Farid was able to manage his grief. The following academic year saw the arrival of a new English teacher at St Catherine's Academy. Stephen Haycraft had something of Abdul Kassab's gentleness. But he was also deeply and intriguingly English, with the informal manners and the stoic solitude that were, in Farid's eyes, the distinguishing marks of the gentleman. Abdul never ceased to remind his sons of the debt of gratitude that they owed, and emphasized that they must look for the things to admire, and not the things to disparage, in the country that had adopted them.

Mr Haycraft was a person to admire: more, he was a person to love, and Farid attached himself to his English teacher with a devotion that was all the greater on account of his still warm longing for Muhibbah. Mr Haycraft radiated a sense of safety; in his presence Farid no longer felt the reverberations of those nightmare years. He was persuaded that a world that contained Mr Haycraft was a world of law, normality and good will. It was inconceivable, in such a world, that a girl could be captured, disgraced and done away with, and in Mr Haycraft's presence he became sure that Muhibbah Shahin was somewhere secure, protected by England even if not quite belonging to it – as she never could belong, since she was a vessel for a pure soul placed in her by angels.

Because he felt this way it was a joy to Farid that Mr Haycraft wanted to learn from him. He went eagerly to school each day in the hope that he would be side by side with his teacher during the lunch break, moving their fingers together along the verses of a bilingual Koran, his going from right to left, Mr Haycraft's from left to right, sometimes meeting in the middle, when they would both burst into laughter.

'All holy things,' Abdul told his sons, 'are only partially revealed to us, for our minds are finite and the light that shines on us is of a dazzling strength. Hence holy things require an effort of interpretation, which the jurists called *ijtihad*. Many of the Sunnites deny this. They tell us that all has been settled eternally and "the gate of *ijtihad* is closed".' In Abdul's view that was pernicious nonsense, which made the Holy Koran not an instrument of peace but a declaration of war against all who reasonably questioned it. Abdul's approach permitted scepticism, and even rejoiced in it, as Rumi rejoiced in disappointment.

So Farid took pleasure in the holy book as he read it with his sceptical teacher. From Mr Haycraft he learned that you could live in doubt and uncertainty and still be protected by law, that this way of life may even be what the modern world requires. There was a path of freedom, which was also a path of loneliness. And this noble loneliness was what Farid perceived and loved in Mr Haycraft. Freedom, doubt and loneliness were not to be feared, but to be triumphed over, as his father had triumphed over disappointment at last, and learned to rejoice in the very fact of it. Then one day, without warning, everything changed.

Chapter 7

Stephen had begun his class on the theme of magic in Shakespeare's *Tempest*. He had printed a hand-out, summarising the art of alchemy as it was practised prior to Shakespeare's day. He had looked up sources in connection with the occult, and with the mystique of the printed book. He had prepared some thoughts about Paracelsus, his life and influence. He had especially studied the use that Shakespeare makes of the idea of healing. He wanted to impress on his class that for Shakespeare healing was a far wider notion than any considered by the National Health Service. It was a notion that touched on the meaning of personal life. At a certain point during the previous evening he had felt certain that, if he stared hard enough into this idea, the goal of his own life would be revealed in it, like a face looking up at him from the depths of a pool. The image stayed with him for a while, then wavered and vanished. Now, trying to recapture it, he stumbled over words, and avoided the eyes of his pupils as they watched him from the sparsely occupied benches. Sharon's absence was like a wound in his thinking, through which the life-blood flowed away. He added words and more words, as though to staunch the flow. But the argument grew weaker and weaker, and was on the verge of dying when she came in quietly through the door at the top of the hall.

The envelope containing her essay and his invitation – written ten days before – lay on the lectern in front of him. Conveying it this far had been easy. Getting it to her would be difficult, maybe impossible. She was trying not to look at him. Her thin-fingered hand was at work on a sheet of paper. Fine blond hair concealed her face; the long neck, unnaturally pale against a smudged school pullover of navy blue, was all that he saw of Sharon's flesh. She had opened her soul to him, but the soul is incarnate and she was now, inescapably, flesh to him. The thought caused him to break out in a sweat. Maybe he should tear up the note he had written. Just hand back the essay without a word. Maybe that's what he should do.

He decided not to decide. And for a few minutes he felt better. He realised that his sentences had become vague, slurred and incoherent. He began again with the topic of Ariel and the idea of a spirit imprisoned in a tree. Imprisoned spirits, he told the class, were of great importance to the alchemists, who specialised in capturing and releasing them. They were a symbol of power and freedom. Once released they were nowhere and everywhere, dis-embodied but with powers beyond the reach of human bodies.

Suddenly she looked up. There was a light of enquiry in her eyes. He sent a quick involuntary smile in her direction. She blushed and turned back to her work. Soon he had reached the point when he could set the topic for an essay; he had already decided on 'Ariel: his character and powers'. But her blush had changed everything. He asked them to write about compassion in *The Tempest*, and the many forms it took. They packed up their books and filed out into the upper corridor. Sharon didn't linger, but went quickly through the door that another girl held for her.

Stephen tore open the envelope, took out the note and pushed it into his pocket. He dropped the essay in his briefcase and left for the staff room. His hands were trembling, and he walked jerkily, like a puppet. In the corridor outside the staffroom Jim Roberts waylaid him, pushing him by the elbow through the door. Most classes had not yet finished and the staffroom was empty. It had a sad, end-of-day feeling. The out-of-date maps on one wall, the broken clock on the neo-Georgian mantelpiece, the portrait in oils above it of the Headmaster, The Rev. Father John McMurty, who founded the school, the worn Edwardian chairs in turned oak and leather, the modern coffee machine on the bench beneath the window of leaded glass and Gothic mullions – all these were already imbued for Stephen with an aura of defeat. This was a place where hope and belief were set aside and where truth prevailed – the truth that must be hidden in the classroom if you were to get through the day. He read this fact in Jim Roberts's lurking eyes and jabbing finger. Jim turned to Stephen and made as though to pin him to the wall.

'It's about Sharon Williams,' Jim said.

Stephen froze. His letter of resignation formed quickly in his mind. Send it now, send it yesterday, send it before all this madness arises!

'What about her?'

'Some information we need…'

Jim tailed off and looked from side to side, as though suspecting eavesdroppers.

'Information?'

Her blushing downturned face. Her small sweet blemished mouth. Her dreams of Ferdinand. 'Chains of enchantment'. He felt sick at heart.

'Well, she's in your class. I thought you could speak to her.'

47

'About what?'

In the rush of relief he looked eagerly at Jim, willing to oblige, to do his schoolmasterly duty in anything, even to speak to Sharon Williams!

'Angel Towers again. Social housing, bloody hell. Anti-social housing rather. The long and short is, the social workers were called in, on account of a shindy involving the woman she calls her mum. Turns out Mrs Williams is not her mum at all, but someone who thought she could make a few quid as a foster parent, when the council were offloading children they had taken into care. Now they have put her on a list of children 'at risk', as they put it. Every fucking child in Angel Towers is at risk. But before they do anything, or rather nothing, as is their usual game, they have asked us to make discreet enquiries – you know, do you love this slut who screams at you and are you happy with her latest cokehead of a boyfriend who is always trying to get you into bed and kicking the shit out of your brothers, who are not your brothers at all but feral primates rounded up by some joker of a social worker who is waiting to release them on the middle classes at election time. Just the kind of job for which you are suited, Stephen, squeezing the secrets from a traumatised child.'

Jim laughed cynically, and jabbed Stephen twice in the chest.

'And supposing she talks to me,' Stephen replied, attempting hesitation. 'What then?'

'We have to provide any information we can gather, to be put in the file, to back up the general decision to do nothing. So that when the girl has been gang-raped, sold into slavery and finally done to death somewhere in Saudi Arabia the social workers can say they did what they could, and in any case they are overworked and underfunded and it is all the government's fault. That kind of thing. When were you born for Chrissake?'

He gave Stephen a few more admonitory jabs, and then swung away with a sigh.

'How did you learn this?'

It occured to Stephen that the story was an invention, maybe a trap. You couldn't be a secondary school teacher for as long as Jim Roberts without wishing for revenge.

Jim looked up at him through tangled eyebrows.

'How do you think? Did I go round to Angel Towers, ring the bell outside a door from which the howls of an abused and abusive menagerie assail my ears, as ready with my polite enquiry as an old Etonian canvassing for the Conservative Party? Or did the social worker turn up in my classroom this morning, leading Ryan Williams, not by the earlobe as I would have done, nor by the scruff of the neck as was once recommended, but by the elbow, with sweet lovey-dovey pushes and melting official empathy, as they call it, asking me to excuse the poor little mite whose absence from school for the last three days could be easily explained if I would grant her a word in private? I mean how the hell does a teacher get involved in this kind of mess for Chrissake?'

Stephen thought for a moment.

'Why is Sharon Williams at risk? Who is threatening her?'

'Who, you mean, apart from the rapists on the eighth floor, the drug-addicts on the sixth, and the slave-dealers in the basement? Could it be, frinstance, mum's latest boyfriend, the knife artist from the defunct Romanian circus that ran out of cash last Wednesday, or the Afghan fathers who are so keen to preserve the virginity of their daughters that they kidnap fatherless girls for their sons to play with, or, let's see…? For fuck's sake, you know the kid. Why don't you ask her?'

'Ask her?'

Yes, ask her, save her, protect her. Stephen was trembling again.

'Why not? She's a sweet kid. Probably sweet on you too: after all, you are the only human being she has ever met. The only gentleman, at least – fancy that!'

Jim's cynical laughter dwindled quickly to a mutter, as he crossed the room to toy with the coffee machine.

'I'll look into it,' Stephen said. He pretended to search for essays in his locker. He snapped shut his briefcase with a business-like flourish. He slowly and laboriously writhed into his overcoat. He sucked air into his dry mouth, and uttered a stifled goodnight. But Jim turned away, and merely smiled.

She was waiting for him in the alley behind the car park. Without a word she fitted her steps to his. They walked for a while in silence. He looked at the wall to either side of them. A smear of yellow light lay along the glazed brick coping. Once this had been the back alley to terraced cottages, housing the workers for a smelting works. Now it shielded a group of ware-houses, which lay silent amid pools of darkness like beached ships of steel. Stephen was going beside her into the unknown, with no one to call on for help.

He carried the briefcase away from her in his left hand, and buried his right hand in the pocket of his overcoat. They entered the car park, and still they had not spoken. Then, slowly, softly, she put her hand into his pocket and wrapped her fingers in his. They walked on a few more paces. It was Sharon who broke the silence.

'It's OK though innit, sir, me thinking about you and me. I mean there inna no harm in it.'

'Not if we don't take it any further,' he answered, and at once regretted the words. 'We' made him part of what was happening. And he realised that she had been hoping for that very word.

'Actually, Sharon, it's best not to talk about it.'

'That's OK, sir. I dunna wanna talk about it neither. Just write it in essays, cause they go special from me to you.'

'But there is something else we need to discuss.'

They were outside the block of flats. The unfriendly door of glass and steel stood before them. To go through it, shutting her outside, would be to make the barrier between them absolute. And he sensed the desolation she would feel, turning away towards Angel Towers. It could not be wrong to invite her in.

He unwrapped his fingers from hers and searched his jacket pocket for the key. He unlocked the door, pushed it ajar and turned to her. She was watching him, her clear blue-grey guile-less eyes fixed on his.

'Do you want to come in for a moment?'

She nodded and ducked quickly beneath his arm. He noticed that her feet hardly sounded on the concrete steps, as though she drifted above them in the air.

Chapter 8

You have washed yourself in the sink, again and again. Your shirt is wet and clings to your collarbone. Your breasts are sore from those hateful hands, and you flinch as you fasten the bra. A wave of nausea sends you back to the bathroom, and then you finish dressing and sit for a long time on the bed, wishing to die.

You again recall your mother in her corner, fixing you with guilty eyes, as though it were her fault he died of a heart attack on your fourteenth birthday. Between that time and Cambridge you hardly grew. Life retreated to some recess deep inside you. You were not to be touched, not to be opened, like some present beneath the Christmas tree, waiting and waiting until Mick arrived and set the tree aflame. But you worked. Nobody worked as you did, at school, at Newnham College, at the College of Law, at the desk where you sat each evening studying accountancy. You would be the angel daughter, shining into the place of darkness where he lay. One after another the certificates came; one after another the promotions. And not even jealous Mick could put a stop to it. But now this! You go tight and hard inside. The tears slide from your cheeks and your hands tremble. Hatred twists and turns like a knife in your stomach.

You have been sitting on the bed in that posture for half an hour when the door opens, admitting a bent old man with pale skin, white hair and electric blue eyes. He is carrying a tray, which he puts down beside you on the berth. On it you see a roll of dark bread, some slices of sausage, an apple and a can of coca cola.

'Can you take me to the captain?'

'No speak English,' the man replies. 'Sorry much.'

He looks at you. His bright blue eyes are prominent and staring, as though painted above his cheeks by Lucian Freud. But his manner is soft. You sense that he pities you, as he has pitied all the girls to whom he has come with food after their ordeal. You begin to cry again. That it has come to this! Now you have only one thing for which to live, and that is revenge.

You get up from the bed and duck quickly past him, seizing the handle of the door. He reaches out for you but he is not quick enough. You are in a tunnel between cabins. At the end is a flight of metal steps, twisting upwards out of sight. You hear voices somewhere above you, and the sound of seagulls. You are running towards the steps, but you slip on the wet floor beneath you and the old man is close behind. He is shouting in a language that sounds like Russian. Now you have a hand on the stair-rail, you are pulling yourself up, two steps at a time. He stretches out to you, he can reach your ankle, but he hesitates to touch and withdraws his hand. You turn to see him crumpled, almost penitent, at the foot of the stair.

You look around. You are on a white metal deck with capstans and hawsers. It is cold. The grey light of morning is stretched like a membrane across the motionless sea, and on the far horizon is land, your land, the home that made you and which you may never see again. You are on the stern of the ship: the propellers churn the sea beneath you and above is the white superstructure of the bridge.

From this angle the ship seems like a doll's house, with vistas into the secret life of adults, as imagined by a child. On each side of you, raised onto the deck by metal casings, are doors, which open and close as though at the touch of some giant finger. In one direction they reveal an officer in a white canvas uniform rigidly seated at a desk, in the other a neat workshop with tools fixed on brackets to the wall as though placed there on display. Above the first door is a wooden plaque with the words *Kabina Bosman* in plain black letters. Above the other door, written directly onto the white metal, are some scribbled words that look like Polish.

There are steps connecting the deck to the bridge, and two men have descended them, gripping the gunwale as they advance towards you. One is young, Asian looking, scantily dressed in jeans and cotton shirt and with short black hair. The other is more Russian in appearance, square faced and burly, with a smudged white sailor's uniform from which his shapeless pink hands emerge like glue from a tube. You back up against the central capstan shouting 'keep away'.

Fastened to the deck beside you is a metal box, and on an impulse you kick open the lid. Inside are hooks, a hammer and an electric drill. You pick up the hammer and wave it before you. The young one frowns, while the other laughs and comes slowly forward. His face is large and sheer like a fortress, with arrow slits for eyes and a great wide drawbridge of a mouth. You decide to hit him between the eyes, but your hand trembles as you raise the hammer and he easily knocks it away. You scream as he grips your wrists, and your legs collapse beneath you. You lie crumpled and sobbing on the deck, the cold metal stinging your thighs as he holds your arms above your head.

'It's OK, man, leave her.'

It is the young one who speaks. He has a Yorkshire accent and he moves towards you with an air of concern. The other loosens his grip and your hands fall to cover your face. The sobbing will not stop, but comes from deep inside you, from a place beyond the reach of your will. The young man reaches down to touch your arm, and you start away from him.

'Don't touch me,' you say, and between your fingers you see him hesitate. His face is regular, with nut-coloured skin, clear brown narrow eyes and prominent cheekbones. From such a face the Yorkshire accent seems like the work of a ventriloquist.

'We inna going to hurt you,' he says. 'We just need you back below. Sod it, man, you'll catch cold up here.'

'Leave me alone,' you say, and he looks at his companion, who laughs, a contemptuous, grating sound that is clearly his only conversation.

For a long time you stay where you have fallen, your skirt ruffled onto your thighs, which are raw from the cold metal of the deck. You are propped against a capstan, your head sunk and your arms beside you, like a broken doll. The men have withdrawn a little, and are looking at you. You try to believe that this is not happening to you, that you will soon wake to your bedroom in Camden Town, with the view of chimney pots and old slate roofs, and *The Wind in the Willows* on the bedside table.

As a child you often prayed, not just 'Our Father' and 'Hail Mary', but the lists of your daily needs for God's perusal. In Church, side by side with Father, you had decanted your soul into the care of angels, and you knew that he did the same. God must be true if Father believed in him, and so you believed in him too. But Father died regardless, and all prayers died along with him. You think of the unanswered prayers of recent times – prayers from people rattling to their deaths in cattle trucks, from peasants starved in their villages, from the emaciated slaves in the labour camps. Dr Goldmark, a wizened Hungarian Jew who was your history tutor, had asked you to study these things, always ending his tutorials with the words 'you see, Miss Markham, that there is no God. But concerning the Devil I am not so sure.' What purpose, after the futile prayers of a million dying children, to report to the Almighty a mere case of rape? You shudder and lie still.

The air is damp; there is a smell of diesel oil. You hear the ostinato throb of the propellers, dragging the shrieking seagulls with the ship. In the distance a spring mist has arisen, hiding the land. Your world is slipping inexorably away from you, and like the slaves on the slave-ships, as they lost sight of Africa, you cry aloud in desolation. You do not resist the men as they lift you. You drag your feet along the deck and down the steps to your prison cell, and when they push you through the door you grasp weakly for the berth and pull yourself on to it. The tray of food is still there. The trapped air smells of paint and grease and vomit. The large man turns his armoured face in your direction, smiles horribly, and leaves with a chuckle. The young man stands by your berth. You try to meet his stare, but are overcome by shame, and hide your face from him. He pulls your hands away and looks at you.

'What's your name?' he asks.

You shake your head in silence.

'Look, I inna gonna hurt you, man. You be nice to me and I'll be nice to you, OK? Like, is there anything you want right now? Frinstance.'

You open your eyes and look at his face. You want to hate him as you hated the others, but something – a stirring of dependence,

56

perhaps, a longing for protection at all costs, maybe just that little flicker of vulnerability that you read in his blinking eyes – stands in the way.

'Yes, you can go away. But first please open that porthole.'

He is still holding your hands away from your face. But with a sudden movement of recoil he drops them and goes quickly through the door into the corridor. After a moment he returns with a monkey wrench, and applies it to the batten of the porthole. It comes open with a crack, and flakes of white paint fall onto the berth. He brushes them away, and puts the wrench on the floor. Sea air rushes in around you, and the sound of seagulls.

'So what's your name?' he asks again.

'Why do you want my name? Are you going to steal that too?'

'Listen, we gotta be friends, see? Otherwise you're in trouble.'

'I am in trouble.'

'Not real trouble, not yet.'

He looks at you. There is a hesitancy in his manner that suggests he is not really part of the gang that has kidnapped you. You are too desolate to exploit this fact. But you notice it all the same.

'Where are you taking me?'

'Normally they hand the girls to an agent in Kaliningrad – a real dump of a place. But you wunna stay there for long. Actually they hanna decided what to do with you. I mean, there was a mistake, see.'

The young man has pushed the tray of food aside and sat down on the berth. The monkey wrench is just out of reach on the floor, and you concentrate all your thoughts on how to get hold of it. But he has made no move, and you must keep him talking.

'Yes,' you say, 'there was a mistake. And you'll pay for it.'

'I mean Zdenko let himself into the flat, and there was the girl on her own, doing her homework just like we told him, because she is a bit of a swot see, and they bring her to Hull as normal and out on to the boat and it's not the right girl.'

He tells the story in a matter-of-fact tone, as though it does not concern you. But it twists the knife in your stomach and you cry for revenge.

'Then you had better get me back to England. Now.'

He looks at you with an air of assessment.

'No, we canna do that. The other girl, see, we done her over. I mean she was ready, and we'd put her off in Kaliningrad and that would be the last we heard of her. You though, you're different. If we dunna do things right you'll make trouble.'

You are trembling now and huddling away from him. But he still has made no move.

'See, the others, they say we'll give her the treatment, she'll be that scared in a day or two she'll just go along with the Russian bit like they all do. I say no, I'll look after her.'

He reaches for the Coca-Cola can and snaps it open. He holds it out in your direction, nodding at you to drink. You shake your head and retreat from him. He takes a sip, returns the can to the tray and suddenly stands up. You reach for the monkey wrench but he quickly kicks it away from the berth.

'What are you doing?' you cry.

'Just be nice, OK?'

He has taken a packet of condoms from his pocket.

'I'll use one of these, see. Then you dunna have to worry afterwards. No bother.'

'No!' you shout, 'no!'

And a sudden blackness falls like a shutter across your eyes.

58

Chapter 9

Justin's first thought was to ring the police. They had given Muhibbah a number to call in case of threats, and he had written the number in his pocket book. He stared at the corner where she had sat. He recalled her curious glances, fleeting touches and enigmatic words. But it was as though Muhibbah were sealed, offering no place from which to peel away the membrane that protected her. Her path through life had been charted on some other planet, and she received instructions for her future in a language that he could not understand. She had gone out of his life as she had entered it, without an explanation.

But the thought of it made him sick. She would be drugged, gagged, kicked and beaten, maybe even raped, then bundled through that dark doorway in Waziristan, the fourth wife of some bigoted slave-master, who would smother her dear face in his stinking beard, and fill her sweet body with his children.

'Impossible,' he said aloud.

He took the phone from his pocket, scrolled down to the number of the mobile he had given her, and pressed the key. As he held the device to his ear another phone began ringing in the office, and his heart missed a beat.

'What the hell...'

He located it in the sleeveless grey coat that hung from the door. He reached into the pocket: the first time he had his hands in her clothing and her clothing in his hands. Pushed down alongside the phone were two pieces of paper. One seemed to be a letter in Arabic. The other, neatly copied out, was a poem. He recognized it as Yeats:

Wine comes in at the mouth
And love comes in at the eye;
That's all we shall know for truth
Before we grow old and die.
I lift the glass to my mouth,
I look at you, and I sigh.

He knew the handwriting, and it was hers. How was it that Muhibbah, who allowed neither wine nor love to cross her boundaries, had found meaning in those words? Was there such a 'you' in her life? He doubted it; indeed he insisted that it could not be true. He replaced the pieces of paper in the pocket with a puzzled shake of the head.

The screen of the phone read '15 missed calls'. The latest showed his number. The others were all from a landline in Yorkshire. He thought for a moment, and then wrote the number down: he would call it from a public phone box, so as not to be traced. He packed his briefcase quickly, adding Muhibbah's phone to his sheaf of papers. Then he locked the office, and hurried into the street.

He came to a phone box; it had been vandalized, and only a stub of twisted metal remained on the wall. He walked on towards the city centre, recalling a public phone in a shopping precinct off South Parade. He could not find it, and by now his heart was racing. There had been few emergencies in Justin's life. Yes, there was the time when his father had been lost in a storm on Cross Fell, and Justin had joined the search party, only to come across the familiar figure almost at once, peacefully striding towards them down the hill. There were a few incidents with the band in which he used to play, but they had petered out as soon as they had begun. And there was Muhibbah, who had entered his life as an emergency but who had remained wedded to her secrets, refusing to be rescued, or at least to be rescued by him. As he pressed onwards through the rush hour crowds, Justin regretted his indolent life and all the shortcuts to comfort he had taken.

'Muhibbah!' he said aloud. He had turned from South Parade into Park Row. The proud facades of the Victorian banks and offices lined the street like uniformed soldiers. Rusticated arches, glazed friezes, buttressed galleries, unblinking windows beneath their brows of carved stone – all spoke of permanence, comfort and the immovable certainty of law. The noble town hall, raising its clock tower high above the rank of giant columns, seemed in its wide sweep to clear away all lesser creations, affirming the right of this city to be forever England. It was inconceivable that in a town dedicated to prosperity, comfort and English order, a girl might simply disappear, smuggled into slavery under far distant skies. But the inconceivable would not be noticed when it finally occurred. His body filled with nausea and dread.

He came across a pair of phone booths on the corner of Vicar Lane; one was in working order, and he typed in the number that he had found on Muhibbah's mobile. It rang twelve times before flipping to an Ansafone. There was a message in Arabic and another, or perhaps the same one, in what he assumed to be

61

Pashto. He hung up without speaking. He wandered in the city centre for a while, drank a double whisky in the Horse and Trumpet and then, with a strange feeling of defiance, set off to her flat, in the sudden hope that she would have given them the slip and made it to safety.

It was dark when he arrived there, but there was a light in the flat and he rang the bell with trembling hand. If she were there she would not forgive his intrusion; if she were not there he would believe the worst. He heard the trip of girlish steps on the stair-carpet, and backed away from the door as it opened.

A thin pale girl stood in the doorway. Her blond hair was wrapped in a headscarf and her blue denim suit was open at the neck, revealing a silver medallion on a ribbon of string. She looked at him from calm grey eyes and smiled enquiringly.

'Hi,' she said. 'Are you looking for someone?'

'I am a friend of Muhibbah's,' he said. 'I was hoping she'd be in.'

The girl looked at him curiously.

'Muhibbah's gone.'

'*Gone?*'

'She left a couple of hours ago: packed up her stuff, and skedaddled.'

'What? On her own?' he asked.

'There was a guy downstairs with a car. He didn't come up. Didn't need to; she had only a couple of bags. But I guess I should know who you are and why you are asking?'

'Can I come in for a moment?'

'O.K. if you can explain why. I'm Millie, by the way.'

She held out her hand and he grasped it.

'Justin,' he said, 'Justin Fellowes. I work with Muhibbah. That is to say, she works for me.'

'So you're the environment guy? I guess that's credentials enough.'

Millie led the way to their communal room and sat him down in the window, just as Muhibbah had done. Nothing had changed since his last visit, except that the issue of *Rolling Stone* was a newer one, and the television was flickering silently in the corner. Millie picked up a remote from the sofa and switched it off.

'I need to find Muhibbah,' he said. 'She left the office without explanation. I worry she's in trouble.'

It sounded very lame, as though he had some other and more disreputable motive for intruding.

'Well that's pretty standard for Muhibbah. Never explains anything. What kind of trouble anyway?'

Millie looked at him candidly. It was an attractive face, regular, soft and quizzical, with pale lips under a slightly prominent nose. Just the girlfriend he would have wished for, had there been room in his heart. Nausea and dread returned, so that he almost choked on his words.

'Kidnap, briefly. I was out of the office; when I returned she was gone, and there were signs of a struggle.'

'Oh? There were no signs of a struggle when she came here: no gun to her head, not even crying. Just the usual Muhibbah, doing her secret things on tiptoe.'

'I know she has been under threat. And she left her jacket behind with her mobile phone and other personal stuff.'

Millie thought for a moment.

'I guess you should go to the police, if you're that worried. But Muhibbah is seriously weird. She's probably gone back to the office to collect her things. And now the two of them are on their way to Timbuktu, to start a new life in the desert. It would suit her very well. She has paid the rent by the way, until the end of next month. I can't say I shall miss her.'

Justin felt the shock of Millie's words. He buried his head in his hands and sighed himself free of their meaning.

'I guess I'd better go,' he said. 'You're probably right. If there's something to worry about, I should report it to the cops.'

Millie looked at him sceptically.

'Look, Justin, I don't know how you stand in relation to Muhibbah. But as I see it, in the culture she comes from, women often pretend they are forced to do what they secretly want to do. And I don't mean sex only. If you lived with Muhibbah you'd know what I'm getting at. She's a walking secret, hiding everything from everyone, including herself. To be brutally frank, she gives me the creeps. And I honestly don't think she'll award you any Brownie-points for interrupting whatever it is she and that guy are up to.'

He shook his head. Such thoughts could not touch Muhibbah. She lay beneath the ebb and flow of them, like a sealed amphora on the ocean floor.

When he left the flat, after exchanging phone numbers with Millie, it was in a state of acute anxiety. He could not accept Millie's verdict, but she had planted a rival image of Muhibbah in his mind. Whatever was happening to Muhibbah now had been prepared over many months; perhaps she had foreseen it, and perhaps the young man who had been stalking her – Justin had no doubt it was he – had banked on her consent. In which case what conceivable role could there be for Justin?

He followed the streets where they had walked in the first mornings of his love, when the office of protector had been his by right. He recalled her self-contained way of moving at his side, her alert interrogations, her laughter at each fact, word, or opinion that was new to her. He dwelt on her perfect shape and perfect face, and on the untouchable enigmatic self that was veiled behind her beauty. The image dawned of Muhibbah broken, violated, enslaved, calling in vain for his protection. And by the time he was climbing the stairs to his flat the tears were running uncontrollably down his cheeks, the first he had shed since childhood.

Chapter 10

Sharon paused on the third step and turned to him. A light from the floor above picked out her features: her face was soft and pale, the lips set in a horizontal line and the blemish to her mouth invisible. Her blue-grey eyes rested on his, and the small white hand on the satchel-strap dropped from her shoulder, exposing the flesh of her neck, like a sacrificial beast inviting slaughter. Stephen's heart was pounding, and he walked quickly past her, saying 'follow me'. He told himself that this encounter was none of his doing, that he was performing a duty imposed on him by his role as a teacher, and that in any case the conversation would be over in half an hour. But as he opened the door of his flat, switched on the light, saw the immaculate testimony to his isolation, and sensed her hovering just behind him, awaiting the invitation that stuck in his throat, he knew that he was on a thin ledge above the abyss.

'Come in,' he said, and threw his briefcase on to the chair at his desk. She did not move, but stood in the doorway, waiting for him to turn round.

'Can I make you a cup of tea?'

He went towards the kitchen. Not turning round was now a policy. Soon she would understand. This is a business meeting, and looks are off the agenda. But he had reached the sink and was filling the kettle before she replied.

'Yes please, sir. Milk and two sugars please, sir. It's reelly nice this place, sir.'

'It answers my needs. Why don't you sit down?'

He turned to her now and saw that her eyes were fixed on him, wide, bright, astonished. He pointed to one of the arm-chairs, and leaned against the other, his two hands resting on the wooden rim of its back. The floodlights in the car park shone through the window, smearing desk, papers, books and chairs with greasy yellow crests. He wanted to draw the curtains, but the gesture would send the wrong message. Slowly, shyly, she moved forward and fell in schoolgirl fashion onto the chair, as though thrown there. The grey woollen skirt of her uniform rode up over the tights, and she smoothed it back across her knees. The skirt was crumpled and stained, and the tights had several holes that she strove to hide from him. As she struggled to conceal her shabbiness he turned quickly round to save her embarrassment.

'I'll just make the tea.'

For Stephen tea was important: he had his own mixture – Assam tips and Darjeeling – which he obtained from a specialist shop off the South Parade in the city centre. As he spooned the leaves into the tea-pot he wondered what the exotic taste would mean to her, for whom tea came with milk and two sugars. He sensed that he was under observation from a place beyond his horizon. Every part of his life would assume some new significance in Sharon's telescope.

When he returned to the living room she was on her knees in front of the bookcase, turning the pages of *The Magic Mountain*. She looked up at him, and sprang to her feet.

'Sorry, sir. I was just looking at your books. Amazing.'

'Well, if there's anything you'd like to borrow, Sharon, don't hesitate.'

'Can I reelly, sir?'

'Of course.'

He set the tray down on the low table between the armchairs, and busied himself with the teapot. She had resumed her seat, and was looking at him.

'I wondered what it's like inside, this place. And now I know. It's so neat and tidy, sir.'

'Well yes. When you live alone you have to be tidy.'

'Wish I lived alone. Just me and books. A whole bookcase full, like you, sir.'

His hand shook a little as he poured the tea.

'Listen Sharon, I won't keep you for long. But I need to ask you a few questions.'

'Dunna worry, sir. I shouldna shown you that essay. But thanks for reading it and not being angry. You inna angry, are you, sir?'

'It's not about the essay I wanted to talk, Sharon. And of course I'm not angry. I need to ask you about something else.'

'What about, sir?'

'About your private life.'

A frightened look came into her eyes.

'I got nowt private life. Except what I invent for myself.'

'Still, you have a place you go to after school; you have a family, neighbours, and friends. You live in a place where there has often been trouble. I just want to know whether things are OK there, and whether you get – well, the support that you need.'

She sat watching him in silence as he drank the tea. He noticed that she was not drinking from the mug that he had placed before her, but kept her hands folded in her lap, the strap of her tattered satchel wrapped around her fingers. Suddenly she was on her feet and going towards the door.

'Sharon!'

She turned in the doorway. Her face was white and her lips were trembling.

'It's all OK, though, innit, sir? Between us, I mean.'

'Not if you just go away when I try to talk to you. I am on your side, Sharon, you know that.'

He was standing now and looking at her. The pale blond hair lay in wisps on her cheeks, as though blown by the wind. One strand touched her lips, and another half shielded her left eye. Her face had a haunted expression, and she gripped the satchel with both hands, as though ready to throw it.

'You dinna ought to ask me nowt, sir.'

'But I'm your teacher, Sharon. And your friend.'

'There's school, see, sir, where you are. And there's Hell, where they are. You inna 'lowed to talk about Hell. If you do, man, they kill you, see.'

'Maybe it is time you talked about it, Sharon.'

She uttered a little cry.

'Then they'd kill you too. It's simple, see.'

She stood in the doorway. He must do nothing. She must be free to go, free to stay. He was the one who watched and comforted, who pitied, but did not desire. A hollow feeling arose within him. He remembered so many mistakes, so many wrong turnings. And now he had put his life in the hands of a child.

'It never harms to talk, Sharon, with someone who cares about you.'

Her hands on the satchel relaxed a little, and she took a step back into the room.

'Do you mean that, sir?'

69

'Of course I mean it; if you don't talk about your fears, they destroy you.'

She was looking at him steadily.

'I mean you caring about me, sir.'

He looked back in silence, and then he nodded. She did not move, but let her satchel drop to the floor.

'I wunna be no trouble to you, sir.'

Her words recalled the dying Dido: 'May my wrongs create/ No trouble, no trouble in thy breast'. Purcell's music sounded in Stephen's ear. He tried to fit Queen Dido's mature and womanly love to the waif who stood before him. How absurd! For a moment he felt able to talk down to her.

'Troubles come, Sharon. But let's try to avoid any new ones, yes?'

He at once regretted the words, which sounded weak and disrespectful. And how strange it was, that this girl who stood as though pencilled on the air before him should demand respect. In her pale face and trembling lips, in her featureless clothes and uncared-for looks, he saw something proud, as though she were protecting what was best in her, refusing to allow it to be destroyed. He pointed to the chair.

'Sit down a moment, Sharon, and drink your tea. No need to talk about things if you'd rather not.'

She came forward, again falling into the chair as though thrown there. She lifted the mug to her lips and then held it away with an expression of distaste.

'You don't like it?'

'Tastes weird, dunnit, sir?'

She put down the mug and then sat without moving, like a patient in a doctor's surgery. There was a stillness in the room. From the car park came the sudden noise of car doors slamming and engines starting, as a nearby office disgorged its staff at the end of their day. Stephen released the back of the chair and went across to the girl. He brushed her hair with one hand. She seized the hand, kissed it, and then let it drop. With an effort he moved away. People passed his door on the stairwell, men speaking gruffly in some Slavic tongue. He noticed she had left the door ajar, and went across to shut it. He turned to address her.

'Now that you know I care about you, Sharon, won't it be easier to talk?'

She was looking at him with wide uncertain eyes. Again she had reached for the satchel and was clutching it convulsively.

'Dunna you spoil things, sir.'

'How can it spoil things if we share our troubles?'

'I better go, sir. Thanks reelly for inviting me in.'

'Won't you at least tell me whether I should be worrying about you?'

They were face to face, and their eyebeams locked. How pale and serious and vulnerable she looked. He pressed his hands to his sides, so as not to reach out to her.

'There's two of me, sir. You dunna have to worry about the one what's yours. And the one what's yours canna talk about the other one, see. And… and if they come asking you, you just tell them you dunna know nowt, right?'

With an abrupt movement she skipped to one side of him and seized the handle of the door.

'Thanks anyway, sir,' she said over her shoulder. 'It was great being here.'

And before he could reply she had run to the bottom of the stairwell and out into the street.

During the sleepless nights that followed Stephen resolved to go as soon as possible to the Council's department of social work.

This resolve was strengthened a week later when, suddenly appearing in front of him as he walked from the lecture hall to the staff room, Sharon thrust out a sheaf of paper, saying 'done another one,' and held his eyes for a moment anxiously. She looked grimy and dishevelled, as though she had slept in her uniform, and when she turned away and walked quickly down the corridor, he noticed that the school jersey, which she pulled low over her narrow hips, had begun to fray along the bottom, so that tassels of wool waved behind her as she walked. He felt a piercing shaft of pity, which quickly turned to fear and then to love, as she ducked out of sight into the library. Jim Roberts had warned him that trouble always comes from Angel Towers; he had not warned him, however, that it could come in this way.

There was only one place in St Catherine's Academy where Stephen could retire with Sharon's essay, and that was the chapel, which was kept locked except for special occasions. The Local Education Authority regarded this place as an anachronism that it would happily have demolished, had it not been mentioned in Pevsner's *Buildings of England* as a quirky but significant example of Victorian Gothic. The key was kept in the staffroom, and Stephen frequently borrowed it.

He sat in a box-pew of dark oak, facing a plain stone altar under a stained glass window, which portrayed St Catherine of Siena in the style of Sir Edward Burne-Jones. The saint, clothed in Dominican habits, held a bouquet of lilies and a crucifix, which she contemplated with downturned sorrowful eyes. No furnishings remained in the chapel, and the light from three lancet windows in the North wall fell evenly, in a soft, gauzy haze that left the barest traces of shadow along the sparse mouldings of the stonework. Clusters of slender pilasters along the walls flowered into a curious vault, where painted angels curled up between the ribs like grazing insects. In the middle of the day, when the distant sounds from the playground were pin-pricks in a tapestry of silence, Stephen felt the trace of troubles far greater than his own, which had sought relief in this place and also found it. Taking Sharon's essay from his briefcase, he glanced up at the serenely sad St Catherine, and felt that he was entrusting his anxiety not to the saint only, but to the vanished congregation over which her image once presided.

Whatever peace he had gleaned from the surrounding atmosphere was shattered at once by what he read. In the neat girl's handwriting that had so often thrilled him Sharon told the story of Miranda and Caliban.

Miranda came to the island with Prospero. And while Prospero was there what could she fear, since he was king over all enchantments? She could save herself for the days of peace and knowledge, the days of Ferdinand, because she felt in her heart that one day Ferdinand would come. Why did they take Prospero away? She never knew; she was a child; her only friend was Ophelia and Ophelia too was a child. No one had warned them against Caliban, and often they would play with the brute, who gave them sweets and toys. Miranda pitied him, took pains to make him speak, taught him each hour one thing or other; when he did not (savage) know his own meaning, but would gabble, like a thing most brutish, she endowed his purposes with words that made them known. And what purposes were they? First, to lie with Ophelia, with which purpose Ophelia agreed because she loved him; and then to lie with Miranda, which Miranda would not do. So Caliban was angry with Miranda, and vowed revenge against her. Now Caliban had friends and family. They lived in their own cave in the same tall cliff-face where the girls were housed. People came from many places to this cliff, and often they made their holes especially dark and mysterious, so as to pursue in secret the customs that they had followed back home.

One day Caliban invited the girls into his cave. Through the door Miranda saw Caliban's fellows, three of them, waiting to make use of his trophy. They were gabbling in their brutish language, and looking Ophelia up and down as though she were a bargain. There was strange music and a sweet smell, and Miranda warned Ophelia not to enter. Be not afeared, said Caliban, the cave is full of noises, sounds and sweet airs that give delight and hurt not. And Ophelia was enchanted and crossed the threshold into that place, from which she emerged silent and trembling. Only on the next day did she cry. But she would not speak of what had happened, and still she would lie with Caliban, who had promised to marry her when she came of age, and who meanwhile gave her those special sweets for which the craving always increases as the pleasure declines.

Then there came to the island a new band of savages, sailors from the Baltic Sea, speaking another brutish language, and offering miraculous gifts of trade. Their goods were people – those imported to begin a new life, and those exported, to work as slaves across the seas. How excited Caliban was to meet them, and for days he strutted up and down on the cliff-face, singing 'Ban' ban' Cacaliban has a new Master, got a new Man'. For the first time money was within his reach, and as luck would have it he had a most precious thing to sell. Just how much they paid for Ophelia there is no knowing. But she went with one of them, who promised her a new life in a place where Caliban would come to join her, and where she would meanwhile be safe. For they had told her that she was in danger: not only for her bad habits, but for breaking so many of the rules that other children – those lucky enough to have parents to look after them – have no difficulty in obeying. Ophelia was frightened, too frightened even to say goodbye to her friend Miranda, or to warn Miranda against evil spells.

So now was the time for Caliban's revenge. Often he waited for her on the cliff-face, enticing her with smiles, saying that with his long nails he will dig her pig-nuts, show her a jay's nest and instruct her how to snare the nimble marmoset. Miranda scorned these promises. At first the woman they had appointed as her mother defended her, shut the door against the monster, told her to resist his temptations, to turn instead to her books so that one day she might flee this place of vile enchantments. But then this woman she called Mum found a new man, a drunken sailor who had come with his crew to install themselves in that place where lodging was free and all the bills were paid. This sailor made no secret of his lust, so that the woman she called Mum pushed Miranda away. She wandered with her books in distant places, visited parks and libraries, wondering all the while how to rescue the true Miranda. A very shallow monster, she thought this Caliban to be. Afraid of him? A very weak monster, a most poor credulous monster… But then winter came, it was cold outside, and where could she go when the door was locked against her?

Setebos forbids his worshippers to touch their women, or his women to be seen with men. He tells the women to stay hidden in their caves, in those dark corners full of spiders' webs and whispers. But girls who do not worship him, girls who have never enjoyed a family to protect them, girls like Ophelia and Miranda, who go unsheltered to school and come unsheltered back again, to a place that is no home – such girls can be captured, either by love as Ophelia was captured, or by force. It happened only twice, that the true Miranda, drugged and despairing, watched the false Miranda squirm in their forced embraces. But she struck a deal with them all the same. Leave her alone, and she will keep quiet about it. Now there are two of her, and the one who keeps quiet is not the one who was defiled. The one who keeps quiet still can say 'by my modesty (the jewel in my dower) I would not wish any companion in the world but you.'

75

Stephen sat shaking in the cold chapel, his tears dropping onto the paper and smearing the ink of Sharon's fountain pen. Above him St Catherine of Siena gazed at the cross on which the god of pity died. And surely, thought Stephen, that god was never resurrected.

'So it has happened,' he said aloud. 'It has happened, and the fault is mine.'

He recalled the first essay she had given him, about Catherine and Heathcliff. It was obvious now that the essay was an appeal for rescue, and he had let it fester on his desk through the long Christmas holidays. She had tried again, and this time with a declaration of love. But because he had done nothing what he dreaded most had already happened, and the damage to Sharon's heart was damage to his. Groaning aloud, Stephen wandered in the cloister and the corridors, clutching the key to the Chapel in one hand, and Sharon's essay in the other.

Chapter 11

Farid Kassab and his brother walked with slow and reverent steps to school, it being seven years to the day since their mother died. In the evening they were to gather around her photograph and recite the Surah Ya Sin, saying 'exalted is He in whose hand is the realm of all things, and to Him you shall be returned.' Meanwhile, their father suggested, it is fitting to pass the day with cheerful thoughts, to be grateful for life and its troubles, and to know that the light that shines brightly on Jamila shines softly also on you. Farid had taken this advice to heart and was looking forward to the lunch-break, when he had resolved to show some of his poems to Mr Haycraft and to enjoy the mysterious solidarity that radiated towards him from his teacher's kind brown eyes.

A shaft of pale January sunlight shone on the brick and grey-stone houses that lined the road to St Catherine's Academy, pointing like a finger to the gate of the school. Farid enjoyed the cold, which reminded him that he lived now in a safer place, that he had a future before him and would pay back his debt. He recalled the oven-heat of Basra, the surges of fear, the angry fighting, the shouting crowds, the noise and fret of their street with its jumbled houses of concrete blocks and corrugated iron. How serene, dignified and self-confident by contrast were the streets of Whinmoore, and even the Angel Towers, which he admitted to be, by English standards, something of an eyesore, compared favourably with the tower blocks of Basra, piled one on the other in defiance of every regulation, and smelling of garbage, urine and fear. Entering the school by the side door, he took those thoughts into the classroom, saying goodbye to his brother who was in the class below. Without a doubt, Farid believed, he was lucky to live in Whinmoore, and only in two respects had life disappointed him – the death of his mother, and the disappearance of Muhibbah Shahin. And from both of those events he took inspiration too, since they concerned the realm of angels.

One of Farid's poems bore the title 'Angel Tower'. 'In the tower of darkness,' he wrote, 'shines the angel. In your room the heart's rose opens to her light.' He described her as a falling star, as the moon drinking sun-wine, as the sun's rays focused in a glass, as a burn etched in the heart, as the wand whose touch brings sight to sightless eyes. He borrowed shamelessly from Hafiz and Rumi, spun images together like candyfloss, piled rhyme on rhyme – towers, flowers, hours – all the time seeing her enthroned in a realm of purity from which she looked down tenderly on his efforts.

Mr Haycraft stopped him in the corridor. He was looking pale and his eyes veered from side to side disconcertingly.

'Farid,' he said. 'Do you have a moment?'

'Yes, sir. I was hoping we might read together.'

'We'll go somewhere private.'

Mr Haycraft had the key to the chapel, and when he had ushered Farid through the door he locked it behind them and gestured to a pew.

'Is it OK to read the Koran in a Christian church, sir?'

'Of course it is. But actually that's not the reason I brought you here.'

Farid blushed, mentally rehearsing all the ways in which he might have incurred his teacher's displeasure.

'Yes, sir?' he asked.

'It's about Angel Towers. We, that is to say the staff, are concerned about something.'

'About what, sir?'

Farid felt a shiver of apprehension, as though his teacher would discover in him some crime of which he himself had not been aware.

'About girls who live on the estate.'

'Girls who live on the estate,' Farid repeated quietly.

'Are they entirely safe there, I mean safe from people who might abuse them, capture them, force them to do things against their will? I apologize for asking this, but I am fond of you, Farid, and I know you will tell me the truth.'

It was obvious that his teacher was referring to Muhibbah Shahin, though for what reason Farid could not guess, since the girl had left St Catherine's three years ago, when Mr Haycraft was not yet on the scene. Farid's instinct was to protect her honour, to deny that the angel of light could be captured, abused or forced against her will into anything, and certainly not into marriage with some diseased old geezer in Waziristan. Here in his satchel, along with the Koran, was the sheaf of poems he had written in proof of her purity. In his confusion he looked down at his hands in silence. It was quite wrong of Mr Haycraft to intrude in this way on something so sacred, something that concerned only Farid, who would protect his angel from all polluting ideas.

Mr Haycraft shifted nervously for a while and then got to his feet and walked up and down the aisle of the chapel. Only once before had Farid visited this place, when Mr Haycraft had given some of the juniors a guided tour, recounted the stories of St Catherine of Siena, and said learned and touching things about the Gothic architecture. Farid particularly remembered his teacher's way of describing the mouldings around the pointed windows, as 'crystallised light'. How he had loved Mr Haycraft then, and how he resented him now. All of a sudden one adoration had been put in question by the other, and the contest was unequal. If he must choose between Muhibbah Shahin and Mr Haycraft he would choose the angel above the man.

Farid looked up at last. A feeling of desolation rose through his body and gathered on the rim of his eyes. He had struggled hard with the Arab habit of weeping, and knew that there were many tears to be shed that evening – sweet, soothing tears, unlike those that were seeking an exit now. He swallowed, tried to speak, and the words would not come. At last the tears flowed, and the words with them.

'A pure girl, sir, cannot be forced to anything. She would rather die.'

Mr Haycraft looked at him long and anxiously.

'I wish it were true, Farid,' he said in a whisper. 'I wish it were true.'

'It *is* true, sir. I know it is.'

'I am sorry. I did not mean to upset you.'

There was a long silence. The boy raised his fists to his face and pushed back the tears. On an impulse he reached into his satchel and took out the poems.

'Sir, I meant to show you these.'

Mr Haycraft shook himself as though wrestling free from demons.

'Not now, Farid. What are they?'

He shot a haunted look towards the boy, who was holding out the sheets with one hand while pressing the knuckles of the other into his face.

'Poems I wrote. About that girl.'

'About that girl,' Mr Haycraft repeated in a whisper.

He took the sheets with trembling hand and turned away while reading them.

'I know they're no good, sir,' Farid offered.

Mr Haycraft was silent.

'I wanted only to say what she means to me.'

With his back still turned Mr Haycraft whispered 'In the tower of darkness shines an angel.' Then, swinging suddenly round he handed the sheets to Farid with a brusque flick of the hand.

'Thank you for showing me these Farid. Let's discuss them tomorrow. There is some lovely, some lovely....'

He tailed off, walked quickly to the door of the chapel, and beckoned to the boy to follow him. As he unlocked it he whispered 'thank you', but so softly that Farid could only guess at the words. And Mr Haycraft hurried away from him into the heart of the school, leaving Farid with the thought that his teacher was after all just an ordinary person, and one whom it would be a mistake to love.

Chapter 12

Jim Roberts could tell Stephen nothing about the social worker who had brought Ryan Williams to school except that she was short and plump, with cropped brown hair and dingy features, and was called Mona, Groaner or Fiona. He imparted this information during a lunchtime talk devoted to 'racism awareness', in which an official from the City Council's office of community relations addressed the assembled staff on the need to deal sensitively with cultural differences. Jim sat at the back of the staffroom, rocking back and forth with ostentatious splutters of amusement, as the official – a young man in casual dress who spoke the same grammarless English as Stephen's pupils – explained that what might be truant in a white kid might equally be home education for a kid from Pakistan. 'Notice,' said Jim in a loud whisper, 'the use of "white" as a term of racial abuse.' The image of the abused Sharon caused Stephen to grip Jim's arm and stare wildly at the mute faces assembled for their hour of ideological instruction – faces of people who had learned to live with the official lies, who knew how unprofitable it was to quarrel with doctrine, and whose triumph was to rescue some child, of whatever race, creed or class, from the pitiless dominion of morons.

'I'm not feeling so good, Jim. I've got to go home.'

Jim gave him an enquiring look.

'You've gone a bit wan. And who wouldn't, listening to this bullshit?'

'I've just the one class. Fourth year English at 2. Are you free then? Can you read them something? Harry Potter, say, *His Dark Materials*. Or show them the video.'

'As long as I can tell them it's shit.'

'Feel free, Jim. And thanks.'

Stephen slipped away, bent over with anxiety. He dialled the contact number for the child social services, and was given an address in George Street, where the visitors responsible for Angel Towers were based. The bus into the city centre was empty and he stared in desolation at the streets of Victorian houses through which it passed – many boarded up, or with front gardens piled with rubbish. Curtains were drawn in most of the windows, and behind those curtains a new form of life was briefly clinging, a nomadic life that had found this niche in a foreign country without discarding its ancient ways.

Stephen was a child of his time: he believed in the value of immigration and half accepted the official doctrine that such conflicts as arose from it were caused not by the suspicion and insularity of the incomers but by the racism and xenophobia of their hosts. Confronted with the intransigent bigotry of the Afghan fathers, however, he had begun to doubt this.

The bus stopped frequently at traffic lights, when he could snatch glimpses through roughly draped curtains of a life that refused to be openly known. In one house the curtains were drawn apart to reveal a television showing pictures of a shouting crowd. But the room was empty of people, and the other windows were dark. Two doors on, gaps in the downstairs drapery revealed bearded men huddled in a circle. A book was open on a low table, and one of the men, whose beard flowed down the buttoned front of his smock to his belly, was running a long finger from right to left along the page. In an upstairs room two women in burqas sat facing each other, motionless, lit from above by a strip-light that edged their black drapery with silver. Women behind veils and nose-guards; men behind beards; children who were gathered behind curtains and who sat in his class as though startled by daylight – everywhere the gaze that could not be met, the eyes that would not be followed.

And on the edge of this mystery Sharon, the foal abandoned by the herd and watched by eyes that refused to show themselves. As Stephen thought of this a groan started within him and sounded through the bus. The driver looked round before driving on as the traffic lights changed. Stephen left the bus at the next stop and walked with troubled thoughts to the address in George Street.

The Department of Community Services was housed in a featureless modern building composed of glass and concrete strips, set among decaying nineteenth-century facades. He found himself in a room plastered with cheerful mission statements and pictures of smiling multiracial children under smiling multicultural suns. He tried to communicate the urgency of his business to the distracted young secretary who greeted him, but he had no name for the person he wished to see other than Mona or Fiona. The rest of his story was one that he found hard to tell.

At the mention of Angel Towers, however, the secretary nodded, as though acknowledging that his tale might have a grain of truth in it, and asked him to wait while she made enquiries. He sat in a plastic chair staring at a notice about benefits. It was hung on the wall between two other notices, one in Arabic script and the other in what seemed to be Polish. Stephen assumed that their message was the same. The sight made him anxious. As a mere Englishman he was, in this environment, one of the dispossessed.

Iona Ferguson was as Jim Roberts had described her: short, plump, in her thirties, with a round unsmiling face framed by short brown hair. She was dressed in a long green tunic of some artificial stuff, which came down over her grey trousers as far as the knees. She looked at him coldly as though he were intruding into her private affairs, and made no move to shake his hand.

'We'll go to my office,' she said, and turned abruptly round, as though her words were not an invitation but a rebuke.

Her office on the floor above overlooked the street, through long metal-framed windows that could not be opened. There was a desk with a computer, a few papers and a telephone. A filing cabinet stood beside the desk, surmounted by a plaster-cast figure of a cat. On the wall facing the window was a large poster, from which four men wearing dark glasses and leather jackets pointed their sightless faces defiantly at the observer. Above them was the word 'Metallica', in which the M and the final A were stretched to form bolts of lightning. He remembered Metallica from his Oxford days, when he had been forced to overhear the sounds of Heavy Metal from the adjacent room on his staircase. It had been a relief when, in his final year, he had been able to move out of college into a house where he was the only undergraduate.

Iona Ferguson gestured to a chair beneath the poster and he sat facing her across the desk.

'How can I help?'

'I'm Stephen Haycraft, a teacher at St Catherine's. I gather you asked my colleague Jim Roberts to make discreet enquiries about Sharon Williams, who is one of my pupils.'

'I did,' she said. She was eyeing him curiously, as though to penetrate his disguise. 'It is a routine matter for every child in care. Whenever it comes to our attention that the domestic arrangements have changed, we try to forestall any trouble. If you have anything to tell us Stephen, it will certainly be useful.'

He assumed that surnames were never used in the world of social work. But it was harder for him to speak, when his status as the one authority in Sharon's mutilated life was so abruptly snatched from him.

'What domestic arrangements do you mean?'

'When we put Sharon with Mrs Williams, when was it, seven years ago now? Mr Williams was still around, and it was as near to a stable household as you are likely to find in Angel Towers. Apparently Mr Williams left quite some while back and there is a new man, a Polish guy, moved in – one reason why the boys are upset. When this happens young girls are at risk, as you will appreciate.'

'I do appreciate. And I wish I didn't.'

'So what has Sharon told you, Stephen? You can call me Iona, by the way.'

She leaned back in her chair and gave an abrupt mechanical smile. He noticed that her small brown eyes, which were closely packed against her nose, had been outlined with mascara. There was a hint of henna in her hair, and her coral pink nails bore the mark of a professional manicurist. There were other signs too, that Iona had tried to improve her appearance, struggling to make the best of nature's gifts, and in the course of doing so, spoiling them. And he thought with a pang of Sharon's quiet blemished beauty, which shone through every coating of neglect.

'She has told me nothing,' he said.

'Well, that's good to hear. I assume you are in a position to ask her the right kind of questions?'

'If you mean can I ask her directly whether she has been raped, then the answer is no.'

She discerned his bitter tone and looked at him for a moment in silence.

'Of course you are her teacher only,' she said. He did not like the word 'only', which seemed to imply that he might be something more.

'I happen to know she has been raped,' he said, and a hot flush suffused his face.

'Oh? By whom?'

'By a gang of foreigners, I suspect Afghan or Iraqi, who live in Angel Towers.'

Iona sighed and wiped a small hand across her brow.

'You will appreciate Stephen that every time we put an Asian family into Council accommodation we have to cope with racist attacks and insinuations. It is our policy not to believe this kind of thing until there is proof.'

'Suppose there were proof. What would you do?'

'Well, we could go to the police of course. But we would first of all move the child to safe accommodation elsewhere.'

'That is what you should do with Sharon. I beg you to do it. Now.'

Iona sighed again and shook her head.

'You tell me she has said nothing. In which case I don't see how we can act.'

'There is a way of saying nothing, Iona, which is also a way of saying everything.'

'Perhaps, if you are very intimate with Sharon…'

He interrupted her angrily.

'She didn't speak to me about it, but I have the evidence in something she wrote.'

He reached into his briefcase for the story of Miranda and Caliban. But he recalled the incriminating words with which it ended, and hesitated. At last he detached the first page and put it down on the desk. Iona held the sheet out long-sightedly in front of her.

'Nice handwriting,' she said.

And she read aloud the first paragraph, pausing from time to time to look at Stephen quizzically.

'Well,' she said, 'this is a clever child with a pronounced streak of fantasy. I am sure she is a pleasure to teach. But you can't honestly expect me to take this seriously as evidence of rape. And listen to this for racist language: *Miranda pitied him, took pains to make him speak, taught him each hour one thing or other; when he did not (savage) know his own meaning, but would gabble, like a thing most brutish, she endowed his purposes with words that made them known.* Strong stuff.'

'It's a quotation,' said Stephen, 'and a very clever one.'

'A quotation?'

'Yes. From Shakespeare, from *The Tempest*, the play that features Caliban and Miranda.'

'So I was right, then. Listen Stephen, you will appreciate that we can't act on something like this. It is not evidence of anything save the girl's fantasies.'

'So you are going to let the matter drop, even though it is you who raised it?'

'Not at all. I appreciate your coming to see me. You wouldn't have come without a reason. And I am going to go back and explore. We'll keep an eye on Sharon, and if there's anything suspicious we will act. If necessary we will alert the police.'

Iona talked on in a relaxed way, referring to other examples of girls at risk, of girls who had gone astray, of girls who had disappeared, so that Stephen could not resist the thought that it is easy to take attractive girls out of circulation by putting them into care. One of Iona's examples especially troubled him. Moira Callaghan had been taken into care at the same time as Sharon, being like Sharon the victim of drug-addicted parents who had neglected and finally abandoned her. Like Sharon, too, she had been placed with a family in Angel Towers, since it was Council policy to look for working class homes for working class children, not least because it was working class homes that needed the extra money. Moira's adopted parents were real racists, however, and took against the Afghans and the Iraqis in a big way, so that when Moira fell for one of the Afghan boys they started spreading stories of rape, and making the girl's life such hell that eventually she ran away.

The Council tried to keep track of her; they knew that she was on the game for a while in Hull, they heard rumours of her involvement with a gang of Polish mariners, and eventually got wind of her from the British Embassy in Moscow, where she turned up one day, with a confused story of having escaped from the mafia boss who was protecting her. The Embassy had been trying to arrange her passage back to England and her adoptive parents. But within days she had disappeared again, and there was nothing further to be done.

Stephen heard Iona's narrative, sick at heart. For clearly it described the girl whom Sharon had called Ophelia, her only friend in times of true adversity. On the bus back to Whinmoore he re-read the story of Miranda and Caliban. Walking from the bus-stop, in a cold winter evening when every huddled figure seemed to turn from him towards comforts that he could not share, he knew that he should pack up and go, leaving behind him forever this situation that he could not remedy and this grief that cut him to the heart. But by the front door of his block, shivering in her flimsy uniform, stood Sharon Williams. She was pale and agitated and made a point of blocking his passage.

'I just wanna say, sir, you shouldna take that last one seriously. I made it all up, sir. And dunna you never show it to no one else, please, sir. Promise, sir?'

She clung to him and he could not meet her gaze. How could he tell her that he had just done what she begged him not to do? More than anything she wanted respect from him. And at every turn he slighted her.

'Of course I won't, Sharon. But really you should be at home now.'

'Home's where you are, sir.'

She hid from him, and he sensed that she was crying. And when she raised her eyes at last, and the blue-grey irises shone on him through the flood of tears, all his defences fell.

Chapter 13

When you start out of the blackness he is standing there, the packet of condoms unopened in his hand, his face puzzled and uncertain. You are shaking still, but there is a little corner in your fear where reason has entered. He finds it difficult to look at you, now that your eyes are open. His own eyes are dark but somehow distant, as though captured by hidden thoughts. The flesh is smooth, nut-brown and boyish, and his pale blue cotton shirt above the jeans is clean and neatly ironed, as though a mother somewhere still looks after him.

'You're alive then,' he says.

'Unfortunately,' you reply. 'And anyway, what do you care?'

His face wrinkles, rejecting your words.

'I'm no' the kind of pervert who can fuck a girl when she's dead, man. Or when she's blacked out neither. Where's the fun, if she dunna know what's happening?'

He assumes an expression of transparent reasonableness, as though inviting you to argue the point. You are thinking quickly now. You have only one chance to find a protector on this ship, and this is it. Keep him talking. But it is hard to talk when you feel sick to the core.

'And where's the fun if she knows what's happening and would rather die?'

He looks at you curiously.

'That's what they say. But they dunna mean it.'

'There are vile creeps who think of women like that. But do you really want to be like them – like those two who tried it out on me?'

'You bad mouth my brother, man, and you'll regret it,' he says through clenched teeth. He is coming forward now, as though the thought of his brother has reminded him that he too is a man. This gives you an idea.

'Just hold it. So you can have a brother and still be an animal? Do you have a sister too?'

'You leave her out of it, or I'll kill you.'

'Feel free,' you say, and fix him with a look into which you distil all that you can of female vulnerability. 'Just don't tell her about it.'

He hesitates, offering you an advantage.

'Look, what's your name?' you ask.

'Yunus.'

'Look, Yunus, before you try it out on me I want you to imagine that you are some great thug of a white man, the kind you have always hated because he takes the prizes that you hope to win, and that I am your sister, whose life is going to be ruined and whose family is going to be dishonoured by what you do. OK?'

He reassumes his expression of argumentative reasonableness. You notice that he has put the hand holding the condoms into his pocket.

'OK, but see the girls normally dunna have nowt family. That's the whole point. We're the only family they has. There's no honour involved, see? Except what we decide.'

'There's the difference. I do have a family. Let's assume it's a family like yours. They are not going to be happy with this.'

'Yeah,' he says with a shrug. 'But I dunna give a fuck about 'em, do I?'

'I'm not asking you to feel anything about my family. Nor even about me. I just want you to imagine your sister, going through what I'm going through.'

His eyes shift uneasily from side to side and he purses his lips.

'So what's your name?' he says after a moment.

'Catherine,' you reply. You have always liked the name, which was that of your best friend at school. Even now, saying it aloud, you feel a soft breeze from the dormitory where you lay side by side, sometimes in her bed, sometimes in yours, reading aloud from *The Wind in the Willows*. It is the first comfort that you have felt on this ship.

'Here's the deal then, Catherine. We dunna talk about families. We leave my sister out of this. And what happens is just between you and me, right?'

You cannot suppress a bitter laugh.

'And if what happens is rape?'

Again his eyes shift from side to side.

'It's rape if you make it rape. For fuck's sake. It's up to you.'

'The philosophy of Yunus, in three sentences,' you return. 'Ask your sister if she agrees.'

It jolts him.

'I said to leave her out of this.'

'Fine, if we can agree the other terms.'

'I'll say this for you. You've got guts. There's none else on this ship would put up with that much fucking cheek.'

'It's why I'm talking to you.'

He looks at you and a kind of experimental acceptance enters his expression. It strikes you that he was not cut out for this career, and you almost feel sorry for him, as he sits on the bunk without touching you, takes his hands from his pockets and folds them in his lap. He is no longer holding the packet of condoms.

'Shit!' he says. He stares at the floor in silence. You notice that the humming of the engines has ceased. The ship seems to be rocking slightly. *As idle as a painted ship / Upon a painted ocean.* With the familiar words comes the image of the classroom where you learned them, at the desk next to Catherine's. You recall her girlish confidences, how she was to marry someone like Coleridge, a poet and a scholar, and maybe make a career as viola in a famous string quartet. You recall her dimpled smile, her quiet laughter and her way of greeting you at the end of each long holiday, putting her arms around your neck and her nose in your hair. Strange that you lost touch when you left for Cambridge and she for the Royal College of Music. Where is she now, you wonder, and has anything like this, anything so unspeakably horrible, happened to Catherine? You weep for Catherine, pitying her imagined woes. You weep and weep, and it is as though the whole world had fallen away from the scene of her imagined violation.

'OK, OK,' he says. 'I'm not gonna do nowt. Just you stop crying.'

There are noises on deck, feet slapping on the metal, machinery cranking, people shouting in a foreign language, Russian maybe, perhaps Polish. You feel a sudden rush of hope. The ship is turning round. The ship has been boarded by the coast guards. The Royal Navy has sent a frigate. There has been a change of plan and you are to be put ashore in a lifeboat. A hundred unfounded stories flit through your mind and put an end to your tears.

'Yunus, can you do something for me?'

He looks startled by your tone and turns to you.

'I'm thirsty. Can you fetch me some drinkable water? And maybe pass me that apple.'

The appeal to everyday considerateness places him in a quandary. You see him struggle for a moment before wriggling from his throne.

'Sure. I'll get some water. No bother.'

He stands, picks up the apple and then hesitates, before throwing it across to you.

'You're fucking cute, Catherine.'

He goes out quickly and locks the door from outside.

What despicable residue of female vanity causes you to get up from the berth and smooth your tear-stained face before the bathroom mirror? What irrational hope of re-joining the world of your ambitions, of putting this vile episode forever out of mind and reassembling not your features only but the neat self-confident soul that spoke through them, causes you to dab cold water on your eyes and on the slight bruise between them, or to take pleasure in the fact, if it is a fact, that no one will notice it? What absurd renewal of trust in your social gifts leads you to accept the presence in the mirror of another face behind your own? And why believe that this Yunus, who is clearly the weakest member of the gang that kidnapped you, has any power to keep them at bay? Why especially now, when you realise with fainting heart that it is not the face of Yunus that stares at yours from the mirror, but that of the man with stringy black hair who had already taken a leading part in defiling you? You spin round and shout at him.

'Get away from me!'

And he laughs.

Chapter 14

A woman with a Yorkshire accent answered Justin's call. She told him that, if Muhibbah Shahin is on their list, they can act immediately, provided they receive a call from Muhibbah. The personal emergency line is just that: personal.

'If you have evidence of something wrong,' the woman added, 'then you must report it to the police.'

'But I *am* reporting it to the police,' he protested.

'I can put you through to them,' she responded.

'Do that.'

After a few rings a man's voice told him to hold the line. There followed late night background noises: a burst of laughter, a woman singing in the distance, and a loud crash as though someone had fallen over. Eventually the man returned to the phone, with the words 'how can we help?' Justin realised at once that the answer was 'not at all'. He explained that his assistant had disappeared from his office, leaving her coat behind, but of course that was no crime; he referred to the signs of a scuffle, but they were paltry and inconclusive; he mentioned that she was an Afghan refugee who had been threatened in the past by her family, but of course that was long ago and he had no evidence that the threat was still a live one. His narrative petered out with the assurance that he felt in his bones that something was wrong. To which he was told to bring those bones along for a closer inspection.

'At least,' the policeman added, 'you canna say this sounds like an emergency. Rather summat for the local force. Where did you say it happened?'

Justin gave the address of Copley Solutions, and the policeman referred him to the neighbourhood police station, which was open for public consultation every weekday between 9 and 5. He promised to alert the staff, and advised Justin to ring them to make an appointment the next morning.

Lying on the black leather sofa that occupied the centre of his living room, piecing together what he had learned from this conversation and from Millie, Justin came to the conclusion that he alone was concerned by Muhibbah's disappearance, and that he alone could rescue her. He clenched his fist and beat hard against the back of the sofa, shouting 'I will do it!' But he had neither the knowledge nor the weapons for the task, and the harder his blows the more hollow and desolate they sounded. He would never have imagined that he could be reduced to helpless grief by losing someone whom he had never possessed. Yet the thought of Muhibbah, staring in stoical revulsion, as the unwanted flesh of an unloved man left slug-tracks of desire all over her sweet body, caused him to cry out in jealousy and rage.

After a brief attempt to drown his grief in whisky Justin lay sleepless on the sofa, sometimes listening to Spiral Architect on his iPod, taking a small amount of comfort from 'Black Sabbath' with its tale of 'fictional seduction on a black snow sky', but ending in the early hours writing Muhibbah's name again and again in his notebook.

97

Arriving for his appointment with Chief Superintendent Peter Nicholson he felt haggard and grim. To his consternation he was shown at once into the Superintendent's office, which was at the rear of the building, overlooking a small garden of shrubs. He had hoped to be held at bay by a secretary, so as to work up resentment towards the person who was keeping him waiting. But the unsmiling officer who rose to meet him put Justin at once in his place, as someone with a heap of qualifications and not an ounce of power. It was not only the round youthful face above the smart jacketless uniform that spoke of Peter Nicholson's rapid rise to the position of Chief Superintendent. There was a brisk application of manner, a way of making prepared statements and impeccable summaries, that revealed a perfectly digitised mind, an advanced piece of office software that was able to replace the fallible human in every conceivable bureaucratic task. Superintendent Nicholson had already absorbed all that there was to know of the case of Muhibbah Shahin, had put together a summary of the relevant law and best practice, and was busily ticking boxes almost before Justin had accepted his invitation to sit down.

'You will appreciate, Mr Fellowes, that our powers in matters of this kind are strictly limited,' he said after giving his expert review of the facts. 'Whether or not you agree with the report of Sir William MacPherson, which accused us of being 'institutionally racist', you will understand that we must now take special care that no well-meaning member of the public can use this charge to make our job impossible. We live in a multicultural society, Mr Fellowes, and we are committed to sensitive policing. Different communities and different cultures among us see things in different ways. You will remember the headmaster of a school, not so far from here, who insisted that Muslim children should obey the same rules as whites, and that the alternative to integration was disintegration. Well, it caused quite a stir in its time, and the imams united in calling for his resignation. Muslim children were, in their view, Muslims first, and British only by adoption. The Headmaster, you will recall, was condemned as a racist and eventually dismissed from his post. Naturally we don't want any of that on our watch.'

'Does multiculturalism mean accepting forced marriage, abduction, honour killing, and slavery?'

'You misunderstand me, Mr Fellowes. We have already cautioned Ms Shahin's family about this. We cannot assume that a crime has been committed, however, until there is sufficient evidence to warrant an investigation. A quarter of a million persons go missing every year, and most turn up in the end. Meanwhile our rule is sensitive policing. The Afghan community has customs concerning marriage and the family that we, or some of us, do not share. You say that there were signs of a struggle when Ms Shahin left your office, and it is of course significant that she left her coat with her mobile phone behind. But you also say that she appeared later at her rented accommodation, in the company of a man, to collect her belongings. For us to assume on such slender and conflicting evidence that she is being abducted would be to invite the charge of gross prejudice. Of course, we can send someone to inspect your office, and to give a professional opinion as to whether a struggle occurred. But there are struggles and struggles, Mr Fellowes. An embrace can seem very like a fight, if you get my meaning.'

Justin did get his meaning, and his gorge rose at the implication. Everything about Muhibbah could be put in question, but not her purity, not the thing she had wrapped up so completely in herself that no one could take it without taking all of her. But behind this vivid thought came another: that Muhibbah belonged indeed to another culture, that all her eager sallies into the modern world had not broached the inner sanctum where the gods of honour and purity reigned. In this the Superintendent was right: to assume that Muhibbah had been abducted was to assume that she had been removed from a place and a life where she belonged. But she had belonged to nothing and to no one around her. Always, even in the most intimate moments, when she had allowed her eyes to rest on Justin and a brief flutter of tenderness had appeared in their depths before plunging back into darkness, even in those moments the real Muhibbah was elsewhere, beyond his reach and unobtainable.

He stared at the photographs on Superintendent Nicholson's desk: the smiling face of a pretty wife, the teenage son in a rugby shirt holding a silver trophy high above his head, the clumsy looking daughter in her graduation gown, the incontrovertible testimonies to success in the art of belonging. Justin had never achieved that success: had never wanted it. And his love for Muhibbah was the proof.

Sensitive policing, the Superintendent reassured him, meant dealing sensitively with Justin too. The police would certainly keep an open eye and mind, would welcome any information that Justin might from time to time acquire, and would be ready to take action as soon as there should be an indication of foul play. In proof of his impeccable intentions, the Superintendent gave Justin a telephone number, which he could call at any time. And as he shook hands he looked glaringly into Justin's eyes, as though challenging him to find fault with anything that had been transacted between them. Then, for the first time, he smiled – a quick, theatrical flash of good humour, which signified 'problem solved'. And the problem was Justin.

All the rest of that day Justin sat at his desk, the plans for the carbon-neutral houses spread before him. He stared gloomily at the chair in the corner from which Muhibbah had gone, rehearsing every possible interpretation of her mysterious behaviour. Only at the end of the afternoon did he recall the clinching piece of evidence, which was that her computer too had vanished. Why had this slipped his mind? He reached for the telephone, and began to dial the number that Superintendent Nicholson had given him. But he quickly replaced the receiver, arrested by a disturbing thought. Would he be reporting a theft? And would the police be looking for her now, not as the victim but as the perpetrator of a crime? From this too he must protect her.

Chapter 15

The two grey-green blocks of Angel Towers stood in an arena of bare concrete, in one corner of which was the remains of a children's playground. Struts that had once supported a metal slide were twisted together like crossed fingers, and the sawn-off remnants of a climbing frame stood vigil over a heap of litter. All the ground-floor flats had been boarded up and sprayed with graffiti. The wheel-less frame of a bicycle lay across the path between the towers, and heaped against the walls were black rubbish bags, plastic bottles, a grease-covered cooker and a disembowelled mattress from which the rusting springs hung out like entrails. Outside the entrance to Block A two shopping trolleys were jammed against the wall in a close embrace. Justin had to hold them back with one hand while pushing on the wired glass door with the other.

The afternoon sun shone into the hallway, glinting on a bank of vandalised letterboxes. Next to them was an intercom with a hundred buttons, five for each floor. Beside each number was a space for a name. One or two of these had been filled in, but most were blank. Muhibbah had once said how nice it was to live with Angela and Millie, after five years on the eighth floor of a Council block. Her family were unlikely to have moved, so Justin had only ten addresses to explore. The first four of the eighth-floor bells in Block A produced no response, while the fifth awoke a male voice that shouted in a language that Justin guessed to be Polish. The five 8th-floor flats in Block B all responded to his call in Yorkshire English, and none had heard of a family called Shahin.

Justin returned to Block A and took the lift to the eighth floor. A corridor ran the length of the building from North to South. On the side next to the lift and stairwell were the two doors of larger flats, which faced the three doors of smaller accommodation across the corridor. It was to the first of the larger flats – number 8/1 – that Justin, after a moment of doubt, addressed himself. The door, which was scuffed and smeared and looked as though it had been repeatedly kicked, was without a nameplate. The bell was broken and made no sound. Justin bent down to peer through the letterbox, but it had been blocked up from inside. He was about to turn away when he heard a slapping noise inside the flat, and a faint sound of music. He knocked hard with his knuckles on the door.

In truth Justin had no idea what to say should he stand face to face with one of Muhibbah's family. He felt no fear, only a deep desolation at the thought that he might never see her again, and a pressing need to speak of her to someone for whom she mattered, even if that person were her enemy. When the door opened at last, he found himself confronting a man whose angular face seemed to be made of hardened steel, with charcoal rubbed into the crevices. Behind him was a dark interior where two large women wearing veils of white muslin were kneading dough on a wooden table. The only words that occurred to Justin were 'does the Shahin family live here?' to which the reply was an intensification of the man's hostile stare.

103

The two women looked up from their work, and a door opened in the background darkness, revealing a dishevelled young man in a T-shirt. The music came from the room behind him – a woman's voice wailing on the word *Habib*, darling, another of the love words with which Muhibbah taunted him, saying she would never allow him to use it in its feminine form, *Habibah*, unless, perhaps, he pronounced it as he should. But the guttural 'Ha' defeated him, and from behind the screen of her impregnable language he sensed Muhibbah looking on his love with mocking curiosity.

He repeated his question and the young man came quickly forward to interpose himself.

'Who are you?' he asked. Justin recognised the even features, the steady eyes, the smooth skin and delicate straight nose of Muhibbah.

'My name's Justin Fellowes. Muhibbah Shahin works in my office; but she seems to have left without an explanation. I gather she used to live here; maybe she has been in touch with you?'

The older man spat disgustedly and turned away.

'We don't know anyone called Muhibbah,' the young one said.

'Oh? But you resemble her so closely. You could be her brother.'

In the hidden recesses two men raised their voices. Justin assumed the language to be Pashto. One of the women was eyeing him across her veil like an alarmed animal. There was a sweet smell of cinnamon in the air, and the walls were hung with lengths of cloth that flapped a little in the breeze from the doorway. The flat seemed full of objects that demanded an explanation and could not provide one. There were some spherical trinkets of silver, on a little cabinet veneered in velvet. A long stick with an ivory handle lay on a narrow table against one wall.

Small cubical boxes covered in gold leaf were stacked in one corner. And on the doors, carefully painted in ornamental script, were passages of Arabic – perhaps verses from the Koran. It was an uncompromisingly inner place, a place of privacy and closure – *Haram*, as Muhibbah had taught him, forbidden, as was everything of herself that she did not explicitly give. A queer vertiginous feeling came over him, as though he stood on the edge of an abyss. He looked in silence at the young man, who returned his look with a frown.

'We don't know her, I said. Satisfied?'

He closed the door slowly, withdrawing his face by degrees and keeping his eyes fixed on Justin, as though to memorise the features for some future use.

Justin stood without moving for a few moments, and then walked slowly away. He descended the stairs with irresolute step; their walls of greenish wash were scrawled all over with graffiti and from time to time he paused to study them, though they made no sense, having only an oblique relation to written words. On the fifth floor he passed a girl going in the opposite direction. She was slim, blonde, fragile looking, and was wearing the uniform of St Catherine's Academy. She was out of breath, and staring fixedly ahead as though in flight. He wondered why she did not use the lift. Afterwards he recalled her pale pretty features with a strange feeling of sadness, as though it were she and not Muhibbah who were asking to be rescued. And in truth he had no more grounds to think that Muhibbah was interested in his protection than to think the same of that girl.

After this visit everything in Justin's life changed. He had glimpsed in that dark interior the antidote to all his dreams. What was the purpose of cleaning the world, when the reality was Angel Towers? Why provide eco-friendly houses for the middle-classes, when the old mess fell into the hands of newcomers determined to exploit it as it was? Why litter the landscape with wind farms and the roofs with solar panels, when the only effect was to encourage the belief that resources were inexhaustible, and mankind could go on squeezing into every available corner of the earth? And why devote your heart and soul to loving and protecting a single person, when that person refused to belong to you or to the place that was yours?

A mood of cynicism overcame him. He began to neglect his work, and to lose interest in the scheme for the carbon-neutral houses. The loss of Muhibbah's computer had thrown the office accounts into disarray, and he could not bring himself to rectify the matter. Instead he spent his days staring into the corner where she no longer sat, and where her accountancy textbook still lay on the desk above a little stack of papers. And in the evenings he would wander from pub to pub until he had drowned the thought of her, or sit with his iPod, listening to his favourite bands.

Ever since his teenage years Justin had treated Heavy Metal as his fortified refuge, into which he would retreat as into a castle keep from the rabble that had breached his walls. Ordinary pop-fans were defeated by the fierce asymmetries of Metal, ordinary guitarists had neither the skill nor the understanding required by the soaring melisma of the solo guitar, ordinary drummers would fall from their perch under the machine-gun kick-back of the drum kit. And as for the vocals and the lyrics that were wrapped in them, these were like venom under the tongue – to be spat, shouted, forced out from throat and larynx like the primeval curse of a once usurped but now revenging deity. Justin had received his musical education at a minor public school, had learned piano, classical guitar and the basics of harmony. But it was only when he encountered the world of Metal that the urge to create, to combine, to plunge into the musical flux and to splash there side by side with his peers and rivals, really took hold of him.

He was not a good singer, but he could croak with the best of them, and at every stage of his life he had found a small band of enthusiasts with whom he could get together for a gig. He loved the feel of the bass guitar on his neck and fingers, he loved the rushing bass lines that would emerge, when the whole tonal spectrum lay bare like a plundered landscape before him, its places of rest wiped out by the savagery of the solo guitar. In Metal, he discovered, harmonies were no longer confined by a key or a mode. The stacked chords in Metallica, for instance, didn't work like the added note chords in jazz, to impart a kind of direction-less haze to the melody. They were destinations, redoubts secured against the enemy, places from which the raid could continue across the whole of musical space.

Justin was not given to hero-worship. But a photograph of the Norwegian bassist Lars Norberg, stepping from black curtains into the searing white glare of the stage, occupied a special place on the wall of his bedroom. He studied Norberg's virtuoso bass lines, aspiring to match them but always falling short. And he listened in wonder to the tracks made by Spiral Architect, the group that Norberg founded way back in 1995. The rhythms in Spiral Architect were not the regular four in a bar of Rock or Indie music, moving the herd forward through pastures of comforting grass. There were bars with five beats, six beats, seven beats or seven and a half. There were frenzied riffs in which a single chord, altered up and down by a semitone, was arpeggiated across bar-lines, flung at the drum kit like a rag doll thrown to a dog, mangled and torn to shreds and yet still retaining its vulnerable and poetic expression like the ghost of the murdered Petroushka.

And then there were the lyrics: not the highest poetry, to be sure, but touching something otherwise rarely visited in Justin, an inward loneliness, a hurt masculinity, a need to assert himself against the soft machine. Already at university, when he first got involved in environmental causes, joined protests against animal experiments, adopted a vegan diet and wore long hair in a pony-tail, there was a Viking streak in his temperament that sided with the warrior bands and the carnivores.

Metal was his way of expressing this. It was the armour in which he sallied forth to battle, singing with James Hetfield and Metallica 'of Wolf and Man'. For his real battles were not with the polluters and the animal abusers, nor were they fought on behalf of the gentle causes that had united the student body against the Chief Executives and the profiteers. His real battles were with himself. He fought against the soft and indiscriminate compassion through which he kept all commitments at bay. He had been happy at Copley Solutions, not because of the work but because, settled into a routine of doing good, he could go on caring for no one but himself. He knew this, and therefore would turn away from time to time, to look inward to the frothing pool of loneliness.

When Spiral Architect sang of 'the kind of lie/ to subdivide, petrify, dehumanize,/ Spinning, twisting, circling on,' he joined in the song and made it his own. He too had been spinning, and the humane causes that fed his complacency were also a denial of his inner self. Women had seen this. It was why Cait-lin had been important to him: it was not the philanthropic businessman whom she had loved but the angry adolescent who emerged armour-plated behind the lance of a bass guitar. And it was from this angry masculinity that his love for Muhib-bah was born.

108

As the autumn drew on, therefore, and the pain of Muhib-bah's exit began to ease, Justin turned ever more frequently to his guitar. He had nimble fingers, and could span the whole range of the bass with the Phrygian scale on E in less than three seconds. He got together again with the band in which he had played, Mike the solicitor and Dave the physics teacher on guitars, and Kieran, who had done time for drugs but was now a successful electrician, on drums. There was a club, the Crustafarian, in the City Centre where they played every other Thursday, and a small crowd of metallurgists would come to hear them.

At first they tried to play numbers that the audience knew. But except for a few solid classics, like Metallica's 'Master of Puppets', in which Mike and Dave had worked the two solos to perfection, the music defied their powers of imitation. Melodies and chords charged into and alongside each other so closely that no line could be easily disentangled from their twisted rope. Justin began to write the words himself, and to sing them aloud in short broken phrases. Kieran would often sing along with him, at a fourth below, and once the others had grasped the chord sequence they would clamber into the flow like eager soldiers falling into line against the enemy.

In his songs Justin ran headlong towards the devils who tormented his Muhibbah; he surrounded her with electric walls and sheets of lightning; he shot paralysing chords and spikes of melody into the imagined bodies of her captors. And from the wreck of his emotions he built the image of a new self, of Justin Fellowes as the primal male. One evening in December, after a day's rehearsal at the weekend, the band performed the song of which he was most proud, 'The Disappeared', at the Crustafarian. It began with a slow accompanying figure on the bass, a web of fourths over two octaves, introducing phrases of jagged melody which suddenly clattered into a full assault, as the drum-kit entered under the crucial words.

You appeared from nowhere
You disappeared to somewhere,
And now there is revenge,
Their revenge and mine, Habibah…

And when singing that last word on B, over a sus chord on E, he at last perfected his pronunciation of the 'Ha' that summarized Muhibbah.

The audience applauded loudly after this performance. One woman, who was in the habit of sitting close to the band along-side the small square of floor reserved for dancing, and who stared intently as though at a religious ritual, made her feelings known with a loud yelp of excitement and a burst of frenzied clapping. Justin had often noticed her, on account of her total involvement in the event: she came alone, spoke to no one, and sat at her table with a gin and tonic, eyes fixed on the band. Her large round face, which she embellished with eye-shadow and powder, had a look of defiant loneliness, and when she stood up and her pale green tunic fell across her substantial form like a curtain, she made a regal impression, as though waiting for the world to bow before her, yet uncertain whether it would.

In the interval that followed 'The Disappeared' she came across to Justin and introduced herself as Iona, a long-time Metal fan, who had been struck by that little word, that multicultural reference, which had lifted Justin's song out of the Anglo-Saxon ghetto and into the real world in which all of us are foreigners. As they talked Justin felt a surge of sympathy for this lonely

110

person who had survived as he had survived, by hiding behind a façade of official philanthropy. And when he learned that Iona's job as a social worker took her frequently to Angel Towers he wanted to be her friend.

They began to meet for the occasional drink or dinner and as spring approached Iona, who lived alone and did not cook, would drive him in her Land Rover to a little place on the edge of the moors. In this place was a restaurant that had become popular by offering a view of farmland criss-crossed by dry-stone walls and punctuated by tree-fringed farmyards of stone. But since Justin had installed the wind-farm next door only a few customers came out from the city.

The place appealed to Iona, because it was situated on the edge of things, and manifestly dying. She made it clear that, unlike those who were stuck in grooves of fruitless nostalgia, she at least was moving on. Justin greeted this information with a comfortless smile. He too was moving on, not from Muhibbah, but from the life that preceded her and which she had thrown into disarray.

He doubted everything he had done, the wind farms included. Did the fear of global warming justify the aesthetic pollution that he witnessed in the failing light from the restaurant window? What if the whole thing was a fraud? The newspapers had been full of stories about the manipulation of statistics by those defending the global warming story. Justin had no confidence that the stories were untrue, and in any case was beginning to revise his attitude to ecology. The environment, he thought, is degraded by nomads – by the people who graze the meadows to death and then move on.

He had sensed this in Angel Towers. But he too was an example: moving from one flat to another, from one girlfriend to another, and always restless, always consuming, always alone. To find the one person who matters, to settle down with her, and then to care for the beauty and the lastingness of the home that you make together – that, surely, was the solution. We protect what is ours, and we do so by loving it: and when we lose what is ours, as the villagers on the edge of the moors had lost their landscape, then we cease to care. Love and beauty, only these two mattered, and he repeated it to himself in the words that she had taught him: *Habb wa jmal*, the two things for which people die. She had said it with a smile, taunting him with that unpronounceable 'Ha', which stood proxy for the unpronounceable being that was hers.

All those thoughts would run through Justin's mind as Iona talked of her life as an active social worker and a passive metallurgist. She had been drawn to both pursuits at a university in the Midlands, where she had studied sociology and where she had been involved, like Justin, in left-wing causes. She had been chairperson for a while of the university Lesbian, Gay and Bisexual Society, not that she was particularly lesbian, she gave him to understand, but because she wanted to work for a new society in which people were no longer singled out for their sexuality or made to feel suicidal because they did not fit in. And she had been a keen follower of Metal for just the same reason, which is that men, in her view, needed an outlet for their macho feelings, so as to let off steam without doing damage.

She had gone into social work partly in reaction to her own dysfunctional family, her dad being a philandering bank manager, her mother a silent couch potato, and her brother a layabout who saw no reason to work when he could lie on his bed in his parents' house and claim board and lodging for free. She had seen the bad effect of selfishness and privilege, and she wanted to play her part in shaping the new society, in helping those who had nowhere to turn to, and in establishing a genuinely multicultural working class.

While she talked Iona fixed her eyes on Justin with an expression of lively interest. For the first two months of their friendship he hesitated to speak of what was on his mind. His encounter with Superintendent Nicholson had left him with the feeling that the official attitude to Muslim immigrants was to leave well alone, for fear of the thought police. He had no way of knowing which side Iona would take, in the conflict between Muhibbah and her family. But he knew enough of social work to conclude that the thought police had its headquarters there.

The official doctrine was a mass of contradictions – so he had learned. We were to be feminists, believing in the rights of women, and also respecters of the sharia which, as Justin saw it, made women the property of men. We were to put freedom, tolerance and choice above all rooted values, but also to offer freedom to the intolerant and choice to the enslavers. In everything there was only one measure of what was right, which was whether the old, settled, British way of life forbade it. So women became property by default, for the reason that it was racist to prevent it.

It was not until a cold evening in March that Justin was led to broach the topic of Muhibbah. Iona was a dedicated carnivore, and had agreed readily to a Chateaubriand for two and a bottle of Burgundy. The wine softened her features, and gave a lighthearted and mischievous look to her small brown eyes. She talked gaily of her difficult cases – most of which concerned children taken into care by the Council, and then placed here and there around the city, often in the sink estates from which they would have to be rescued again. She too, over the years, had become cynical, holding on to her beliefs only by default and because no better ones had appeared to replace them. Nevertheless she was adamant that Britain was a racist society, and that we must still do what we can to protect each generation of immigrants from the deplorable desire – which she had witnessed in her parents – to send them back where they came from.

She spoke that evening of a boy, a young Pakistani, with whom she had been involved at university and who, before dumping her in order to a marry a girl from his community back home, had taught her a thing or two about Muslim men.

'For orthodox Muslims the masculine and the feminine are separate spheres, which touch only at the perimeter. It says in the Koran that men are guardians over women, while the virtuous woman is obedient, protecting the man's interests in the home. It is there, for your information, in verse 35 of the Surah called Woman, *an-Nisa'*. I don't say I go along with that. But in my job you have to be aware of cultural differences, and this is the great-est cultural difference of all.'

'But don't you want to rescue girls from that kind of domination?'

'Yes, if they want to be rescued. But most of them don't. It is only domination if it feels that way. For some girls it feels like freedom – to be protected by your parents, and then protected by a husband, sounds like the perfect deal, especially when you are in a foreign country where no one is to be trusted.'

'But what do you do if they *want* to be rescued?'

Something in Justin's tone alerted her, so that she sat back, raised her glass to her lips, and peered at him across the red meniscus with an expression of professional interest. She took a sip, put down the glass and then leaned towards him, her elbows on the table and her face resting on her hands. He was suddenly struck by an attractive quality in her. There was, in her dancing eye and large soft face, a kind of hard-won confidence in her role that had no doubt appealed to that Pakistani boy, and which had been a support to him in the great enterprise of not belonging – the enterprise that was also Muhibbah's.

'Is there some particular person you have in mind, Justin?'

'Yes, someone employed in my office. She might even be known to you, since her family are in Angel Towers. They have already made an attempt to kidnap her. She was managing to live a normal life as a normal modern girl. But she disappeared from the office last summer. I want to find her.'

'And why do you want to find her?'

What was it about Iona that made him tell the truth? The calm, even voice, perhaps, the fact, decided tacitly between them, he didn't know when or how, that sex was off the agenda, the knowledge that things had once gone badly for Iona as they had gone badly for him, and that she, like him, had entered a stage of lonely scepticism, encumbered by stale convictions that she could not quite discard. Whatever it was, he returned her friendly look and said

'Because I love her.'

'What a mistake,' she replied.

'It's a mistake that many people make.'

'But if she has made no effort to be in touch?'

'Maybe she can't.'

'Or maybe she won't.'

'Well yes,' he admitted, 'there is that possibility.'

The thought was cold and cheerless. But Iona had earned the right to her cynicism, and he did not blame her. He told her the basic facts. He described his failed encounters with the police and with Muhibbah's family and he learned that Iona knew a lot about the Shahin family, which was high up in the Afghan community and well connected with the mosque. He learned that Muhibbah had two difficult brothers, who had flunked school and entered the criminal underworld. Nobody in his right mind would mess with a family like that, certainly not Iona, who valued her reputation as an anti-racist and had a branch of her department to run. Once more Justin stared at the truth – that he alone had a motive to rescue Muhibbah.

'But don't you see what she has done to you, Justin?' Iona said, with a measure of urgency.

'What exactly has she done to me?'

'She has captured you, used you, precisely because she could never belong to you. Even if she has run away from a forced marriage, she nevertheless sees marriage as Ahmed saw it when he chucked me – namely, as a contract between families, not a union of hearts. Meanwhile she has to bundle her sexuality into herself, so that it can exchange at the proper price. And that's the bit you can't resist: the call for total protection, and the box of secrets opened at last, just as the contract says.'

She said this not bitterly, but with a slight shaking of the head, to indicate a truth learned the hard way. And she stared down at her hands, wrapped around the glass on the table. Despite all the evidence, Justin rejected her verdict. His love was so pure and unwavering that he could not think of Muhibbah, except as a woman who had already locked his image into that box of secrets that she held against her heart.

'You see,' Iona went on, looking down at her glass, 'we have tried to make a world without sexual difference, a world in which women and men do the same things, obey the same rules, mingle publicly on equal terms. And to do this we have had to suppress our feeling for the other sex. We give up on courtship; we stop trying to make men mysterious to women and women mysterious to men. And the urgency of our passions seeps away. With them it is entirely different. They hide the private from the public, the home from the world outside, the body from its clothes. So the mystery of sex remains. That's why we have such trouble with the vulnerable kids that we take into care. Place a girl with a family of whites and she will immediately fall for the Muslim boy next door, hoping to enter that mysterious world as I did, and doomed to be chucked aside like a puppet when the passion has been spent.'

He recalled the lyrics of 'Master of Puppets': 'Master, master, Where's the dream that I've been after? Master, master promised only lies…' And he became lost in thought.

'Earlier this year,' Iona was saying, 'I had to deal with such a case, another problem festering in Angel Towers. It was a school-teacher came to see me, adamant that one of his kids had been raped. And the proof? A fantasy story about the Asian boy next door, the same old story. And he begged me to intervene, to move the girl elsewhere, as though safe accommodation were to be had for the asking, when all the girl had to learn was the truth that you learn the hard way, as I learned it, namely that there can be a multicultural society, but never multicultural love. Still,' she added, looking brightly up at him, 'I like you so much, Justin, that I am going to help you find your Muhibbah. And who knows, she may be the exception that proves the rule.'

They drove back to the city through the Edwardian suburbs, Iona chatting about the unprecedented demographic changes that had made her job so exciting and so difficult, Justin lost in sombre reflections on the meaning of what she had said. It was at the moment of waving goodbye to her, as she drove away from his flat, that his mobile telephone rang, and he fumbled for it in the raincoat that he carried over his arm, convinced that it would at last be a call from Muhibbah. When he finally extracted the phone it had ceased to ring. But there was a voice-message.

'Justin. It's Millie. Please ring me. It's urgent.'

Chapter 16

Sharon broke away at last, hiding her face in her hands. Stephen stared at her in silence. And then, because she was shivering, he wrapped his coat around her shoulders.

He stood by the door of his flat, at the threshold between the outside and the inside of his life. For three months now he had not known to which of those sides Sharon belonged. All his feelings pleaded for her, and he held on to his shreds of reason with no confidence that they would save him. He watched his hand reach out to brush the hair from her forehead, and it was as though it were the hand of someone else, mocking him with a mimicry of his own desire.

'Listen, Sharon,' he said, 'I can't offer you a home. But if you need protection there are ways of obtaining it. I just need you to talk.'

'I dunna ask for nowt, sir. I only says what I feel.'

'So why can't you talk to me?'

'I only wanna say, sir, the bad things, sir, them things dunna happen to me, not the me what's yours, sir. You inna crying, sir, are you?'

He turned away. In each of us, he thought, is a lake of tears, and a boat, always waiting, moored at its edge.

'Only see, sir, you mustna tell no one nowt, and then I'll be all right. It's what I come to tell you, sir.'

From the corner of his eye he glimpsed her beseeching face, the face of a traumatised child, wrestling for the first time in her life with love and longing. If she would speak to him they might make a sensible plan for her rescue. But she was a girl of keen intelligence; her plan was to have no plans, so that when the crisis came – and surely it was coming soon – she would have no other refuge but him.

'I'll be all right, see. Mum's on her own now. She'll see I'm OK.'

'That's right, Sharon. That's how it should be. I'll walk you home.'

'Like I said, sir…'

'To the place where you live, Sharon.'

She took his coat from her shoulders and held it out for him. He wrapped it again around her and gently urged her down the steps towards the street. She went meekly, like a defeated thing.

Often at the weekends, tired of reading, tired of music, tired of beating his head against the unseen walls that surrounded him, he would walk in the neighbourhood. He enjoyed the firm stonework of the Victorian and Edwardian houses and sometimes sat in the small park behind the Anglican Church, built in stone by an apprentice of George Gilbert Scott. But he had never walked past Angel Towers, and a growing aversion prevented him from looking in that direction. He ushered the girl before him along the alley. They emerged into an arena of concrete, lit by orange sodium lamps that were flickering into reluctant life in the dusk. The two towers rose from a sea of rubbish, their lights glowing high above him behind curtains of grimy lace. Some boys were skateboarding on an improvised ramp of wooden doors. Another was sitting on an old mattress in tears.

The boarded-up windows of a ground-floor flat announced 'Cal Gaffrey is a perv' in orange spray-paint. The vista was forlorn beyond anything he had imagined, and he pressed his hand against the coat that covered the girl's shoulder, overcome with protective emotion.

'Which one's yours, Sharon?'

'Dunna matter, sir. You leave me here.'

With a sudden movement she broke away from him and thrust his coat into his hands. She stood for a moment, her pale skin translucent in the twilight, her eyes fixed on his. Then she ran to the door of Block A, disappearing through a pair of shopping trolleys like a will o' the wisp through reeds. Stephen turned back the way he had come, recalling her provocative words: 'home is where you are, sir.'

Two weeks later there was turmoil at St Catherine's Academy. It was a turmoil that Stephen had seen coming since the beginning of term. Junior boys who attended early morning lessons at the madrasah of the mosque, and who failed to memorise their verses for the day, had been arriving in school beaten and tearful. Mrs Gawthrop, a middle-aged lady as Victorian as her name, who taught history and biology to the juniors, had made a point of protesting to the parents. It had become her personal stand against multiculturalism. She had even gone to the mosque in order to remind the imam that corporal punishment is illegal. The imam refused to talk to her, so she had complained to the police. The imam too had lodged a complaint, saying that it was offensive to his religion and his office to be addressed directly by a woman. Now the elders of the mosque had arranged a demonstration, which had been backed by the sociology department of the local university. The young and controversial Professor Rosebud, acting head of department and professor of social work, had even written to the local paper, denouncing Mrs Gawthrop as a racist and her school as a hotbed of Islamophobia.

Stephen did not accept Mrs Gawthrop's view of things. Of course it was wrong that children should be beaten – though a few months as a schoolteacher had somewhat dented Stephen's conviction in this matter. In any case the controversy was more about the subject of knowledge than the means for acquiring it. When parents regard their faith as their most precious possession, surely they were right to pass it on to their children? And since the school could not do it, the mosque had the right and the duty to do it instead.

So Stephen believed, and he arrived at school that morning half sympathising with the sparse crowd that had gathered in the forecourt. A few men with beards were dressed in the jalabiya and headscarf of the mujahidoun. But most wore English-style suits beneath raincoats and spread umbrellas. A placard declared that 'Islam is the solution' and another, neatly written out on a wooden board with a felt-tipped pen, and held by the polite Mr Ismail, owner of a corner store close to the school, announced that 'the heart of knowledge is the knowledge of God'. Stephen greeted Mr Ismail, who stared for a moment in embarrassment but then smiled and said 'Good Morning'.

In the drizzle of a cold March day the men strove to maintain their serious looks. But squinting and blinking endowed their damp faces with a theatrical appearance. It was as though they were rehearsing for the real event, which was to occur in better weather on another day. The driver of the bus they had hired preferred to stay in his vehicle, which was parked outside the school gates. He would occasionally lift vacant eyes from a heavily ornamented copy of the Holy Koran, look round him as though assessing the weather, and then return to his finger on the page.

In Stephen's view of things, these people had other grievances than the one placed in their minds by Mrs Gawthrop. In countless ways they had seen their customs, their values, their family ties and their religion marginalised, despised and even spat upon. They had come to this country looking for material prosperity and moral dignity. And they found themselves without work, and surrounded by a corrosive nihilism. Surely their first concern must be to protect their children, to implant in them the respect for faith and custom that Stephen had witnessed in the Kassab brothers, but which was – let's face it – absent from the average British child. Were they not right to cling to the tried and tested source of wisdom that they carried with them everywhere and which they would never trade?

As he greeted Mr Ismail, however, Stephen became aware of another contingent of demonstrators, who had emerged from a bus that was disappearing towards the city. Young people in jeans and donkey-jackets, led by a long-haired man in a duffle coat, were converging on the school in a serpentine phalanx. Among them were girls wearing headscarves, surrounding a figure covered from head to foot in a burqa – recruited, Stephen supposed, to show the commitment of the university sociologists to the fight against Islamophobia. Two of the boys held a placard saying 'Don't tolerate intolerance'; others had begun to shout 'Gawthrop, Over the Top' in a rhythmical chant. In matters of the greatest importance, Stephen believed, it was debate and not threat that was needed. And if one side to a dispute should begin to shout abuse, disqualifying all opposing views as a kind of 'phobia', Stephen's instinct was to close his ears against the noise. He walked on quickly into the school, alarmed at the thought of how things might develop.

The Headmistress failed to awaken much interest from the police, who made a routine showing and then retired to a patrol car. She therefore decided to close the school, sending home any pupils who had made it past the blockade. The children were frightened, and Stephen spent the morning conducting them in groups through the shouting melee, reassuring them, as best he could, that the threats were in no way directed at them, and that there had been a misunderstanding which would soon be resolved. After an hour of this he returned to the staffroom with trembling legs and palpitating heart, unable to rid himself of the insults that had been crammed into his ears like corn into the gullet of a goose: racist, abuser, even 'rapist' from the person in the burqa who screamed at him through the cloth and who, to Stephen's hearing, was almost certainly a man.

He took the key from the staff-room and let himself into the chapel. He would sit it out there until the noise had subsided and the crowd dispersed.

The Christian religion was a fleeting and uncertain visitor in Stephen's life. He was the only child in a family of atheists, who viewed worship as a hobby of simple people, like stamp collecting, clay pigeon shooting or model railways. At the time of his parents' divorce, when he was studying for his A-levels in a North-London grammar school, he had read the New Testament and taken to visiting a Roman Catholic church. Later, at Oxford, he had attended evensong in the college chapel, partly to enjoy the singing of the choir, but also in search of a peace that he needed and which always seemed to lie just out of reach: the peace that passeth understanding, as he learned from St Paul and the Book of Common Prayer.

By then he had acquired, from Bach and Haydn as much as from the study of English literature, an acquaintance with the Christian faith and its cultural meaning. He had joined the extensive crowd of believers in belief. The Christian religion, he decided, was the heart of our civilisation. This heart had grown old and weak, and culture had been put in the place of it. But the heart transplant didn't take, and our civilisation, after gasping for a while, had died.

In the opinion of Harry Fisher, the long-haired expert on Virginia Woolf who had been appointed as Stephen's tutor, Stephen was busy with the work of mourning. He was conducting the spiritual exercise through which the grief over one loved thing becomes a welcome extended to the next. 'And that's great, Steve,' Harry had said, 'but after religion what next can there be?' Stephen had no idea. Along with the millions of civilisation's orphans, he was waiting for a revelation that he knew would never come. Yet, in the real troubles nothing else, he believed, had ever offered consolation. For in the real troubles it is not the body but the soul that is threatened. Such, if it deserved the name, was Stephen's faith.

There had been few real troubles in Stephen's life: his parents' divorce, yes, which left him bruised and guilty, believing himself to have played an obscure part in causing it; a love affair at Oxford, which ended in bitterness and jealousy when a rival appeared; his father's sudden death during his final Oxford year; but otherwise only the routine difficulties that lie across the path of a poetic but indolent bachelor. Sharon, however, was different. Here desire wore a mask of duty, and duty forbade desire. Sharon needed help, and refused all other ways of obtaining it: he alone could protect her. But she also wanted him, with an urgency that her situation fully justified, and which tore through the rules like a hornet through a spider's web.

He had begun to imagine himself alone with her, escaped from their situation, able to plant his kisses on that adorable adoring face, and to drive all her demons away. But imagining this he also summoned the jealousy that she did not deserve, the pain of what they had done to her, which was a sword passing through her body into his. And then the tears would flow: tears of anger and humiliation, and an urgent desire to place all this before her, to beg her forgiveness and to show the respect that she longed for, and which was, he knew, the only salve for her hurt.

He looked up at the solemn face of St Catherine, a face expressing another kind of love, in which neither sex nor selfishness had a voice. Humans, he thought, could not rise to such a love by their own efforts but would always need the help of prayer. 'Thrice blest whose lives are faithful prayers/ Whose loves in higher love endure.' So Tennyson wrote. But prayer is effective only for those who believe in it. He wondered if Sharon prayed, if she had ever been taught the words that would break those 'chains of enchantment' that had been thrown around her.

The image came of himself in the role of father, the father she never had, putting her to bed with a prayer. He rehearsed the words of the Hail Mary, imagining that he spoke them above her tired form, that she felt the warmth of his protection and that she fell into a dreamless sleep from which she awoke fresh, pure, to 'a life that leads melodious days', like the girl she wanted to be and whom she tried to create in her beautiful essays. And this image, which seemed to justify all that he felt for her, accused him too of an illicit desire, told him he must find another way of loving her than the one she had slapped down before him as a challenge.

And then a strange thought came to him. As he reached back into Sharon's life, thinking of what she might have gained had faith and piety protected her, why, he asked himself, should that faith have been the Christian one? Suppose she had been adopted by a Muslim family: by the Kassabs, for instance. Wouldn't her chances have been better? Protected by a code of honour and surrounded by an electric fire of prohibitions, she would have repelled her would-be abusers. This weird thought troubled Stephen greatly. He could not think of Sharon as other than the vulnerable, free-minded, poetic creature that she was; to imagine her wrapped and mummified in a spiritual burqa was to imagine another person entirely – and certainly not a person whom he could honestly love as he loved that girl.

He sat for an hour or more with those thoughts, hoping from time to time that some plan of action would emerge from them, but lapsing almost immediately into a corrosive doubt. To do nothing was impossible. But if Sharon kept strict *omertà*, and forbade him either to discuss her case with others or to know in detail what it was, there was nothing – nothing legitimate – that he could do. Maybe the social workers would step in to save her, but after his encounter with Iona Ferguson he had no confidence that such a thing could happen. And to wait for the police to take an interest would be to wait too long. Moreover, to discuss things with the cynical Jim Roberts was unthinkable. So the problem was Stephen's, and the solution nowhere to be found.

The light was fading, and there was silence now outside. He lapsed into mental vacancy, his eyes resting on St Catherine, his hands folded as though in prayer. Gradually it dawned on him that there was another person in the chapel, breathing quietly at the back. He stood up, hesitated and then turned. The oak door was closing, and he watched the heavy keeper of the latch settle against the catch-plate with a clunk of wrought iron. He went out slowly, and took time in locking the door.

He found her crouched in a corner of the cloister that led to the main building of the school. She hid her face from him. Her slight form was pressed into a niche of stone, the knees drawn up, and the arms wrapped around the shins. He prayed that no one would see them like this. But he could not ignore her. When she looked up at last it was with a face rigid and white.

'I werena spying on you, honest, sir. Only I saw you go in there and…'

'And what, Sharon?'

'It's them, sir. Outside. I canna go past them, sir. I was waiting for you to take me. Only you dinna come. I had to find you.'

'You can't sit like that, Sharon. Get up and talk to me properly.'

She jumped immediately from her cocoon and stood to attention before him.

'Sorry, sir.'

'That wasn't a reprimand. I just want us to speak to each other as equals.'

Sharon looked at him for a moment in silence.

'I know that, sir.'

She straightened, fitting herself into her body as though for inspection.

'Surely they have gone by now,' he remarked.

'Most of them, sir. Not all.'

Best not to enquire. Best to take her out now, catch sight of the ones that scare her. But then what? To track them down? To kill? Such thoughts frightened him. But they suggested a more honourable path than the one that she was urging.

'OK, let's go. We'll walk together as far as my place, and you'll go on from there to Angel Towers.'

She reached for her satchel, which she had stuffed into the niche out of sight, and went before him towards the front door of the school. Someone had sewn up the loose hem of her pullover and he noticed that her hair too was more tidy than usual, with the wisps that blew across her face held down with Kirby grips. Perhaps Mrs Williams had remembered her adopted daughter at last. Perhaps she was defending Sharon from the men who had targeted her. It was a comforting thought, but he did not pursue it since it was clear from her every gesture that Sharon was scared. As they approached the door she began to hold back; by the time they arrived there she was cowering behind him, emitting little moans of fear.

The door was on a Yale latch and swung shut when opened from inside. He turned the latch firmly and strode out onto the gravel forecourt. Sharon followed with little steps, clinging to his jacket.

The bus hired by the visitors had been driven away, and there was hardly a sign of the day's demonstration: only a few crushed plastic bottles, a couple of Tesco shopping bags and a broken umbrella. The gravel had been scuffed into heaps and would need combing out by the gardener. A branch had been torn from the old hornbeam that was growing on one side of the forecourt, and Stephen was saddened by this, because the view of that tree from the staff-room was one of his consolations. Then he noticed a group of men dressed in Western clothes, loitering on the corner beyond the school gates. They were eying him curiously and one of them was holding what seemed to be a rolled up banner as though it were a sword, thrusting it from time to time into the air, and uttering a low guttural cry. Sharon was moaning and pressing against him. He thought with alarm of the possibility that some lingering member of staff might be watching their progress across the forecourt.

'It's all right, Sharon,' he said. 'Just walk normally. Nobody will hurt you.'

128

'Canna, sir. Canna walk past them. You gotta take me another way.'

So those were the men, the ones whom he had come to hate, as he had hated no human being in his life before. He looked at them. They were two hundred yards away, four men in their twenties, two with Asian features. They were scowling now, from dark eyes that contained no flicker of friendliness. One of them, taller than the rest, had a squint, and wore a black woollen overcoat; he lounged against a lamppost, his hands in his pockets in gangster pose. Sharon's fear communicated itself to Stephen. He steered her away from the men, towards the old canal that passed under the street a quarter of a mile beyond the entrance to the school, and which was now silted up and clogged with weeds. Alongside this canal there was a towpath, by which they could re-join the road that led to the network of warehouses behind Stephen's flat.

Conscious of the eyes that followed them he walked with awkward steps, veering from side to side and beginning to push against Sharon as heavily as she pushed against him. Reaching the canal, they dropped down some wooden steps off the road-bridge. When her feet hit the towpath Sharon broke into a run. She pulled at his jacket and he began to run beside her. At the next bridge they mounted the wooden steps on to a road that ran parallel to the one they had left. Stephen paused to look behind.

'There's no need to run, Sharon. No one's following.'

She stopped to look at him and in her eyes he read both fear and elation: fear of the others, elation at being in danger with him. Things constantly happened to deepen the intimacy between them, and he wondered how much she intended this. There was no doubt that her fear was real, but had it been necessary to run in that way, side by side, as though in flight from an invading army? He wondered.

129

They walked slowly now. He asked who the men were and why she was afraid of them. As expected, he received no reply. But when they entered the car park behind the flats she suddenly began to speak, whispering between tight lips so that he had to bend to hear the words.

'Bogdan's away now, gone to sea, collecting the goods. It's OK with mum when Bogdan's away. Only today she dunna come home till six. I could sit in your place, sir. I wunna disturb you, just sit there, read your books. Please, sir. Nobody will know.'

'Look Sharon, all this is very irregular.'

Once again she had trapped him into using the wrong words, the truthful words. For 'all this' meant so much more than 'this'.

'Yes, sir. But there canna be nowt harm in it.'

Sharon was true to her word. She sat down at the dining table that he never used and took out the folders from her satchel. For half an hour she bent over her work. Then she took a couple of books from the bookcase across to her place at the table. She read in complete silence, sometimes pausing to write on a piece of paper, while he sat at his desk pretending to work, striving to think of something other than the quiet presence behind him. When he turned at last he saw that she was nodding to herself. She seemed to have recovered from her fear. He asked what she was reading.

'Yeats, sir. 'Byzantium', what you told us to read.'

'How do you find it?'

'It's huge, sir. But it gives me words. Unpurged images of day: that's just how it is, sir. But with me they dunna recede: those images that yet fresh images beget.'

'I know that, Sharon. It is why you should talk.'

'Canna, sir. Better go now.'

130

She rose quickly and had packed her satchel and reached the door before he could get up from his desk. The fear had returned and she stood looking at him with rigid features.

'I'll see you home, Sharon.'

'No, sir. This is home.'

'As you wish, Sharon.'

'I do wish it, sir.'

'I didn't mean…'

But what did he mean? To take her back to the place of destruction, when she was his, a thousand times his? He stood with one hand on the desk, fighting himself. And he remembered the man with a squint, who leaned in his overcoat against a lamppost, eyeing him like an enemy. Suddenly it came home to Stephen that he was engaged with this man in a mortal struggle, that if he lived this man must be destroyed. And with that thought came a great surge of relief. It was as though he had made a decision, and at last was free.

When Sharon turned quickly and slipped with a whispered 'goodbye' on to the stairs, Stephen waited for a moment and then took his coat and followed her. He had to walk quickly to keep her in sight, and by the time she reached Angel Towers, where she melted through the abandoned trolleys into the foyer of Block A, he was out of breath.

He stood by the lift, which was occupied. The illuminated panel showed the carriage stopping at the fifteenth floor. He pressed the button, and studied the ranks of bell pushes on the graffiti-covered wall to his left. Most of the name-tabs were blank or illegible, and he could see no 'Williams' on the fifteenth floor. He entered the lift nevertheless, propelled by a reckless desire to move in her shadow, to find her as she truly was, to trap her and to cut off her flight.

131

The lift smelled of sweat and urine, and its walls were covered in obscenities scrawled in black with a felt-tipped pen. On the fifteenth floor two large flats faced three smaller ones across a corridor. The walls seemed to have been freshly painted in bright yellow, but had already been sprayed here and there with illegible squiggles of graffiti. There was music and someone was shouting at a child. Two of the smaller flats had nameplates beside their doors, and one of them said 'Williams' in Sharon's neat handwriting. Underneath, pasted to the wall, was a lozenge of white cardboard with the name 'Krupnik' scrawled in biro.

Stephen lingered outside the door, not knowing what his next step should be. There was a sound of television, and two of the Williams boys were arguing about the programme. Pots and plates were being moved about. Then a woman, Mrs Williams he assumed, raised her voice above the noise, saying 'turn that thing off, I'm on the phone.' Stephen walked quietly away. Someone had called the lift, so he decided to take the stairs, which were lit by fluorescent lights set in walls of greenish concrete. All the surfaces were covered with the same black graffiti, a repeated pattern that, in its meaninglessness, seemed to exude a bestial anger. It was as though worms had been spat on this wall, spoiling its unclaimed spaces, and preventing any human thought from breeding there. The sight infected Stephen with a chill. To be a teacher of literature now: what a picture of futility. And yet there was Sharon.

He came across her on the eleventh floor. She was crumpled in a corner of the stairs, crying silently. The books from her satchel were spilled on the concrete landing. There were two folders, a battered edition of *The Tempest*, and his own copy of Yeats, which she must have smuggled from his bookcase.

'Sharon!'

He was on his knees beside her. She held her hands close to her face, shaking her head and refusing to allow him to prise her hands away. There was blood between her fingers and the sleeve of her jacket was torn at the wrist.

'Listen, Sharon. I'll not allow this to happen to you. You must tell me who did this and why.'

She dropped her hands suddenly. The blood was flowing from her cheek, which was red from a sidelong blow and cut against the cheekbone. He took a handkerchief from his pocket and dabbed the blood away.

'Why are you here, sir? Dunna let them see you.'

She was moaning again and struggling to her feet. In order to hide his pity he began to gather up her books. She was leaning on the wall, holding the handkerchief to her cheek, and reaching out with her free hand for the satchel. He took the hand in his and led her towards the lift.

'No, sir. I'll walk up.'

She was shaking, and he held her beneath the arm to steady her. She spoke in a whisper.

'Take me to the fifteenth floor, sir.'

He took the weight of her body on his arm and helped her step by step on the staircase. At the fifteenth floor she turned to him.

'You dinna ought to have followed me, sir,' she whispered. 'It was because of you he hit me. And dunna you never go in that lift.'

'Why is the lift so dangerous, Sharon?'

'You go now. Please.'

He stared at her, confused and wretched. She walked alone to her door, where she turned and pointed to the stairs. He hesitated, and then descended with a bleak sense of having intruded without right into Sharon's life. Why did his attempts to respect her end like this, as though the presumption were his? Maybe it was always like that with a precocious child. But it was too late to back off, too late by far. Sharon was his and would be his forever.

Chapter 17

Abdul Kassab had written a letter to the local paper supporting Mrs Gawthrop and St Catherine's Academy. Following threats from local Islamists, he had warned his sons to stay away from school on the day of the demonstration. But Farid's curiosity had proved too great. From the gardener's shed where he was hiding he had a good view of the front of the school, and a sidelong perspective on the crowd.

He accepted Abdul's view, that religious education is not a matter of learning the Koran by rote, but a matter of opening the heart and the mind to illumination. And he acknowledged that the divine light enters through many pathways, the Christian Gospels being one of them, the poems of Rumi another. But how, he wondered, can you convey this tolerant vision to people who believe that faith lies in recitation, ritual and the five times daily utterance of words that Allah must surely be fed up with hearing by now? He did not despise the crowd of protestors, though he found it hard to believe that Islam meant anything very much to the belligerent young people who had joined them. And as for that woman in a burqa, his blood boiled to see her, as she shouted disgraceful words that no woman should use, while hiding her mouth behind a screen.

Abdul viewed the burqa and the niqab as forms of unforgiveable rudeness and he approved the French law that banned them from the public realm. In the society that has offered us protection, he told his sons, people are face to face, confessing to their faults, meeting each other's eyes, and in general showing that they are free, fair and accountable. We commit a terrible offence by hiding our faces when others so openly expose themselves to judgment. The headscarf, yes, but not the veil. Farid thought of Muhibbah Shahin, who had worn neither garment, but nevertheless held her face away from the world, as though she would return your look only in some private sphere to which you were not – yet – invited. That, in Farid's eyes, was purity – a quality instilled in the flesh, and not worn in a strip of cotton.

There was a commotion, and the noise increased to a roar. The door of the school had opened and Mr Haycraft was standing on the steps, four frightened children in the St Catherine's uniform clinging to his jacket. His face was pale, and he put his hands out in front of him as though to soothe a pack of dogs. Then, holding his head high, he walked towards the gates of the school. Farid had not entirely recovered his feelings for his teacher. Given the opportunity to enter the sacred sphere where Muhibbah Shahin was sovereign Mr Haycraft had decided instead to desecrate it, and Farid had found it hard to forgive him. Nevertheless it had been tacitly decided – by whom Farid was not sure – that their readings of the Koran would continue, and Mr Haycraft had even, on one occasion, volunteered some comments on Farid's poems, suggesting that florid imagery of the Persian kind is not enough to lift a mortal human subject into the realm of spiritual perfection. Being a fair-minded person Farid took this criticism to heart, and set about improving his style.

As Mr Haycraft led the children past the crowd, therefore, receiving the insults as though leaning against a storm, Farid was able to look on his teacher objectively, as an imperfect but in many ways admirable human being, a gentleman who lived by the rule of kindness, and who was now exhibiting a rare dignity and courage. For a moment he was tempted to come out of hiding and walk beside Mr Haycraft, just to show these hooligans the contempt in which he held them. But, unlike his teacher, he would be the legitimate target of revenge, and revenge, he knew from his Basra years, was both a way of life and a pact with the Devil – the Devil from whom Colonel Matthews had rescued them.

The teacher left the children at the bus stop. Seeing him return the crowd abandoned the small amount of restraint that the children had inspired in them. The woman in the burqa had somehow got the word 'rapist' into her head, and was shouting it through the cloth in a rhythmical chant. Others were hurling more cogent insults. One smooth-shaven man in a two piece suit and tie repeated *la illah ila allah* in a tone almost too soft to be heard, but with a constant admonitory wagging of his finger in Mr Haycraft's face. The teacher entered the school, returning instantly with another six children. He was visibly flustered now, and ushered the children before him as though they might protect him from the worst. After five trips to the bus stop Mr Haycraft returned through the crowd with bowed head and shaking hands, and Farid's heart went out to him. He cursed the tormentors of this innocent man and for a moment meditated revenge against them. But his father's strictures against revenge again took up their habitual place in his thoughts, and he sat on the gardener's pile of hessian sacks in a fit of melancholy, dreading what this conflict might mean for the school and for his own hopes of a solid English education.

He sat thus for an hour. The crowd gradually dispersed, most of the men climbing into the bus that had been parked beyond the gates. When he judged it safe to emerge, Farid pushed the glass door of the hut ajar. But to his surprise Mr Haycraft was once again standing on the steps. A girl in the school uniform pressed against him, clutching his jacket and hiding her face in its folds. When she looked up at last, her face emerging like the small head of a tortoise from its shell, Farid saw that it was Sharon Williams, the frail sixth-former who lived somewhere in Block A at the Angel Towers. He watched as they advanced with wandering steps towards the gates.

A group of men were loitering in the street beside a lamppost and Mr Haycraft was being pulled away from them by the girl. The two kept colliding awkwardly as they stumbled along. There was a peculiar intimacy in her way of pulling at her teacher, and also in his way of falling against her, with his arm constantly around her shoulder, and his head bowed over hers. On reaching the road they did not turn right towards the Angel estate. They went in the opposite direction, towards the canal, a place of ill repute where no pure girl would ever go.

Farid waited a while before taking the direct route home. A strange thought had occurred to him, and he entertained it as you might entertain a visitor with whom you hoped for no future connection. Suppose Mr Haycraft were in love with that girl. And suppose he wanted to believe her to be an angel: the faint English shadow of Muhibbah Shahin. Would that not explain his mad assault in the chapel, his desperate search for reassurance, his need to prove that a girl can be pure without fighting for her purity with every inch of her being as Muhibbah Shahin would have fought? And would he not know, in his heart, what a mistake he was making?

Abdul Kassab had often reminded his sons of St Paul's advice: 'whatsoever things are true, whatsoever things are honest, whatsoever things are just, whatsoever things are pure, whatsoever things are lovely, whatsoever things are of good report; if there be any virtue, and if there be any praise, think on these things.' And only on these things, Abdul always added. So Farid dismissed the thought that had briefly visited him. Nevertheless, he cast a glance at the two receding forms and shook his head.

Chapter 18

The man had taken up position like a sentry at the bottom of the stairs, his black overcoat buttoned over his chest, his arms folded across it. His dark hair fell across his brow in greasy strings. The cheeks were clean-shaven, the mouth curled and cruel. He fixed Stephen with one eye, while the other roamed as though dissociating itself from the business. Stephen was suddenly struck by the absurdity of his situation: his new life as a public-spirited teacher ending like this, in a fight to the death with a criminal.

'You leave my fucking bitch alone, man, OK?'

Stephen, who had half expected an *allahu akbar* and a knife in the heart, was taken aback by the broad Yorkshire accent. When he found words it was as though he were reading from an official summons.

'It's you who need a lesson in leaving people alone.'

The man laughed contemptuously.

'Is teacher going to give me a lesson?'

'In this country assaults are matters for the police.'

The man stepped forward and put his face into Stephen's.

'You go to the police and she's dead, see?'

'What a simple worldview.'

Stephen, exhilarated by his own contempt, prepared for blows. But they did not come. Instead the man looked at him with something like astonishment.

'You wanna be dead too? I'll put you on the list. No bother.'

A woman carrying shopping bags entered the foyer, and crossed to the lift. Stephen ducked past his opponent, saying 'then we'll meet again'.

The man walked slowly up the stairs, singing a tuneless phrase to the words 'Smack my bitch up'. If, at that moment, Stephen had had a weapon he would have used it. He lingered for a second and then went back with grieving heart to his desk and his laptop. He searched the Internet for the words the man had sung, and brought up the video clip of the Prodigy. It showed scenes of assault, rape, defecation, drug injection and nudity in which women are jostled, thrown about, scorned and humiliated, over an accompaniment of computerised rhythms, and with the four words tunelessly repeated from time to time as though by a disembodied observer. This was the world of Caliban, the world that existed all around him, into which his poor Miranda had been dragged. Stephen sat at his desk in a state of impotent rage and sorrow.

A few things had become clear to him nevertheless. Mrs Williams had a lover, Bogdan Krupnik, who was in the shipping business and often away. Krupnik had targeted Sharon, so that, while he was at home, the girl was cast off by her adopted mother. Meanwhile Sharon had been assaulted and raped by at least one of a gang of men: a gang that had already abused and destroyed her only friend. In the culture where this gang was at home, the Holy Koran and the Prodigy were of equal and opposite standing. The same person who recited the words 'Mankind, fear your

Lord, who created you from one soul and from that soul its spouse', words the beauty of which had pierced Stephen to the core when Farid Kassab had recited them in Arabic; the same person who respected women of his tribe as sacrosanct and untouchable – that same person sang in tuneless contempt of the women whom he met outside the home. When it came to the English girls in neighbouring flats his philosophy was summarised in those four shameful words: 'smack my bitch up'.

He had assaulted Sharon in the lift, so that she avoided the lift, climbing fifteen flights on the stairwell, where there was some chance of protection. He had seen her fleeing with her teacher from the school where he had gone to demonstrate. He had waited for her, taken the lift ahead of her, and met her on the stairs coming down, there to strike this poor innocent across her frightened face, and to accuse that face of the only thing in it that he could not destroy, which was love. And he, Stephen, who had caused this love, must now respond to it.

At Oxford Stephen had studied the *Duino Elegies*, in which Rilke ponders the all-enveloping plenitudes of being through which our lives are perfected. These are the moments of visitation, the moments of the Angel. And yes, for a solitary poet like Rilke, that is surely how angels must be: an order of reality altogether superior to the human, which nevertheless enters and transfigures our world.

In the Koran too there are angels, beings that move among us invisibly, bearing divine commands. In the Surah of the Virgin Mary it is the Angel of the Lord who stands by Mary, as she clings in her pain to the trunk of a palm tree and wishes that she were already forgetting, forgotten – *nasian, mansian*. Stephen remembers the words, sounding in the voice of Farid. 'The Angel comforts Mary and tells her to shake down the dates from

142

the tree, so that she might go with the infant Jesus refreshed into the world of men.

'Angels patrol the pages of our holy books, always sweeping in with aristocratic ease and unblemished immunity to suffering. We cannot call to them, cannot command their help. As Gabriel says in the Surah of Mary, "we descend not, save by command of your Lord".' He recalled Farid's innocent poem, Angel Tower: the angel whose light opens the rose of the soul. For a moment, in his distress, Stephen had imagined the poem to be about Sharon, and he recalled the moment in a hot flush of shame. But of course, Farid was merely snatching fragrances from the Islamic perfume-chest. Sharon's essence could never be captured in that way. She belonged to another, more believable order of angels – the order of victims, beaten into corners, holding on, through their humiliation, to their inner purity of heart. Such an angel might be sent with the same redemptive task as those higher beings of Rilke or the complacent go-betweens of the Old Testament and the Koran. Such an angel might bring a message, 'special from me to you', as Sharon did: the message of love, carried unsoiled against her heart through all the assaults and terrors of her journey.

But then there was the man who claimed her as his bitch: was there more to their relations than force? Suppose that, like Kundry in *Parsifal*, Sharon was the humble angel in one life, only because she was the trampled whore in the other. Stephen could not refute the idea, but he could not live with it either. It brought into his heart a wretchedness beyond any he had encountered. He slammed his fist on the desk; he paced around his living room; he flung himself on the bed and groaned aloud in torment. But the idea remained and he knew that he must act to extinguish it.

143

He rang Iona Ferguson, who agreed to meet him the next morning, when Stephen had a half-day's break from school. She came at once to fetch him from the secretary's office and sat him down with slightly flustered gestures. Without allowing her to speak he recounted in outline what had happened when he had accompanied Sharon home from school. He did not mention the hour-long interval in his flat. Iona nodded as she listened, and seemed altogether better disposed to believe him. He noticed that her office was in disarray, with files heaped on the desk. Her brown hair was tousled and her face without make-up, to Stephen's eyes a great improvement, for this woman was not a doll but a life-force, someone who shone a light of her own across the swamp of human failure, and seemed both to lament and to rejoice in what she saw. She leaned towards him as he spoke, her fingers stretched out on the desk.

'Your story figures, Stephen. You appreciate we can do nothing direct until the girl is prepared to testify. But there is something nasty going on at Angel Towers and that girl is caught up in it. I will arrange a visit and see what Mrs Williams has to say. And as for the guy, we already know about him. He is one of two brothers; they came here as refugees from the war in Afghanistan. But they have Yemeni passports, are more Arab than Afghan, and are not refugees at all; they are certainly not entitled to Council accommodation, and we are going to eject them, when we can. Meanwhile I shall alert the police, who I guess will want a witness statement from you, should they decide to act.'

'And why wouldn't they decide to act?'

She looked at him grimly and shook her head.

'For the same reason I wouldn't decide to act, if I were in their shoes, which I am not quite.'

'And what reason is that?'

'Look, Stephen: we are dealing with closed communities, people who are driven to the edge by the white majority. Who wants to be accused of racism or xenophobia at a time like this? Certainly not a policeman or a social worker. It would be the end of the line for a superintendent, and not much different for me.'

'So we have to sacrifice innocent girls to political prejudice?'

'I wouldn't call it prejudice, Stephen. Just a commendable habit of seeing the general in the particular.'

Stephen absorbed her message as best he could. It had only one important implication, which was that he alone could rescue Sharon. He must act now or not at all. He went to school that afternoon in the hope of finding her, not knowing what he would say when they met, but hoping that it would all become clear, once they were face to face on neutral territory.

She was not in class, and the few remarks he had prepared about the Brontë sisters fell flat, precisely because she would have understood them and taken them to heart. He had come to depend on her, not only in his private life, but also in his work. When she was there he recovered his interest in English literature, his delight in words, and his belief in culture as a redeeming force. When she was not there the ghouls of modern life returned: not Facebook, Twitter and the chattering swarms in cyber-space only, but the things that he had been discovering in recent days – the things that passed for music, entertainment and literature in the world of his pupils, and which were accurately summarised in those four vile words: 'smack my bitch up'. Only through the Kassab boys had he acquired any sense that poetry had a place in his pupils' lives. But it was the poetry of another time, another place, another language – and most of all of a religion that sat uneasily in the world that Stephen knew.

When the lesson was over he wandered in the school for a while, listened to a rant from Jim Roberts about the previous day's demonstration, and then made his way home. She was waiting outside the block of flats, standing to attention as though posted there. As he approached she did not look at him. Her left cheek was red and swollen, with a plaster stuck at the top. Her expression was taut and withdrawn. And when he stood before her she suddenly shot out a hand, in which a little sheaf of papers was held far out as a hot coal might be held with tongs. He took it, and she turned away, ignoring his calls as she ran across the street and disappeared into the alleyway.

There were several sheets, loosely folded together. Some were illegible scribbles; some were fragmentary quotations from poets in a scrawled version of her hand. The pages were crumpled and tear-stained. One of them contained a laconic poem:

On floor number eight,
You meet your fate.
On the fifteenth floor
You can take no more.

On the final page the writing changed to her neat, firm classroom script, and took the shape of a letter:

Dear Stephen,
Am I allowed to write your precious name? I think so, because this is
the last letter I send you. Soon things will end. Therefore I must tell you
what I feel. You think I am a child. No, Stephen. I am a woman, your
woman. I have known this for half a year now: I have known it from
the light that shines from your face, from your words, from your smiles.
(I am sorry that I blush when you smile at me.) I have grown as a gift

146

for you – a surprising gift in a horrible place, like a golden ring on a
dust heap. When they have finished, there will be nothing left to give.
But for this last moment I am entirely yours.

I should have braved them yesterday, and left on my own. Truth is,
I was jealous. I had seen all the others leave under your protection, and
I wanted that protection too. I wanted it so badly. I loved running with
you by the canal. I could have died then. This is not silliness, Stephen.
It is truth.

It was a love letter, a suicide note, and a final bid for help. If
he did not act now, it would be too late to save her.

Chapter 19

Fainting is not an option. All you can do is scream. He clamps his coarse hand across your mouth and pushes you on to the bunk. He is tearing at your shirt, your skirt, your knickers, and his loose eye seems to swivel uncontrollably, as though set in frenzied motion by his lust. In the corner of the cabin the monkey wrench is lying where Yunus kicked it. But your arms are pinned. Somehow he has managed to wriggle out of his trousers, and with one thigh he is forcing your legs apart.

You avert your eyes from his face, your thoughts from what is happening. You imagine this as the moment before death, the moment of those prayers relinquished long ago. Again there is the image of your mother. She had a way all her own of looking hurt by your behaviour, as though it had been aimed expressly at her. She would curl up in her corner, pull her books, magazines and needlework closer as though to affirm their status as her last reliable defences, and then complain softly with downturned eyes. Never did she raise her voice. Always she would speak as though calling the universe as witness to her patiently suffered trials.

Another thought follows. This monstrous insect gripping you and smearing you has not said a word. When he briefly takes his hand from your mouth you do not resume your screams. Instead you ask 'Do you speak English?' like the demure Alice, confronting some inexplicable monster in the forest of her dreams. He pauses, and a glint of astonishment enters his functional eye.

'Course I speak fucking English.'

'Then tell me by what right you are doing this.'

'Because you fucking asked for it, bitch.'

'When did I ask for it?'

'When you fucked my brother, bitch. Yunus inna having nowt I dunna have, man.'

'Did Yunus say he had done this to me?'

'Shut the fuck up,' he replies, clamping his hand across your mouth. 'Yunus and me, we share everything, right?'

He begins to jab at you like a terrier digging a rat. Soon he will be inside you. This thing that you gave to Finn (a bad mistake), to Mick (a mistake too in its way) and yes, you mustn't deny him, that sweet boy Michael whom you met on holiday in Spain, who was studying to be an architect, who followed you back to England in vain and who was probably not a mistake at all – this thing that must be given since it is the whole of you, is about to be stolen and trashed. You manage to scream through the slipping fingers around your mouth. There are footsteps running. Someone is opening the door from outside. Yunus is shouting, angry words with that strange sound of a finger stuck down the throat.

'*Ya Hassan, aish ta'amal?*'

Hassan rolls quickly onto the floor. He locks the door from the inside. In that moment your strength returns. You too are off the berth, you have the wrench in your right hand and hot hatred in your heart. When you bring the wrench down on his right ear it is with all the force in your body. He falls against the bunk with a groan. You hit again in the same place, and blood wells from the ear. You let go of the wrench and reach across with trembling hand to unlock the door. It is immediately kicked towards you. Yunus stands for a moment, a bottle of water in one hand, a mug in the other. Then, dropping them both, he falls to the floor and puts an arm round his brother.

'You fucking bitch. You've killed him. You've killed my brother.'

He reaches out to slap your face and you duck away from him, throwing yourself shaking and weeping on the berth. You had placed what little hope you had in Yunus. Now the fate of Laura Markham, MA, ACA, Junior Partner Milbank and Co., is sealed. But to your surprise Yunus, who has lifted his brother against the side of the bunk, and applied a towel from the bathroom to his ear, does nothing further to punish you. Instead he goes out into the corridor and shouts a few words in Arabic. Hassan's dingy companion comes running to his master with a patter of canine footsteps, and together the two men lift Hassan on to the bunk, Yunus pushing you out of the way as though you were an intrusive pillow.

'Stop crying, bitch. What's your trouble compared with his?'

You curl up in the corner of the bunk, and fiddle with your torn shirt and bra. Your breasts are sore and there is a taste of blood in your mouth, where Hassan's hand had pressed the flesh against your teeth. Hassan is conscious and muttering, his head lolling slightly from side to side. Yunus picks up the wrench from the floor and shakes his head before handing it with a few words to the dog, who goes with it down the corridor.

Yunus looks at you, still shaking his head. There are tears in his eyes.

'You dinna had done this, Catherine. I coulda been good to you. Now we're fucked. Hassan!'

He puts his head in his hands.

'He asked for it. I didn't mean to kill him.'

You realise as you speak that it's a lie.

'We've got to get him to hospital. Iqbal!'

The dog comes running. Yunus mutters a few words, and he again disappears down the corridor. Now Hassan is moaning and holding his ear. Catching sight of you, he gives a threatening grimace, and attempts to move in your direction. Yunus holds him down.

Iqbal reappears, followed by a large, pot-bellied man in a uniform of smudged white canvas. He has a broad face in which the eyelids seem to have been cut in as an afterthought, the watery pupils barely visible behind their rims. His hair is long, greasy, unkempt, and his thick lips and broad squashed nose contrast oddly with the tiny slits of his eyes.

'Ya you fuckvits,' he says, spitting the words. 'I get only trouble since you come. Contract says collect in Kaliningrad two days' time. Now you vant I turn back to Hull. Vot the fuck this about, you tell me.'

You are off the bunk and standing firm before him.

'Are you the captain?'

He laughs. It is a sinister, hollow sound, as though a door had been opened on some other creature laughing deep inside.

'You call me captain, ya. I give ze orders.'

'Do you realise I've been kidnapped?'

'You telling me I don't know vot goes on in my ship? Listen, slut, these fuckers make a big mistake. Pick up the wrong bitch, see. Don't tell nothing till ve're half vay to Denmark. Now they're vorried, say ve gotta stop. And next thing one o' zem is damaged.'

It is Yunus who speaks. He is crying, tears of fear and rage.

'You get us back to Hull right now, Bogdan, OK?'

Bogdan laughs again.

'You want rewrite our contract, kid?'

'My brother is hurt bad. He dies, I kill you.'

'Talk tough to old sea-dog, you make friends with sharks.'

Bogdan's brow wrinkles and his fists clench in readiness. But he is clearly assessing the situation, his eyes shifting from one to the other and his lips moving slightly as though doing mental sums. Hassan groans again, and raises his hand to the towel around his smashed ear. Yunus holds him around the shoulder.

'OK,' he says at last. 'I put you two off this ship.'

'And Iqbal too,' Hassan says through clenched teeth.

'No Iqbal. How I talk to ze new cargo when zey load zem up?'

'This girl too,' Yunus says. 'She comes with us.'

'So I get to Kalinigrad, big Boris comes on board, says "vere's ze juicy bitch I paid for?" I shrug my shoulders and say she vent overboard off Gdansk. Nice one, and a belly full of lead for Bogdan.'

Yunus looks at you, and then at Bogdan. Something in his manner recommends silence.

'OK, Bogdan. But just get moving yeah?'

Bogdan swings away, nursing a private smile. Iqbal follows him. You pick up the bottle of water from the floor and drink from it, standing against the wall under the porthole. Iqbal returns with iodine, bandages and a packet of pain killers; he and Yunus bandage Hassan's head and prop it against the pillow. The ship is vibrating again, and you feel the surge and groan of the propellers as it turns for land. Yunus beckons to you, and you run past him on to the deck.

Your feet are bare, the deck is cold, and a light drizzle wets your shirt. Despair billows out before you, dragging you like a sail filled by wind. You scrape past bulkheads and stanchions, are held up at last against a kind of cabin in white metal. Yunus has pulled you to a standstill with his hand on your arm. You try to wriggle free, but he turns you around and presses you up against the metal wall.

'How far did he get? Tell me.'

'Leave me alone.'

'Tell me.'

'No further than you. And he got what he deserved.'

'You're mine see.'

'I'm not yours or anyone's.'

'If Hassan dies I'll kill you.'

'Good.'

Yunus's eyes seem to wander. He reaches his hands above his head as though summoning help from on high. Clearly family relations are not his strong point. He is rival and double of his brother, protector and accuser of his sister. Where you fit in is unclear. But he is nonplussed, because he wants you as a lover, not a slave.

'Anyway he's a tough fucker,' he says. 'When he gets better you'll be meat on the pavement, man.'

'I thought I was meat in any case. Apparently Boris has paid for a consignment.'

A pained look crosses Yunus's face.

'I seen the kinda cunt you are. You'll wriggle out of it some-how and be back making trouble. We're in deep shit, Hassan and me. They're gonna ask how he got hit, people are gonna look for you and you gonna make trouble anyway. We gotta have a deal. You say nothing about all this and I'll get you off the ship, OK? Yeah, and maybe you'll give me some cred and we can get together.'

You laugh bitterly at this.

'So tell me your plan, Yunus. Without the getting together bit.'

'We'll be offshore in Hull this afternoon. Now you go down out of sight.'

'I'm not sharing a cabin with your brother. Unless you want one of us dead.'

'But you gotta stay below.'

You look at him defiantly.

'I'm not taking orders from you.'

He hesitates. There are tears in his eyes again. How can there be room in your heart for pity? Yet there is something bewildered in Yunus, a kind of plea for indulgence that has never been properly answered, unless by the sister who is too sacred to be mentioned, and whose icon exists in some inaccessible inner space. Always you have had the gift of solving problems, of seeing in a flash what is wrong and how to rectify it, and that is precisely why you are the thing you are – or were, before *this*. Now too you see things clearly. Yunus has never respected women, unless he can hide them in an enchanted inner world, as he hid his sister. Now he has come across a woman in the open. You are the reality that he has always denied.

'Shit, Catherine, I'm on your fucking side. I wanna get you back home, like I wanna get Hassan to hospital. If Bogdan sees you walking around the deck you're fucked, man. Get in there – OK?'

He points to a door in the metal bulkhead where you stand.

'Why in there?'

'That's our cabin, me and Hassan. I'm staying with him below. I'll bring your stuff. You gotta be ready.'

He pushes you towards the door, but with gentle, uncertain gestures, perhaps afraid you are going to scream. You are in a cabin now with two berths. Men's clothes are scattered across the

154

floor and there is a smell of male sweat. There is a CD player and a heap of CDs, mostly hard rock. In the corner under the porthole is a suitcase. Both berths are unmade, but you sit on one of them, shaking still, your mind empty and your stomach sick. The door opens and you start back in fear. But it is Yunus, holding your jacket and shoes in one hand, a bottle of water in the other. He looks nervously to either side of you, then places the objects on the other berth.

'Couple of hours we're in the roads at Hull. Get ready, OK?'

He vanishes, closing and locking the door. The throb of the engines in this deck-level cabin is somehow amplified. You feel it in your thighs, and in the lower part of your body. You writhe away from it but there is no escape. Your heart is gripped by it, your mind is gripped, your soul too. You are reduced to this mad unceasing throb; you have become part of the mechanism, a gear of human flesh, a tender nerve stretched across metal cogs. Sometimes you weep. Sometimes you start up in anger. Sometimes you just sit on the bunk and stare in desolation at an Oasis T-shirt that lies discarded on the floor.

There are footsteps on the deck. There are cries in some Slavic tongue – Polish, maybe Russian. Sacks are dragged on the deck, someone is hammering metal on metal, Bogdan is shouting. There is a sound of winching and suddenly the ship seems to tilt to one side and to lurch round in a tight circle. Yunus is standing in the open door, his dark eyes beseeching, his hands open and held out to his sides. You wish you could hate him, but you can't.

'For fuck's sake get your things on. And stay with me.'

You follow on wooden legs. Out on the deck a breeze is blowing. There is a light of afternoon, with the docks of Hull ranged on both sides of the road where the ship is idling. A thin sliver of red sunlight daubs the grey-green gantries along the seawall. A

boat is suspended from chains and swinging in the air. Hassan
has been placed in it. He is still clutching his ear, and his face is
pale and weary. The chains unwind and the boat slides down to
the water. The bent old sailor with pale skin busies himself with
the pilot ladder, attaching it to hooks in the side of the ship and
letting it fall into the boat. He grips the gunwale and swings himself with surprisingly agile movements over the side. Yunus has
pushed through the crew, who are gathering up the chains on to
the two capstans that house them.

Bogdan's voice sounds from the bridge.

'You stop zere Yunus fuckvit. That slut stay viz me.'

He adds orders in his own language, and two of the sailors
step forward, one tall and burly, wearing white canvas and with
an unpleasant leer, the other small, dressed in jeans and an oil-
smeared pullover, who wipes his face on the back of a dirty hand
before staring at you and reaching towards your body. Bogdan is
descending the stairs from the bridge at a run. You are beyond
tears now, beyond screams, almost beyond awareness.

The two sailors move aside for their captain. Bogdan reaches
out to you, his eye-slits closed tight by the angry swelling of his
cheeks. Suddenly Yunus is there between you, face to face with
Bogdan. He has a knife in his hand.

'You touch that girl and you're dead. She's coming with us, see.'

Yunus pushes you behind him and backs step by step to the
gunwale, the knife held out at arm's length.

Bogdan stands perplexed for a moment, and then bursts into
hollow laughter.

'Ya. So you take ze bitch. You tear up ze contrak. Great. Ze
parting of ze ways. And zis cargo waiting in Kaliningrad: zey
wait and zey wait. And look what trouble old Yunus is in, when
ze big boss in Kabul learn all about it.'

156

Yunus stops for a moment. Your hands behind you touch the gunwale. In a moment you can be over and on to the pilot ladder. But an unaccountable feeling of solidarity attaches you to Yunus. It seems more important to understand why you have ceased to hate him than to figure out your escape.

'OK, Bogdan,' Yunus says. 'I'll bring the other girl, the one you wanted. Just give us a few hours, OK? I'll get Hassan to the hospital and be straight back with the bitch. Marcin can wait for me.'

Yunus pushes you against the gunwale and, understanding the gesture, you swing yourself onto the pilot ladder. There is a vertical drop to the boat below, where the man you hate, still clutching his ear, is looking up at you. Your head is spinning; a hot flush of shame confuses you. How absurd, after all that has happened, that you are more troubled that Hassan can see up your skirt than by the danger from which you are escaping. There is a scuffle against the metal rail above you. Yunus is shouting 'back off', and Bogdan is giving orders. More shouts are exchanged, you are in the boat now, and Yunus is clinging with one arm to the ladder, while fending off the two sailors with the knife. Somehow he gains the boat as the sailors swing themselves, one after the other, on to the ladder. Bogdan is shouting to the old man, but Yunus has him by the throat with the point of the knife below his ear. In a moment Yunus has kicked the boat away from the ship, and taken charge of the outboard motor, steering towards the docks.

You sit in the rear, Hassan in the prow, the old man muttering curses between you. Yunus stands behind you at the tiller, steering with the outboard motor. He lands the boat outside the dockland area, in an oily backwater beside an old warehouse, a shadowy place with no sign of human life, where the sea scrapes its crust of plastic bottles monotonously against the land's concrete rim.

He begins to lift his brother on to a flight of stone steps that you can just discern, and which lead up from the water to an old stone platform. The sailor watches you, and in the fading afternoon light his eyes take on a violet hue, seeming to shine from his skull like lamps. Suddenly you are afraid of him. You must get off this boat at once. Yunus is calling to you.

'Catherine, for fuck's sake, give me a hand.'

The thought of touching Hassan fills you with loathing. But once the brothers have disembarked, the old sailor will take the boat straight back to the ship, with you on board. You have no choice; you are attached to Yunus, and without him you are lost. You go across, and together you lift Hassan out of the boat and on to the steps. Hassan scowls at you, but says nothing. There is that smell of engine oil; you recall the impatient jabbing of his sex against you and again there is the image of a terrier, poking the hole of a rat. You almost succumb to nausea and stumble as Yunus turns back to the boat.

'See you here, Marcin. Tomorrow midday. At this place, OK?'

'No speak English.'

'Yeah, yeah, that's what you say. Just be here tomorrow midday, OK?'

The old sailor shrugs, and remains sitting in the middle of the boat. Yunus leads you away from the water, his brother leaning against him, along a path beside the warehouse. He has taken a mobile phone from his pocket and is giving instructions in a language that you do not recognise. You emerge onto a main road through derelict warehouses, where two taxis are waiting. Yunus manhandles his brother into one of them and turns to you.

'OK you hit my bro, and I dunna like that. But he's a moron and a bastard. I apologize for him. You and me, we could be friends see. Here.'

He reaches into his pocket and takes out a mobile phone and a set of keys.

'These are yours. And this too.'

He hands you the wallet that had been pressed against *The Wind in the Willows* in your pocket. You look at him in silence. In the yellow light of the street lamp his smooth shadowless face seems curiously vulnerable, like the face of a child. You notice the difficulty he has with eye contact. He looks at you as though you were not revealed in your face but hidden somewhere behind it. You see that he wants to touch you, but doesn't dare. Maybe it is the first time in his life that he has been caught in this dilemma.

'Look. You had a fucking bad time and I apologize. If you tell anyone then that's going to mean big trouble for me and my bro. I'm not threatening, see. I'm too fucking scared, man.'

Still you look at him in silence. He takes a piece of paper from his pocket and hands it to you.

'I wrote my number on this. You can ring me when you want. I gotta go now. Dunna say nowt, OK?'

He opens the taxi door and tries to take your hand as you slip inside, but you shake him off. A hurt expression crosses his face.

'You tell him where you wanna go. He wunna charge.'

The taxi draws away and you watch as Yunus shakes his head sadly and then goes to join his brother. You give the address from which you were abducted; the taciturn driver nods and drives into the night. Two hours later you are back on the concrete staircase of the block of flats, letting yourself in to the poky foyer with shaking hands. You are in the bedroom, lying on the bed and sobbing violently, your face pressed into the pillow. And yes, there is another person in the flat.

Chapter 20

It was several minutes before Millie was able to explain herself. Perched on the edge of the sofa, with her hands gripping the fabric, she searched the ceiling with outraged eyes for the words she needed, and her lips trembled over the inadequacy of what they found. The floor was covered with CDs and magazines, scattered from the shelves that had harboured them. The Picasso reproduction had been taken down and propped against the wall. Cushions had been flung from all the chairs. And on the window seat where he had watched as Muhibbah wove her spells around him, was a heap of files, their lever-arches opened and their pages scattered. They were the notes she had made for her course on accountancy.

'Yale locks are no obstacle to professionals, and there was this guy with them, Polish or Bulgarian or something, who looked as professional as they come. I came home to this: the three of them just standing there like they were the landlords. There was the one who was with her when she picked up her things. And another, older and taller, with coarse black hair and a squint. No apologies of course. Simply angry stares, as though *I* were to blame for trashing the place.'

'Did they think Muhibbah had come back here?' Justin asked. For a brief moment he allowed the image of Muhibbah fleeing from her captors: the hair swept back, the dark eyes set on the road, her hopes fixed on Justin.

'Not a bit of it,' said Millie with a shake of the head. 'They were asking whether I had seen an unmarked CD she had left behind. I asked them why they had broken in. They said they were her brothers and were within their rights. After all, she had paid rent she had never used.'

'And did they tell you where she is?'

'Yes, because I asked. And the reply (expletives deleted) was Afghanistan, and none of your business. The taller guy began to ogle me, and that really bugged me. He had a disgusting leer, and for a moment I thought of calling the police. But I dropped the idea, thinking that maybe this information would be useful to *you*.'

'Not exactly useful,' Justin said grimly. 'Except in the way that unwelcome truths are useful.'

Millie looked at him softly.

'I confess I never believed your story about kidnapping,' she said. 'Now I am not so sure. But God what a rotten lot you have got yourself mixed up with. The secretive Muhibbah was bad enough, but when you discover the world she was concealing you can begin to understand why she took so much trouble to hide it.'

Justin sat through this narrative in a state of resigned disengagement. It was the final humiliation to learn that Muhibbah had not, after all, escaped the fate from which he had tried to rescue her, and perhaps had been preparing for it all along. Of course the other men in her life were not lovers but brothers, spreading the seed of their migrating tribe sideways through the host community, treasuring their sister as the price of new alliances, roaming the world with predatory indifference to the pleasures snatched along the way. He resolved to rid himself of his obsession, and to look for the person who would replace Muhibbah in his feelings – Millie for instance, who had such a practical and neatly presented allure, and whose breasts, bubbling at the lip of a low cut blouse, reminded him of the many months of abstinence that his futile love had caused.

'Ah well, Millie,' he responded, 'I guess I knew. Thanks for telling me, and please…'

He began putting the lever-arch files together while Millie gathered up the CDs and the copies of *Rolling Stone*. At the sight of Muhibbah's virginal handwriting he suffered a pang. But she had abused him and abused his love. She was to join his rank of villains, along with the rest of her family. At the end of twenty minutes, when the flat had been restored to order, he felt bold enough to ask Millie for a date.

'Phew,' she said, 'rebound at last. We could go somewhere now, if you like. I want to get out of this place.'

Iona approved of Millie, when she met her at one of Justin's Thursday gigs. Most of all she approved of the change that came over him, as the image of Muhibbah receded. But she had news for him too. They were sitting together in the Horse and Trumpet in the city centre, which was near to her office and had a young and modern clientele among whom Iona felt at home. She was treating Justin to her opinions in the matter of the Sharon Williams case, concerning which she now had a substantial file. As Iona saw it the girl was a target for sexual abuse, and there were three people about whom she had her suspicions.

'Isn't this a matter for the police?' Justin asked.

Iona laughed cynically.

'For Superintendent Nicholson? Don't make me laugh. Remember his attitude to Muhibbah? Is he going to risk a charge of racism, just because of a rumour? He needs evidence, and the evidence must be so overwhelming that he can say that he had no alternative but to act on it.'

'Are you going to tell me that the Shahin family are involved?'

'One of my suspects is the elder brother, Hassan, the one with the squint. He has been making a fuss lately on behalf of the Koran and the Prophet, Peace Be Upon Him, demonstrating in front of St Catherine's Academy, and threatening the teachers. Methinks he doth protest too much, if you get my meaning. Though I'm not sure what he is trying to cover up. Maybe sexual abuse is only a side-line. We have served notice on the family that they are not entitled to Council accommodation. And this means that he has been round to our offices too, accusing us of racism, Islamophobia, human rights violations, insulting the Prophet, eating pork, shaking hands with women and so on and so forth. It brought back some poignant memories.'

Justin squeezed her hand, as he always did when the conversation turned to their two disasters, the one that had closed her heart to the opposite sex and the other that had done something comparable to him. But he did not want to hear more about Muhibbah's family. He no longer visited the sanctuary that he had erected around her image, and if from time to time he paused at the entrance, it was only to notice the cobwebs that now hung over every part.

'So who are your other two suspects?' he asked.

'Oh, there is the Polish guy who has moved in with the adoptive mother. And then…'

'And then?'

'And then there is her teacher, who to my mind has an interest in the girl that is not, you might say, healthy. To put it simply, he is hooked on her. A pretentious bastard too: imagines that he lives in some poetic universe, way above types like you and me, and that she has somehow managed to join him there. He wants her body, so he has invented her soul.'

'Poor sod. So what's the girl like? Does she justify all this attention?'

'She is pretty, slight, frail, vulnerable – just made for abuse. And she is clever too. The bore is I shall have to interview her, and I know she'll clam shut, with a few tantalising snippets hanging out of the shell. But back to the Shahin family…'

'Must we talk of them?'

'Have you not asked yourself why they were so anxious to find the CD that they were looking for in Millie's flat?'

Of course he had asked himself. And he had veered away from the question, as he had veered away from so much else that had happened in the wake of Muhibbah's departure. The hole that had emerged in Copley Solutions' accounts, for instance; the collapse of the scheme for the carbon-neutral houses, following erratic deliveries of Lithuanian timber; the growing awareness, as he spent his days staring from his desk at the place where she should have been, that his projects were in disarray, and that the green agenda no longer had any appeal for him – all these things seemed connected. But to think of them was to think of Muhibbah, and that was not allowed.

'Well,' Iona said, dropping her chin into one hand and resting her elbow on the beer-splashed table, 'here is what I reckon. That girl and her slimy brothers were all along in cahoots. Maybe she tried to run away from them at a certain stage. And maybe she was serious in wanting to live as a modern woman.

164

But something drew her back, and that thing was business. Not legitimate trade, but a shady business involving her brothers, for whom she was keeping accounts. Why else should she have walked off with the office computer, when her brother came to collect her? Have you thought of that?'

'Listen, Iona, I have thought of every explanation, and none of them casts credit on Muhibbah. So all I can do is forget about it. And that's what I am trying to do. If there is something shady going on, then that's not my problem.'

Iona laughed again.

'What I am telling you, Justin, is that it *is* your problem, as much your problem as Sharon Williams is my problem. And it could even be – who knows? – that the two problems are connected.'

'How so?'

Iona's eyes were shining, with the inner glow that he had often seen, and which entirely transfigured her so that she became, in her own way, almost beautiful. When her face came alive like this it was as though she were taking electricity from some transcendental source and passing it on. For a few months now Justin had been plugged in to her, dependent upon Iona for the energy that kept him alive. He nodded, not wanting to hear what she was about to say, and also wanting her to say it.

'Look at it this way. There is the perfect sister, the shining treasure shut away in its box, to be exchanged only for something beyond price – for instance, for an alliance of families, a tribal bond, a source of indefinite social power. All around there are the abused and frightened girls, who cost nothing more than lying promises, and who exchange on the market at the going rate. And then there is the Prophet, PBUH, who in their view ratifies both types of exchange, the priceless and the priced, and who provides the perfect cover for all transactions.'

165

'The perfect cover?'

'Yes. When deals are authorised in that way the guys who make them have no motive to question them. And we cannot question them either, since for people like Superintendent Nicholson and me that would be political suicide. In short, here is a girl brought up to believe that human beings, women especially, divide into the priced and the priceless, and who puts herself in the latter class. Wouldn't she go along with her brothers, when they ask her to apply her brain, her contacts and her knowledge to the profitable business of people trafficking? What obstacle would she see?'

'The obvious one: that she herself will be a victim.'

'Not if she adheres to the one conviction that you discovered in her, which is that she is beyond price.'

'And in your eyes, Iona, that makes her worthless.'

'I wouldn't say worthless. Just a waste of time.'

'Yes, I got the point. So are you going to pursue this daft line of enquiry?'

'I might. After all, I promised to find her.'

'But I no longer want you to find her. I have moved on.'

'I doubt it, Justin. But you see, I don't believe what they said to Millie, that she is back in Afghanistan. I think she is close by and dangerous.'

Justin was glad when the conversation shifted to Metal. Someone had transcribed the two guitar parts of 'Cloud Constructor' and placed the result on the Internet. He was amazed by what he read: two measures of 4/4 and then lost in the rhythmic jungle, with fifteen, eighteen, even twenty one equal notes to the bar. He told Iona he would make variations of his own, find some better words than those that Spiral Architect provided: it would be a new song. Maybe he would dedicate it to her.

'Surely you should dedicate it to Millie,' she said with a wry smile.

'Oh, that…'

In truth things had not worked out with Millie. It had been a solace after months of tortured isolation to spend time with an honest and plainspoken English girl. It had been flattering to be asked to explain his former life as an environmental activist and to show how she could follow in his footsteps at the end of the year, when she had her degree in chemistry. He had enjoyed talking to her about his music, playing endless riffs while she watched admiringly from the black leather sofa in his flat. He had felt a surge of protective affection, as he gently reproved her taste for the Pixies and the Kooks, and explained the difference between routine and rhythmical drumming. But when, after what he assumed was a normal prelude of contrived hesitations, she yielded to his kisses, and slipped all hot between the sheets of his bed, he felt, in the moment of pleasure, a strange, bleak loneliness. Afterwards he rolled over and sat for a long moment staring at the carpet from the edge of the bed. She was sweet, concerned and affectionate, but she suspected he was thinking of Muhibbah and the offense went deep. From that moment onwards Justin and Millie were just good friends, a fact that he was too embarrassed to explain when Iona insisted on treating them as a couple.

He knew that he was drifting. He avoided his flat, often, on leaving the office, going directly to a pub, to spend whole evenings drinking with people whose names he had forgotten by the next day. He sometimes went alone to the cinema, and apart from his Thursday gigs and Sunday rehearsals he lost contact with his former friends. Once a week he and Iona would go out to dinner, or eat a Chinese takeaway in his flat. And from time to time he would meet up with Millie, when they would exchange erotic kisses and look at each other quizzically before making vague arrangements to meet again.

The worst part was the day in the office. With Muhibbah at his side, spurred on by her lively curiosity, he had contemplated from his desk the serene landscape of their mutual future. He was going side by side with this woman into a new world. They were making plans for a carbon neutral society; and also for their own carbon neutral, nation neutral, religion neutral home. His eyes turned to the desk she had abandoned and which he did not dare to touch. And he was overcome by a sense of hopelessness and unreality. New projects came to him, accumulating in piles of half read documents. There was a contract to install solar panels on all the municipal housing in the north of the city; a scheme to introduce a first degree in environmental management into the university, with Copley Solutions PLC as consultants; a request for a water-flow assessment and contamination tests for a suburban sewage system – and all such projects, which would once have kept him at work eagerly and late in the search for the right solution, seemed overcast with dreariness and futility. Yet, as his interest declined, so did his responsibilities increase, since he alone could get results, and no one at Copley Solutions had the authority to take the work elsewhere.

It was in mid-April that things began to change. The financial year had ended, and the CEO in Amsterdam raised questions about the accounts that Justin could not answer. Before an audit was done, the CEO told him, a proper investigation should be undertaken, and Justin was to find a reputable firm of financial investigators who could act quickly to stem any leaks or to identify sources of dishonesty. After a day of searches Justin came across the website of Milbank and Company, with the profile of their junior partners. Looking at him demurely from the screen, blond hair neatly parted across her brow and blue eyes sparkling with humorous intelligence, was a girl whose beauty was the equal and opposite of Muhibbah's. His enquiries suggested that no one was more suited to the job than Laura Markham, and arrangements were quickly made to bring her to Yorkshire.

It was a crazy feeling, that he might, by falling in love with this unknown girl, cure himself of his fatal attachment. But he hoped for some such result, and if, through her investigations, Ms Markham were to implicate Muhibbah in wrongdoing, and perhaps even confirm Iona's suspicions about the Shahin family, then would that not make it all the simpler finally to transfer his affections, and to start life again?

So it was that when he met Laura Markham from the London train on a pleasant afternoon in April Justin was, for the first time in many months, in a state of eager anticipation. He had invented a story about the need for a plaçe that would be secure against the leaks and breaches that arise in hotel guestrooms. And he had found a furnished flat not far from the office, in a pleasant suburb blighted only by the two stark blocks of concrete panels known as the Angel Towers, which you could just see from the kitchen window. He had asked for two sets of keys, only one of which he intended to pass to Laura, not knowing whether he would find a use for the other set, but hoping nevertheless that something would happen to give him the right of entry into her space.

Laura Markham did not disappoint him. Her pretty girlish features shone with a ready intelligence, and she seemed as interested in him as he in her. Not that she was forward: there was a demure quality to her enquiries, and when she smiled at him it was with a little flutter at the corners of the mouth, as though she were awaiting his permission. But they were immediately at ease together, and as he showed her round the office his enthusiasm for his work suddenly returned. He steered past Muhibbah's vacant space without a qualm, and explained the project for the carbon neutral houses without withholding any relevant fact, even confessing that one member of staff had, on leaving, taken her office computer with her, so making it difficult to trace the transactions that she had placed on it.

The hour spent with Laura over a glass of wine was the best he had spent in many months. She was interested in music, preferring classical in general and Mozart in particular, and her taste in modern poetry – Yeats, Larkin, Hughes – coincided with Justin's. She loved her work for both its human contact and its intellectual problems. She was self-confident, optimistic and yet with a poetic streak that was withheld from ready exposure. Justin was sure that she had been much loved as a child, had retained the indelible image of home and happiness, and was working to find them both again. By the time he dropped Laura off at the front door of the block of flats, he was half in love. He went cheerfully home and did as he had once been in the habit of doing: he picked up groceries from the corner store, cooked himself a meal of lamb chops and peas, and opened a bottle of Rioja.

When she did not appear at the office next morning he rang the mobile number she had given him. There was no reply. By midday he was seriously concerned, and drove round to the flat, sounding the buzzer without eliciting a response and finding a use for his spare set of keys that he had not anticipated. He called her name into the silence. There was a disconcerting hospital smell, suggesting the aftermath of a serious accident. But he found no trace of Laura.

The suitcase flung on the bed in the bedroom looked as though it had not been opened, and the only clear sign that she had installed herself in the flat was a file from Copley Solutions, lying open on the table in the living-room window. He was surprised by this, since he had not seen her take the file from the archive. It dated from the weeks before Muhibbah's departure, and dealt with a consignment of wood from Lithuania, delivered via Lesprom. He came across the little illiterate note, inserted between its pages – 'complete off-shore until delivery. MS advise. Reference Squirrel', followed by a mobile phone number, beginning 0048, which he knew already as the code for Poland. And the narrative that then unfolded before his mind filled him with fear.

Chapter 21

There was only one place that Stephen could begin his search for her and that was the Angel Towers. He took the stairs to the fifteenth floor of Block A, with the faint hope that he might find her in a corner somewhere. From behind the doors came shouts in many languages and the sounds of loud TVs. But on the stairs and in the corridors there was an eerie emptiness. At one point he passed two urchins in a corner of the stairs, who scowled at him. On the twelfth floor a woman in a burqa appeared from a half-open door and then hastily withdrew. But elsewhere there was only absence, the absence that was Sharon.

He stood outside the door inscribed with the names of Williams and Krupnik. A TV was relaying the six o'clock news. Someone was hitting a pan with a spoon. A deep male voice cried 'Ya fuckvits, you stop zat noise'. And then he rang the bell.

Immediately the TV was turned off, the banging stopped, and there was silence. Even before the door was opened it was clear that he was an intruder into a space that had no open dealings with the outer world. He had the image of her tormented face as she struggled with the noise and commotion in that prison. For three months now he had known of her suffering and done nothing to relieve it, expecting her to make a clear statement of her case when nothing was more wounding to her pride than a clear statement of her case. He rang the bell again, clutching his brow in bitter self-reproach.

The door opened to reveal a thin, sallow woman in a flowery cotton dress, who stared at him from large grey eyes. Her brown hair was pinned up above her brow, and she held a pale right hand across her chest. Her demeanour was anxious and fugitive, and she addressed him with the one word 'yes?' behind which 'no' upon 'no' could be heard to resonate. Some trace of her girlish attractiveness remained, but it was clear to Stephen that Mrs Williams had been a lifelong loser in her encounters with the opposite sex, and that the broad-shouldered, pot-bellied man in a denim suit who sat at the kitchen table and turned slit-like eyes in the direction of the door had had no difficulty in imposing his will on her.

'Mrs Williams?'

'Yes,' she answered, though he felt again the reverberating 'no'.

'I am Stephen Haycraft, Sharon's teacher.'

'Oh, Sharon. She's not here. What's happened?'

'Do you know where she is?'

The man had risen from the table and was advancing to the door.

'No. Bogdan, you saw her, dinna you?'

'Ya, I come home, she in corner writing, then out she go, not say a vord. So vot's your problem?'

It was not a threat, merely a recognition of Stephen's profound insignificance in the life of Bogdan Krupnik.

'Have you any idea where she went?'

173

Stephen addressed the question to Mrs Williams, who looked at Bogdan apprehensively.

'She willna tell us where she goes, will she, Bogdan? But what's wrong, Mr...'

'Haycraft. Stephen Haycraft. She is – well she seems worried by something. She left a note for me. I need to discuss it with her.'

Lame excuses. And clearly there was nothing to be got from standing there in the doorway, listening to Bogdan Krupnik.

'Zat girl she make trouble everywhere. Around here come ze social worker, fat cow, now ze teacher, and to us she say nothing. Vot's going on I like to know?'

Mrs Williams accompanied Bogdan's diatribe with frightened looks, waiting until he suddenly swung round and marched out of the kitchen into the interior of the flat. Then, without looking at Stephen, she quietly closed the door in his face.

As he stepped off the bottom stair into the foyer he saw Mrs Williams, emerging from the lift. She came shiftily across to him, and addressed him with a fragile look, as though begging to be treated kindly.

'I know things's not right for Sharon here,' she said. 'I canna do nowt. She's no' mine, see. And there are the boys and Bogdan. It worries me. She's frightened of Bogdan, stays out late when he's here, but there's no need to worry see. That's what I told Mrs Ferguson from Social. But they could put her somewhere else. That would be best see. She'd be happier too. I wanted to say all that, only Bogdan gets mad at me. Maybe you can do something.'

He took two leaves of paper from his diary and wrote on one of them.

'Here is my phone number. Let me know as soon as you have news of her. And give me your number too.'

'Do you think something's happened?'

If Mrs Williams was anxious, it was on her own behalf. She was begging him for the thing that Sharon was too proud to ask for. She was begging him to take the girl away.

'Where does she go when she is out?'

'We dunna know, see. She dunna have no friends to speak of. She just picks up her books and goes out, see, and then comes back when the kids are in bed. If you can do summat, get them to put her with another family like, get her away from this place…'

'Well… I'll make some enquiries… That's to say…'

Across the concrete yard, in a patch of scrubland behind the ramps where the kids were skateboarding, there was a figure running: Sharon! He set out after her. He sped through some trees, which were struggling to survive in a patch of trodden earth. A twisted bike wheel crowned a bush of hawthorn on which the first buds were appearing. Food wrappings and shopping bags clogged the railings behind the trees, and in the dusk their shapes were like a gathering of curious animals. He was running towards her and also away from her, fleeing what was now inevitable, racing through a dream, and the shouts of the children came from a space that did not contain him. He ran through an iron gate that had come off its hinges, on to the street that led northwards away from the Angel Estate.

Someone else was running behind him. Above him the towers stood like two giants who had fought each other to a standstill. There was a buzzing in his ears and his heart was pounding. At the corner of Duke Street, where Italianate villas lined the pavement, he caught sight of her in the distance, fleeing with panic-stricken steps, clutching books beneath one arm, her blond hair streaming behind her and glowing in the light of a street-lamp. How frail and mouse-like she looked, and how fierce the breathing that was approaching from behind.

175

He turned quickly, his hand raised to avoid the blow. But the man ran past him muttering, his mop of black hair flopping around his swivelling eye. Perhaps he had not noticed Stephen. Perhaps he was too intent on his prey.

Sharon reached the corner that led to the canal. Stephen knew of an alley that joined the towpath where she was bound to pass. It was fully night when he reached the place, and the orange glow of the city on the horizon was the only light in the sky. The back gardens of Victorian houses were fenced off to one side, the weed-choked canal lying black and slimy on the other. There was no sign of Sharon. A chill north wind cut through his cotton jacket. In the gloom he made out the form of a man, walking carefully towards him as though afraid of stumbling into the water. Stephen was between the man and Sharon, defined at last in the role of her protector. He blocked the towpath and stood his ground.

They faced each other in silence. In the gloom the cast of the man's dud eye was no longer visible, and the sharp features above the leather gear gave him the appearance of a gangster, who had tracked his victim to the place of revenge. Stephen was not a coward, but he had made a policy of avoiding physical encounters, arguing to himself that people with brains have a duty to protect them from people without them. All the troubles of the world stem from our inability to sit quietly in a room: so Pascal had written, and Stephen agreed with him. But the thought of Sharon banished the impulse to escape. This man was a special case. This man had appeared in Stephen's life as a mortal enemy, already marked out for death. It was only when Stephen had lashed out with a blow to the face that he saw that the man had a knife.

It was the left eye that swivelled, and Stephen dived to the right of it, hoping to become invisible. The blade swooped through the air above him and dug into the wooden fence where he crouched. Now the man had turned and was looking back at Stephen along the towpath. He had pulled the knife from the wood and was pointing it at Stephen's stomach.

'You stupid fucker!'

The man stepped forward, withdrew his right arm ready to lunge, and gave a cruel smile. At that moment a scream sounded behind him and he turned. Stephen kicked out at the hand that held the knife and sent it spinning onto the towpath.

'The fucking bitch!'

The knife had fallen to the man's left, and he was fumbling on the ground with his hand in search of it. Stephen seized it, and cast it out into the canal. Again they were facing each other, and in the distance someone was running. The man lunged at Stephen, who felt tired now as though all his limbs had doubled in weight. He moved as in a dream, with reluctant legs. The man came forward to administer a kick, overshot and stumbled against the fence. The situation struck Stephen as entirely theatrical. He almost laughed at the absurdity of it. If he were to kill this man, it would need better planning. And clearly the man thought the same. He was breathing heavily and supporting himself with one hand on the fence. They stood facing each other in postures of total fatigue.

'OK,' Stephen said. 'Enough of this.'

'Stay out of this, you fucker. I've got plans for that bitch.'

'Well, as it happens, so have I.'

Stephen walked with heavy legs along the towpath. The man stared after him, not shifting from his station against the fence, his chest heaving within the leather jacket like a bellows. Stephen knew that he had not scored a victory, and that the man really did have plans for Sharon. The important thing was to find her and to get her to speak. Then, but only then, could he take revenge.

He found her wandering by the steps that led to the school road. She walked past him in silence. Her face, caught by the street-lamp on the bridge, was pale and drawn, and although she glanced in his direction as she passed there was no light of recognition in her eyes.

'Sharon!'

She stopped and stared fixedly in front of her. He walked quietly towards her and took her free arm. She went suddenly limp and leaned against him.

'I wanted him to kill me,' she said at last. 'But not you, sir.'

'If we handle this right, Sharon, he won't kill either of us, and he'll spend a long time in gaol.'

She was crying now, sobs that welled up from the depths of her suffering, and which shook her whole frame as he held her.

'You dunna know them, sir.'

'Let's go, Sharon. We're not safe here.'

'We're no safe anywhere.'

'That's what we're going to change, Sharon.'

He led her up the steps on to the road. They walked towards the school. Her trembling form beside him filled him with pity and desire. His whole being was given to her now, and what the world said or did had only the faintest voice in his plans. He called for a taxi on his mobile phone, and asked to be picked up outside the school. As they waited by the gates her tormentor appeared, and stood watching from a distance as they climbed into the car.

'I'm taking you home,' he said, turning to her.

'Where you are, sir?'

'Where we both are.'

She gripped his hand silently, while Stephen mentally composed his letter of resignation to the Headmistress of St Catherine's

Academy, deciding to place it in her hand next day. A wave of indescribable happiness washed over him. Quite suddenly it was all resolved; he would start life again, far from this place, with Sharon beside him, studying to be the brilliant figure – a professor of literature perhaps – which he knew she must become one day. Together they would wash out the stain of her abuse, bring peace to her soul and justice to her tormentors. And the world would accept them in the end, knowing that he had acted rightly and that there was no alternative to doing what he now must do.

But what exactly must he do? Nothing hasty, nothing that would ruin what he longed for with all his heart. Back in the flat, he looked at her where she sat across from him in the moquette armchair, her hands trembling around a cup of sugary tea, and saw that he should not touch her – not now, not yet. He must win her confidence: not confidence in him, but confidence in herself, in her life, in the hopes that had been so brutally torn from her and trampled upon.

How scruffy and beaten down she appeared, but how lovely too. He told her about her adoptive mother, who had begged him to find another place for her. He indicated, as delicately as he could, that he understood the situation with Bogdan Krupnik. He outlined a plan for her security, and she sat through all of it, trembling and silent until the conclusion, which he announced bashfully, getting up and pretending to look for food in the kitchen. For the time being, he said, and until matters were settled and her safety secure, Sharon was to stay where she was, in the place that she called home. He turned round to find her standing in the doorway, whispering 'thank you', and then reaching out to touch his lips with the fingers of one hand.

179

'Yes,' he continued with a tremor, 'we can make up a bed for you here on the couch, and I will let your mum know what is happening. Of course you'll need some things and I suppose I must go over to the Angel now to pick them up.'

'No!' she cried. 'Not there!'

He looked at her pityingly.

'But you'll need things for the night, clothes for the morning, your school work…'

'I'm OK like this.'

Eventually it was agreed that they would go out in search of the things she needed. He left a message on Mrs Williams's phone, saying that he had found Sharon, was looking after her and would let Mrs Williams know when the girl had been re-housed. They took a taxi to the 24-hour Tesco in the city and returned after two hours with pyjamas, a new shirt, tights and underwear, toiletries and a satchel for her schoolwork. He was embarrassed in the shop at first, since he was clearly neither her brother nor her father nor a friend. He didn't even have the standing that Humbert Humbert acquired towards Lolita.

But she was so happy in his company, so crazily involved in the abnormal project of being normal, so full of wonder that the respect she coveted was after all available for purchase and that the man beside her was ready with the cash, that he began to respond to her hilarity. It was only in the taxi back that their mood became more sombre. For she was trembling again, leaning against him, whispering that she ought not to be with him, that they would be discovered, and that both of them might soon be dead.

Getting her through the door of the flat was difficult. She would swing back and try to duck past him onto the stairwell. Eventually she allowed herself to be led to the armchair, and sat quietly as he began to prepare a supper of sausages and peas. Then she got up and came across to watch him. She was like a dog, following every one of his movements, but saying nothing. He offered her a glass of white wine. She drank it with gulps and grimaces, and then looked at him for a long while from blue-grey astonished eyes.

That night Stephen lay sleepless. Occasionally he heard her turning on the couch next door, and once she cried out as though from a nightmare. In the early hours the door of his bedroom opened, and she stood on the threshold watching him. When he rolled over to face her she fled, closing the door. He got up later to find her already dressed, sitting at the living room table reading *The Magic Mountain*. She listened attentively while he explained the book's significance and the significance of Thomas Mann in the literature of Europe.

'Yes, sir,' she said quietly. 'But Europe was a place then. There's no places now.'

Getting her to classes was also difficult. To arrive together was out of the question. But she would not go alone. Eventually he ordered a taxi, and put her out of it a hundred yards from the school. The process of soothing and protecting her was demanding and also beautiful. She watched wide-eyed as he made his preparations, submitted to his decisions with gentle reluctance, and then smiled awkwardly when things seemed right. He had two keys to the flat, and he entrusted one of them to Sharon, causing a gasp of protest.

'What if I lose it, sir?' she cried. 'What if they get it from me?'

'But what if you need to get in and I am not there?'

'Always be there, sir. Please.'

Eventually she accepted the key, dropping it into the bottom of her satchel as she left the taxi.

All day Stephen was in a state of euphoria, and his class on *The Great Gatsby* was a special event, involving a heartfelt analysis of the novel's central character. Stephen portrayed Jay Gatsby as an outsider whose soul only visits the bright parties on Long Island as a spectator, while belonging in the Valley of Ashes, where contrition and penitence are the rule. Stephen himself was Gatsby, concealing what others would condemn as a crime for the sake of a pure and innocent love. His eloquence grew as he watched her from the corner of his eye. She was covering her pages with notes and looking up from time to time, entirely absorbed by what she heard, rescued, for these moments, from the remembered torment of her life.

Soon her rescue would be complete, and he planned it with wild and chaotic scenarios. They would flee together to London. He would borrow money, start again as a writer, support her through her studies; he would watch her as she grew up and vanquished her timidity, confronted her past and her trauma, surrendered to the truth, to the hope that he was offering, and to their life together. Then they would take revenge.

So absorbed was Stephen in those thoughts that he did not get round to writing his letter of resignation. It was a busy day at school in any case, with more trouble from the imams, who were now demanding the dismissal of Mrs Gawthrop, and threatening a mass withdrawal of Muslim pupils if their demands were not met. It was known that Stephen got on well with the Iraqi boys and often discussed the Koran with them, so that the Headmistress asked him to take a special class for the juniors, with the intention of expressing, illustrating and amplifying the official policy of respect towards Islam. And his euphoria grew, as he contrasted the message of the Prophet with the behaviour of those who purported to follow him. Sharon's revenge, when it

182

came, would be entirely personal, and he would show the imagined spectators that the man whom he punished was not only a criminal but also a traitor to his faith.

They left school separately, and by the same arrangement by which they had come. It was too late to make an appointment with Iona Ferguson, so he was obliged to postpone the question of Sharon's lodging. He visited the nearby supermarket, returning to make a meal of salmon and rice. She was curious as to his habits, asking whether he always had such delicious things for tea, and whether he drank wine every day. She anticipated his replies, excitedly describing Stephen's life as she had imagined it, and all the little places where she would be of use to him if he allowed. She especially wanted to write down his classes, and perhaps make a proper book of them.

They sat quietly after supper, he at his desk, she at the table. And later, when she emerged from the bathroom in pyjamas and settled beneath the blankets on the couch, he went across to kiss her on the brow. She moved her face as he did so, and their lips met. Only with the greatest effort did he draw away.

So it was for a week. Each day he set out to write his letter of resignation, but each day something arose to prevent it. Each morning he made the decision to ring Iona Ferguson and each afternoon he revoked it. And each evening he cooked for her and read to her, trying to turn the conversation in the direction he sought. If she would go with him to the police, make the kind of statement that a prosecutor would need from her, and allow him to say what he knew, then everything would be above board and his happiness would be perfect. But each time he approached the topic she veered away in panic. After a while he valued the peace between them so much that he refrained from questioning her. And then the Easter vacation came, and it began to seem as though everything in his life apart from Sharon was unreal. All was beginning to fall away, leaving the two of them as though caught in a spotlight on a wholly darkened stage.

Cut off from his old routines, however, Stephen experienced the occasional twinge of apprehension. It was too late now to visit Iona Ferguson. To have rescued the girl and offered lodging for a day or two would have been an understandable act of kindness. To have kept her secretly at home for two weeks would be construed as a crime. Meanwhile the Williams boys would be sure to relay the news that she was no longer at home. He was irremediably committed to her, and yet had only half decided on a plan. He composed his letter of resignation, ready to give to the Headmistress at the beginning of term. And he spent days in the local library in order to convey to Sharon the provisional nature of their arrangement, which he knew in his heart not to be provisional at all.

She fretted when he was absent and would not leave the flat. He returned home in the evening to find her at the table in the window, a pen in her hand, a book open in front of her, and an expression of joy as though she had given up hope of seeing him again. She still called him 'sir', and seemed to have forgotten entirely the delirious declaration of love addressed to Stephen. But she was beginning to talk to him in the same idiom as her letters, adjusting her grammar to his, and giving voice to her impressions.

Once, when they took the bus out of the city, and walked for several miles across the moors, she entertained him with a version of *Wuthering Heights*. She spoke in a whisper, her sentences coming from somewhere behind her mouth. In the story she was Catherine, roaming in search of her Heathcliff across 'grassy pillows, buttoned down with sheep'. And when she found him,

184

they sat in silence together 'like two dolls on a shelf'. 'That's you and me, sir,' she added, and there the story stopped.

Often, in the evening, she would be writing, and he longed to know what it was, and especially to see the change that might have occurred, now that she was happy.

For that she was happy he did not doubt. As the days of the vacation drew on it became apparent that Sharon was not by nature the taut, withdrawn and half-crazy waif who had first made her appeal to him, but a normal and life-affirming girl, who – but for the experiences that she had undergone – would have been advancing through life with the minimum of trouble. She had implored him to respect her, had held out for his respect against all the odds, and had laid bare her soul in those extraordinary spasms of honesty that burst the shackles of her despair. And now she was free.

He saw the result in her face. The look of withdrawn astonishment gradually faded, and in its place came an eager alertness, as though she were discovering the world of human relations for the first time. She would sit at the table, her little pile of books beside her, a sheet of paper in front, and look across to where he worked, frequently putting her elbows on the table top and the fingers of one hand in her mouth. She asked questions about books, about student life in Oxford, about the kind of music he liked, which she was beginning to like as well. And although she still clammed shut should he make a personal enquiry, she listened intently to all the stories of his past.

He told her about his parents – his mother a high-flying business woman, who had begun life as an actress but now ran a head-hunting agency of her own; his father a good-for-nothing who had tried and failed at many trades, eventually becoming a peripatetic teacher of cartoon drawing at the London art-schools.

185

He described the trauma of his parents' divorce, visiting feelings that he had never expressed before to another person: his sense that he, an only child, was to blame for his father's black moods and his ever-increasing absence from the house; that his mother's tears were a response to his failings as a son and his inability to be cheerful in the long evenings of their mutual discontent. He wondered whether she had felt anything like this, but she merely shrugged her shoulders and said 'dinna have no parents, dinn' I?', urging him instead to keep going with his story.

He told her of his father's death, which occurred during his last year at Oxford. Mr Haycraft had been found with a broken neck, at the foot of the steep stairs leading to a private club in Soho where he was in the habit of drinking. Foul play was not suspected, and the funeral was attended by a large number of people, almost none of whom Stephen knew. The trauma of this event meant that he did not gain the first class degree that was expected of him, so that he had to relinquish his hopes of an academic career.

Sharon listened intently to Stephen's stories, always looking at him with wide-eyed sympathy and once getting up from the table and coming across to lift his hand to her lips and kiss it. He was emerging from his shell, as she had emerged from hers, and he experienced, in her presence, a sweet feeling of peace that filled his heart as nothing had filled it before. As a result he constantly put out of mind the urgent need to report Sharon's whereabouts to the Department of Social Work, and to arrange his resignation from her school.

It was an evening in mid-April that everything changed. They had eaten their supper and cleared away the dishes. They had read for a while from *The Merchant of Venice*. A blackbird had just ceased to sing in the car park, and a quiet, placid dusk was veiling the suburb in shadow. When she asked if she could have a bath he nodded without moving from his desk. It was only the second time she had made this request, baths being a luxury in the Angel Towers. But he studied to take no special note of it. For that, he assumed, was how to put her at ease. He listened to the bath water running, noted a cry as she tried the temperature, and then went back to the *Sonnets to Orpheus*, closing his ears to her splashes.

He stopped reading, sensing that she was standing in the doorway of the bathroom, looking in his direction. And when he turned to confront her, she let the bathrobe fall from her shoulders onto the floor. Looking back at this moment across all the ensuing grief, he remembered it as the last moment of happiness in a life which had been properly happy only this once.

'This is yours, Stephen,' she said. 'I kept it for you.'

Chapter 22

Justin rang the number from the office telephone. A man's voice answered, with the word '*tak?*' rudely spoken.

'I'm ringing about Lesprom business,' Justin said.

There was a silence.

'It's about a shipment,' he added. 'One between Kaliningrad and Hull. The reference is squirrel.'

There was another silence.

'OK, so you tell them no shipment, OK?'

The accent was Polish.

'I don't understand.'

'No shipment without money.'

'And the girl?'

'I don't know about any girl. We want compensation. Otherwise no shipment. Two days lost because of this girl you talking about.'

'There was a mistake,' Justin said. His mind was racing, and he saw the whole scenario clearly before him, the abused girls going one way, the robbed refugees the other, and Iona left with the wreckage. The only unexplained detail was Laura: why should they have picked on her? And, worse thought, was he not to blame, having placed her in that block of temporary lodgings instead of a proper hotel?

'A mistake, ya. But that's not our business, see. The ship off-shore any time now. Zdenko come collect the money.'

'How much?'

'It's gotta be twenty grand.'

'Twenty! Far too much.'

They haggled for a bit, until Justin got the sum down to fifteen.

'So where will he come?' he asked.

'The same place,' came the reply. Justin listened for suspicion and heard none.

'Sometimes we use a new address.'

'Fuck that. Buckton not safe?'

'Of course it's safe.'

'So Falkin's Yard, tomorrow midday, we collect the cash.'

'OK,' said Justin and rang off. Should he report Laura Markham as a missing person? His experience argued against it. It was more important to go at once in search of her kidnappers. He rang Iona, told her what had happened, and where he was going. She was to come looking for him if he was not in touch by seven.

'I hope you know what you are getting yourself into, Justin?'

'Of course I don't,' he replied.

'Well I do. People trafficking is a nasty business. And I advise you to be careful.'

It was Iona's way of saying that she supported him. And he trusted her, because she was as disillusioned as he was.

Buckton was a small village on the edge of the moor. The rhythms of the city were barely audible here. There was a church of grey stone with a spire and perpendicular windows and next to it an old rectory half hidden by beech trees and surrounded by lawns with bright borders of spring flowers. 'Home Farm' and 'Manor Farm' both abutted on a neat village green, where three serene Georgian houses in weathered brick competed for eminence along the edge. A pub, 'The Wild Boar', elbowed its way into a street of stone cottages, and a village shop, with a Victorian glazed facade, was conducting its precarious trade with a few respectable pensioners. The scene was studiously English, as preposterously idyllic as any backdrop to an Agatha Christie murder. And Justin reflected with sinking heart on the possibility that he had stepped into just such a story.

He parked the car in a little square, where a central plinth surmounted by a war memorial bore a plain cross of stone. Falkin's Yard, he was told, lay on the edge of the village, and consisted of the defunct buildings of Falkin's Brewery, one side of which had been renovated and converted into holiday lets. The building was Victorian. There was a cobbled yard in front of an industrial facade of stone, into which had been inserted four attractive dwellings, each presenting two windows and a door. It was outside the season, and three of the dwellings were vacant, with shutters across the windows and padlocks on the doors. The fourth, at the far end of the yard, had a forbidding appearance, with drawn curtains and sacks of uncollected rubbish against the wall.

There was a frosted glass panel in the door, which revealed only more darkness. When Justin rang the bell it was some time before a light went on in the hallway, and a figure swayed in the glass. The door opened, and she stood as though dazzled by the light.

'Muhibbah!'

She backed away from him with her fingers bent against her mouth and her eyes wide with astonishment.

'So it was you!' she said.

'Can I come in?'

'Yes. No. *Bismillahi*, how did you know?'

'How did I know what?'

'Let's go for a walk.'

She turned quickly away from him, took a canvas jacket from a peg and threw it over her turtle-neck and trousers, the same outfit that she had always worn, as though nothing in Muhibbah could change until everything changed. Soon they were walking out of the village and on to the moor. But no, something had changed. He had never seen her cry before, and he put out an arm to comfort her. She did not remove it, but leaned just slightly towards him.

'So it was you,' she said again. 'You who made that phone call.'

'Isn't it time you explained things to me? I can't believe you are mixed up in this business.'

'Oh, Justin, you rescued me once. You won't want to rescue me again.'

'Just tell me one thing, Muhibbah. The girl who was kidnapped, is she safe?'

'What girl?'

'The girl who came to investigate our accounts.'

'No idea about that. Did this happen recently?'

'Yesterday, I think.'

She shook herself free of his arm and looked at him. Her face was tight now, self-contained, resisting him.

'I don't think they would do such a thing,' she said emphatically.

'They? Who do you mean?'

'My brothers. *Allah yaghfiru lihum!*'

191

They walked on in silence. Justin felt fear in his stomach, certain now that the worst had happened and that he would never see Laura again, certain too that this woman who walked at his side was as dangerous as Iona thought her to be. After a while they sat on a lichen-covered boulder. Beside them was a five-bar gate, mounted with iron hinges on a gatepost of stone. The sunlight of a spring afternoon danced in the breeze-blown grass. A flock of sheep grazed in the meadow at their feet, and in the distance rose the grey-green hills of the moorland, with their dry-stone walls and sheep pens. Here and there a cottage was sheltered among pine trees.

It was a scene of pastoral beauty, such as had drawn him years before into the fight for the earth. And he had lived in defiance of this thing that he so much loved. He had campaigned against sheep, which reduce the landscape to a monoculture of grass and parasites. He had fought against the nimbys who protect their beloved fields from wind farms and who see modernity as a livid scar. His passion for a sustainable environment had cut across his life, turning everything in a new direction. And this woman too had cut across his life. She sat there, as alien to this landscape as any metal wind turbine, her perfect beauty aimed at his heart.

'So they didn't send you to Afghanistan?'

'You rescued me. Remember?'

'But you are with your family again. It was your brother, was it not, who took you from our office?'

'He didn't take me. We left together.'

'But there were signs of a struggle.'

'Yes. I tried to stop him taking the computer. But he is stronger than me.'

'So tell me what this is about.'

She looked at him. Her eyes were still, the irises like black olives, but with a light of their own, a light shining from regions as remote as her soul. Slowly tears formed in each of them and ran down her cheeks. He wiped them away with his forefinger, and she did not resist.

'Please, Justin, you tell me. Then perhaps I will know what to say.'

He told her about Laura Markham, commissioned to examine the discrepancies in the firm's accounts. He told her about Laura's disappearance, about the file on the table and the note with the phone number lying loose in it. He reported on his conversation with the Polish man who had inadvertently given the address at which he had found her. And he suggested that Muhibbah could cast light on all these things, and especially on the question whether Laura had been kidnapped, and if so by whom. She shook her head, which she had buttoned down from behind as was her defensive tactic. He could find no expression there, no corner that he could peel away to reveal the vulnerable woman beneath the perfect integument of skin.

'I know nothing about this girl who disappeared. But I do know about the file, about the phone number, and about the holes in your accounts.'

'Then tell me that at least.'

She began a story. She did not look at him but either stared at the earth so as to whisper into its ear, or looked up at the sky to blurt out some note of self-justifying triumph to the sun.

It was a curious story, about her two brothers, one by her father's first wife who was an unruly psychopath, the other, by her father's second wife and her own mother, whom she loved more than anyone in the world. She whispered of her childhood in the old Yemeni town of Tarim, where her father had brought them from Afghanistan. She evoked her first years with images one after the other like pictures in an album. There was the beautiful old house with its cool courtyard and tinkling fountain. There were the two mothers, creating peace, halwa and wisdom in some dark recess. There were trips to the rocky desert for worship in the open air among men with guns. There were formal visits from tribesmen who looked at the Afghan visitors as though trying to settle whether to kill them or to die for them, and who always left with the question unresolved.

'But we had come as fighters, Justin, as *mujahidin*,' she said, addressing the sky. 'We were the elite, the *zahrah*.'

Somehow it had gone wrong. The money ceased to come, and her father left with his wives and daughter for England, waving his Afghan passport and claiming asylum for some fictitious cause. The boys, however, who had Yemeni passports, were left behind. And that is why everything changed for her. In all the troubles of a Muslim girl – the threat to send her back to Afghanistan, the offers of marriage from disgusting old men, the moment when she was taken away from the Tarim Girls' School and locked for a week in her room – her brother Yunus had fought for her. She was a stone of the desert, pure, clean, dry and hard, and he would not let that stone belong to anyone except the man who could mount it in gold. And she had fought for Yunus too, had kept him at home when their father and Hassan had left with their gaggle of gun-toting tribesmen to take paltry revenge on the world as it is, the world made in America. Again she raised her eyes to the sky.

'There are flowers in the desert, blooming suddenly when there is rain, otherwise buried, hidden and impossible to destroy. Our love was like that.'

And then she whispered of her desolation, a twelve-year old refugee, struggling with the language that she and Yunus had begun to learn from the television, going each day to St Catherine's Academy, and coming home to that grim cave where her father sat motionless like a deposed god, and she was shut away with frightened females. She begged and begged for them to bring Yunus to her. She threatened to kill herself. She refused all food. And so at last he came.

It costs a fortune to smuggle people from Yemen to the drained marshes of Iraq, from there through Turkey to Azerbaijan, through the Russian Federation to the Baltic coast and thence to England, social housing and benefits. To achieve it they had to work closely with the Poles who had been housed by the Council in the Angel Towers, and also with Afghan and Iraqi families who were prepared to pay for their relatives to be brought across. By the time Yunus and his troublesome half-brother arrived the Shahin family were well into the business of people smuggling, in conjunction with a Polish ship operating out of Kaliningrad.

'I'm telling you something, Justin, that you shouldn't know. And I have lost every right to swear you to secrecy.'

She looked at him and again the two perfect tears welled up in her perfect eyes and stayed like pearls on her cheeks until he quietly removed them with his finger. And when he had done so he leaned forward and kissed her on the lips. She did not move, did not close her mouth or open it further than it had opened from her flow of words. But her eyes narrowed slightly as he moved away.

'I don't know why I did that,' he said, embarrassed.

'Don't you?'

He looked down in silence. Why was she telling him this story? And why was he listening, when he should be actively searching for Laura, the girl who was to rescue him from Muhibbah's malevolent charms, and who was now in danger? And yet he listened. He heard of the trouble caused by Hassan, and his gang of Iraqis who picked up vulnerable English girls, promised marriage, and then sold them on to the highest bidder. She whispered the verse of al-Baqara in which it says that there is nothing wrong in any allusion to marriage you make to a woman, and that Allah knows that you will say things to them. But the verse does not permit the things that Hassan did, and which he encouraged Yunus to do as well.

Yunus was a failure. He left St Catherine's Academy without any GCSEs; he had tried for jobs and never held one for more than a week; and he clung to Hassan as his guide. Together they could live on the edge of this decaying society, exploiting the residue of doubt, guilt and repudiation that made the English in general, and their girls in particular, such easy prey. He had said that England was no place for a decent Muslim girl and that she should return to a country where girls were respected. He repeated the message several times, saying that it was a matter of honour. And then he wept for an hour on Muhibbah's shoulder, telling her that he hated what they had done to a girl called Moira and that nothing like that could happen to this hard jewel from the desert, which he had polished for year upon year.

'And that,' she said, 'is why Yunus would not help me, when the marriage offer came from that bloke in Afghanistan.'

So that was when she had fled, and Justin had saved her, she did not deny it. She owed everything to Justin, and if she had not loved him as he wanted then he must recognize that she could love only the person to whom she belonged. But to belong she had to be given, transferred, as Yunus might have transferred her.

'I am not something to be bought and sold,' she told the sun. 'I am a gift or nothing. That is how I have always been and nothing can change it.'

After she left, she kept contact with Yunus, whom she had never ceased to love and whom she wished to detach from her family, and from Hassan in particular. Hassan, she whispered, had joined a group of madmen with beards who called themselves *muhajjiroun*, the ones in exile, who were going to install the reign of the Prophet in these kafr lands. What is it with psychopaths? For most of the time they act as though they had no conscience at all, needed no-one's forgiveness, not even Allah's, and then suddenly they get religion and decide that their relationship with Allah is the only thing that counts.

He started dressing up in a jalabiya and a chequered ghutra on his head. He let his beard grow into a tangled worm-infested bush, and the sight of him, with his loose blind eye and his mop of thick black hair in a dirty dishcloth, would be enough to cause any passing policeman to call immediately for reinforcements. He made trouble everywhere, organised protests about Iraq and Afghanistan, protests about the schools, protests about the Council. And then overnight he changed back to his hooligan persona, shaved off the beard, dressed in leather and a big black overcoat, and took up again with girls. Always Muhibbah was beseeching Yunus to get away from this madman, to set up house with her, and one day she saw how it could be done.

The people business was precarious. Some of the Iraqis were blackmailing the Shahins, saying they would report the whole thing to the police if their families weren't brought in for free. And the deals were in cash, with no documents to explain them, or to explain what a Polish ship was doing anchored offshore at the mouth of the Humber. Muhibbah loved her work at Copley Solutions, because it was so neat, so clean, and so perfectly accounted for, with files of letters explaining every deal, and figures balancing each other in double-entry books. And that gave her an idea.

197

She whispered to the earth how she and Yunus, together with the Polish captain called Bogdan, had set up the bogus firm of Lesprom, which made shipments of wood to Hull and was paid by Copley Solutions. And the money that Copley paid was secretly collected by Yunus and passed through the accounts by Muhibbah. Often there would be a real delivery of wood, but Muhibbah worked things out so that nothing would be noticed. Soon they had their own business going, the three of them, of which the Shahin family knew nothing, and Yunus promised to leave as soon as was reasonable and move in somewhere with Muhibbah. And then they would make the business entirely legal, offering a package deal to refugees, with an EU passport, easily obtainable in Poland, a passage to England and the chance of social housing.

'How could you do that without me knowing?' Justin asked in astonishment.

'Because you were looking straight at me and not asking yourself what I was doing,' she replied quickly.

'And do you think you had the right to put my business at risk for the sake of you and your good-for-nothing brother?'

Muhibbah gave a tight, thin smile.

'It was for your sake too, Justin.'

'For *my* sake? How come?'

A lark sang high above them. A west wind was driving fluffy clouds across the sun, and shadows danced on the meadows like dolphins on the surface of the sea. And here beside him was the hard dry spirit of the desert.

'How would it be possible for us to marry, if I had no brother to make the gift?'

'I see,' said Justin in astonishment. 'So what happened?'

'Hassan, of course. Yunus couldn't keep our secret from him. Hassan insisted Yunus take me away from you, destroy all the records of what I had been doing through your office. The business was to go on as before, as a secret thing, full of shady corners. And I was to have nothing more to do with you, since that way lay danger.'

'And you let this happen?'

'I let it happen, Justin. Which is why you won't want to rescue me now, from the mess I have got into.'

'I don't understand what the mess is.'

'When you made that phone call our Polish contact got immediately in touch with Yunus. So my brother knows there has been a leak. He rang me to say that Hassan has had an accident, hit his ear on a metal spike, and that the ship has turned back. He had to threaten Bogdan, and the whole deal has been put at risk. It is likely there'll be scores to settle and attempts to settle them coming our way from Russia and Afghanistan. You don't really think we have fifteen grand in ready money do you? Yunus was frightened, Justin, and so am I. If we don't get out of this somehow it is either gaol or something worse.'

'And you want me to help you get out of it?'

'I didn't say that, Justin. No, I just felt that I owe you the truth.'

He looked at her, a long, searching look that she returned. And a deep trouble stirred within him.

'In the Surah al-Imran,' she said, 'God blesses those who are *sabin*, you have a good word for it, yes "steadfast", and those who look for forgiveness before the dawn. I am one of those who look for forgiveness before the dawn, one of the *mustaghfirin al-asHari*, and there's that 'Ha' again that you can never pronounce. That's all that's left of my religion. You used to play that R.E.M. song in the office, you remember? 'Losing my Religion'. I thought of that verse from the Koran whenever I heard it, and I think of it now.'

199

'Do you miss your religion, Muhibbah?'

'I have not made a good job of life without it.'

'Would you have made a better job of life with it?'

'Of course not.'

They sat for a while in silence, as the sun began to go down. Then she turned to him, her face alive as though with a sudden idea.

'You know something, Justin? Until a moment ago I had never kissed a man on the lips.'

'I apologize,' he said, and again the trouble stirred in him.

'What is there to apologize for? I wanted you to do it.'

'Did you?'

'Yes.'

She sat still, her face turned to his, waiting without excitement for whatever he might do. When he pressed his lips to hers she raised her arms slowly to his neck and buried her fingers in his hair. She drew gently away with downturned eyes.

'Justin,' she said. 'I've been so stupid.'

It was getting late and he knew he must telephone Iona. But they lingered side by side and silently as they returned to the village. It was dark when they entered Falkin's Yard. A blue Volkswagen was parked outside Muhibbah's holiday cottage.

'My brother!' she said.

'Which brother?'

'Yunus of course. He's back already. Quick, you must go.'

'When will I see you?'

'Why should you see me?'

'Many reasons, Muhibbah. But one in particular. Together we could sort out those accounts. Then there would be one thing less you have to worry about.'

She gave him a long and steady look. Again the tears welled up, and again he wiped them away.

'Thanks, Justin. I'll come to your office tomorrow morning. You'd better get hold of that file.'

He rang Iona from the village square, and she insisted that they meet at once. Nothing that he recounted surprised her. But the only advice she would give was to go to the police and get the whole bloody lot of them arrested, Muhibbah included. He didn't dare suggest that he had formed the opposite intention, and that he would do what he could to save her.

'And Laura?' Iona asked.

Yes, and Laura, what of her?

Chapter 23

You stifle the impulse to scream. Someone has just let himself in to the living room, there is the sound of a chair moving, as though he were sitting down at the table. It must be nine o'clock. Fear stifles your sobs, and for a moment your body makes a secret of itself, like the body of a hunted animal. You find you are tip-toeing to the bedroom door and shutting it quietly. You find you are supporting yourself on the wall, sliding around the room on trembling legs, until you are in the bathroom, locking the door behind you and staring at a blanched face in the mirror above the sink. Whose face is it? Not yours. Not the face of that ambitious, clever girl who was on the verge of a career as an investigative accountant, whom so many men had wanted as a lover and who had re-made herself after two stupid mistakes. The face you see belongs to a brutalised victim, one who has not yet taken her revenge, and who owes the salvaged remains of her body to a confused slob of a boy who had been unable to take her by force because some spark of love had been suddenly lit in him. Maybe it is Yunus in the next door room. Maybe he cannot stay away from you. Maybe you have to repeat the whole miserable dialogue, to point out to him yet again that, whatever chance a vulnerable immigrant without education might have had with you was lost at once when he thought of possessing your body without your soul.

Thinking of this, however, a measure of courage returns. You won that battle. And you won it because the human being in you awoke the human being in him. You are not, after all, without weapons. You smarten up the face that you see in the mirror. You go quietly into the bedroom and change into a clean cotton skirt and blouse. You pick up your mobile phone, ready to make an emergency call, and you walk noisily through the bedroom door, out into the corridor and into the living room. A man starts up in astonishment from the table in the window and swings round with a gasp.

'Laura! Thank God!'

'Justin! What in Heaven's name…'

'I do apologize. I let myself in, I kept the other set of keys in case we needed, in case the work required, you never know…'

He peters out, stares at you for a moment, and then resumes.

'I was so worried about you, when you didn't turn up this morning, so I came round to see where you were. Obviously you had other things to do. I have given you a terrible shock. How awful.'

You look at him as the words tumble out in disarray; for a moment you feel you might faint. He comes across quickly and hands you to an armchair.

'Thanks,' you whisper.

'Thank God!' he says again. 'I can't tell you how worried I've been. I thought you had been kidnapped or something!'

He laughs hysterically. And you laugh with him. The very idea! You, Laura Markham, kidnapped! All of a sudden the images of your ordeal flood back: the hands on your ankles, your mouth, your breasts. The slime of Hassan's sex on your neck.

You get up and rush to the bathroom. You retch into the bowl but no vomit comes, only a thread of white saliva. And then you lie on the bed, exhausted, eyes closed, trying to turn your mind away from the horror. You remember Catherine again. She used to sing the Willow Song from Verdi's *Otello*. And in those days you played the piano well enough to accompany her. How stupid to have given up, just for the sake of the law exams.

'Are you alright?'

Justin is standing in the door of the bedroom, looking down on you with concern. He has fine blue eyes, a slightly receding brow, but a clear, honest, manly expression. This is a man you could like. You nod, and try to smile.

'A bug,' you say. 'But I'll be OK in a minute.'

He retreats and after a while you get up, take a quick shower, drink some water, and return to the living room, where he is reading through the file on the table.

'Sorry this day has been a write-off,' you say. 'But we start properly tomorrow.'

'Not a write-off at all,' he replies. 'God knows how you put your hands on this file, but you have solved the problem.'

He gives you a questioning look. You must try to be normal, look as though nothing untoward has happened. For whose sake you have to do this you do not know. But it is significant that your thoughts return to Yunus and the image of his slender fingers on the knife with which he kept that Polish captain at bay. And then there is Justin: the last thing you want is to appear in his eyes as a victim, a degraded object of a stranger's lust. He is to see you as a clean, competent professional woman, and one who is free, should she choose, to bestow her heart on a man.

'I picked it up from your office yesterday – it was under some books and papers in a corner, as though someone had wanted to hide it. I meant to work on it this morning, but I wasn't feeling too good – went out for a walk, must have missed you when you let yourself in. I tried to ring,' you lie, 'but you were out of the office.'

He begins to relax.

'Yes, I was out all day, as a result of this file. But maybe I had better leave you now, Laura. I am sure you need to get some rest.'

'Actually I could do with some food. If you haven't eaten could we go out somewhere?'

Normal courtesies, normal appetites, normal business dealings, normal surroundings – how necessary they are, and how soon you feel normal too, as you sit in the little Italian restaurant with a plate of pasta and a glass of Frascati. For a blessed moment it is as though it never happened, a nightmare with no roots in reality. When, from time to time, the black thoughts return, they take a vengeful form, urging you to complete what you began with the monkey wrench. And one day you will.

Justin's story is like a picture that has been clipped round the edges, so that the shadows are cast by absent people and the expressions are without a visible cause. Was Justin in love with this Afghan girl who worked for him? Is he hoping to excuse her conduct, by explaining that she never intended to cheat the firm, but only to find a legal route for her family's dodgy business? You cannot tell. All you know is that Justin has more emotion invested in this case than he ought to have, and that someone – himself, perhaps, or the girl – is going to get hurt. Still, you agree to meet her next morning, and to see whether it would be possible to rewrite last summer's accounts with the alien transfers removed from them.

Later, in bed, the unpurged images of day do not recede. But you wrestle them under the pillow. For a while you get by with *The Wind in the Willows*. Then you try singing 'Tambourine Man', which brings a flood of sudden tears. You think about Justin, picture his bachelor life, and wonder whether there is room in it for a real woman, or whether he will always feel safer with some buttoned up refugee determined to cheat her way past the normal barriers. Towards morning you fall into a restless sleep, and start awake at eight, your dream-hand groping for a monkey wrench, your memory telling you that it was not just a dream.

Chapter 24

Justin lay on the leather couch, with 'Insect' in his ears. He could not make sense of anything – of Muhibbah, of Laura, of himself – and the crazy lyrics mimicked his mood. 'Insect spawning, hybrids crawling/ In spinning cluster skies we're soaring'. He reached down for the tumbler on the woollen carpet and raised it to his lips. To drink the whisky he had to sit up straight; the iPod earphones fell from his head and were swallowed by the silence. It was past midnight, and the sleeping city emitted only a few motorised snores. He went back again over the day's events. Something was missing, some vital piece of information that would tie the narrative together and show what it really meant. Was Muhibbah's story the truth? He doubted it. And her kiss, the first that she had ever bestowed: did it have some other motive than desire? He recalled the image that had flashed through his mind as he made that phone call: the image of a kidnapped girl, shipped in misery and humiliation to a life of sexual slavery. In some way slavery and honour were connected in Muhibbah's world. Her rock-hard purity had to be paid for, and not paid for by her. 'I am a gift or nothing' she had shouted at the sun. But gift-giving cultures depend on covert deals, and in covert deals Muhibbah and her tribe were experts, not troubling to distinguish between the deals that were legal and those that were crimes.

Once he had wanted to fight for her against every threat. But maybe, as Iona said, the real threat was not to Muhibbah, but from her. It was in such terms that he should interpret that kiss. In itself it was a sign only. But it promised something vast and engulfing in its fullness. It was the avatar of a complete bodily entwinement, a nuptial melting together from which there would be no return. Did he want that? Once, perhaps, he had wanted it. But only because, in his infatuation, he had not examined what it meant.

And then there was Laura, whose beauty was the opposite of Muhibbah's and who had seemed, at the first encounter, exactly what he hoped for – honest, open and engaged, with none of Muhibbah's secret corners: the one who unravels mysteries, not the one who creates them. But meeting her again, after the strange and only partly explained day of her disappearance, he hardly recognized her. She was nervous, distracted, uncertain of herself. Her face had a bruised and slightly swollen look, as though she had been taking drugs. Yes, she was beautiful, exqui-site in her way. But she seemed to have lost all interest in the job for which he had hired her. It was as though she were warning him off. Maybe she suffered from some debilitating disorder – bipolar syndrome, perhaps, which would send her plummeting to the depths of a familiar and dreaded depression. Yes, perhaps that was it. He felt sorry for her, but not so sorry as he felt for himself, who had invested his hopes in Laura, and once more lost them all at a go.

He woke with a start, his head befuddled by whisky, his body on fire from a dream of Muhibbah's kiss. It was eight o'clock and his mobile phone was ringing beside the bed, into which he had heaved himself six hours before. The voice that spoke in his ear was Muhibbah's.

'I've got to see you right away. It is urgent, I'll come to the office. Please be there, Justin. Please, as soon as you can.'

She was waiting in the street outside the office, the knuckle of one finger in her mouth, her thin shoes drumming on the pavement. They went in silence to the lift. As the door closed she uttered a dry sob and fell into his arms. He felt her hair on his cheek, her breasts against his body; he smelled her dry sandalwood smell. But they had reached the third floor and the door had opened before he could kiss her. As they went across to the office she averted her face.

'I have no right to ask you for anything, Justin. I owe you already so much.'

They were the only people in the office, and she was sitting across from him at his desk. Outside the spring sun was dusting the rooftops with gold. Her sleeveless coat was hanging on the back of the door behind her. Justin was astonished by this, and wondered whether the letter and the poem were still in the pocket. His brain was not working properly, and the most ordinary things were mysterious.

'You owe me nothing, Muhibbah,' he said. 'Maybe an explanation though.'

She put her hand to her mouth, stifling a sob.

'It's Yunus,' she said. 'Something's happened on that ship, something terrible that he won't talk about. And now he has to flee. He says he must disappear by tonight.'

'For good?'

'Yes, for good. And before they catch up with him.'

'They?'

209

'His partners in the business. Hassan has had an accident, a burst ear-drum and a cracked skull: he's in hospital in Hull. Likely to be there for a month or more. Hassan has ways of collecting money – he could have found the cash they are asking for. But Yunus has no, what do you call it, no leverage. He is just a boy. And there's something else too. Yunus won't tell me what it is, but something they want from him – something that he cannot give. So he's going to slip away, back to Yemen, melt into a warrior tribe as our father did. And I am to go with him. Britain, he tells me, is no place for a Muslim girl.'

'Not possible, Muhibbah. You simply can't. And anyway, who says you're a Muslim girl?'

'But who is to prevent me?'

'You yourself,' he replied.

She looked at him narrowly and nodded.

'So you haven't understood what I told you yesterday, Justin.'

'What do you mean?'

'You could prevent it. I cannot.'

'Explain yourself.'

She got up and began to walk around the office. At one point she stopped by the desk she used to occupy, picked up her accountancy textbook, and gave a wry smile. Then she came across and stood beside him, one hand on his shoulder.

'Look at me, Justin.'

He did as she commanded, and the beauty of her face disarmed him. She was watching him from a region that he could never enter, where the rules by which he had lived did not apply.

'I am talking about people who have no standing in your society Justin, illegal immigrants, criminals, people who live in the shadows, who have to enforce their deals by means that you need never use. I am the only part of Yunus that they could punish. If he goes then no one else in my family will lift a finger to protect me. You are all that I have.'

'You *might* have had me, but you rejected me.'

His voice trembled, and against his better judgment he laid a hand on the hand that still rested on his shoulder.

'You are wrong, Justin. I did not reject you. I was never in a position to reject you, or to accept you either. Of course I had a chance to free myself from the world I come from, to be a modern British girl, Justin's girl, for however long he might be interested. But that would not have been right for you or for me. When the crisis came and I had to choose I made the wrong choice. I should have told my brother to back away from me. But I didn't and you don't forgive me.'

She stated it as a matter of fact, part of that world of rigid law and custom, which a solitary girl has no power to change.

'So what are you asking, Muhibbah?'

'Isn't it obvious? If I were to marry someone it could only be you. As your wife I would be safe; as Yunus's abandoned sister I would be punished in the normal way of the girls who have fallen foul of them. So I have three possibilities: to go with Yunus into the desert, to stay here with you, or to kill myself. Which is it to be?'

'You make marriage sound like a move in a game of chess, like castling, or something. But I was brought up to think that marriage is about love.'

'*Bismillahi*, Justin, isn't it obvious that I love you?'

Justin, to whom it was not obvious at all, nevertheless pressed his hand on hers, and nodded silently.

'All these months, shut away in that place, with neighbours who looked at me as though I were a terrorist or something, keeping house for Yunus and dealing with so many mysteries, all with a single meaning which is money, can you imagine what I felt? I longed to be back in the office, listening to you talking about your music, about poetry and painting and land-scapes and all those peculiar English things that I wanted to know, like whether the Queen could sack the Prime Minister or why there are two archbishops and not three or one. You know I joined the travelling library that comes twice a month to Buckton, and I read the novels that you talked about – have you not noticed how my English has improved? Well, I did that because it made me close to you again. And although I was shocked and frightened when I heard that a stranger had dis-covered what Yunus is up to and where he lives, it was a joy to discover that the stranger was you. At last I could put things right, and do what I should have done all those months ago, which is to join myself to you.'

She did not look at him as she spoke, but addressed the wall of the office, as though testifying before an imaginary judge. Justin regretted the whisky he had drunk the night before, and which was impeding his thoughts. He recalled Iona telling him that there can be a multicultural society, but there cannot be multi-cultural love. And he wondered whether Muhibbah's words were a proof or a disproof of that maxim. She could have let him know months ago that she wanted the closeness she now was claiming; she could have made an effort to be in touch from her village hideout; she could have broken away from her criminal brother at any time had she chosen to turn to Justin for help. But it was only now, when he was the last recourse and the least of the three evils confronting her, that she was declaring her love for him. And whether she was discovering her love or inventing it he could not tell. Nevertheless, he rose to his feet, turned to her, and held her beautiful face in his hands. She looked at him steadily, as a proud desert girl looks at her fate, be it love or death. And she returned his kiss with a passion that surprised him.

'So what are we going to do, Muhibbah?' he asked as he broke away.

'It is up to you, Justin. Here I am, if you want me.'

'And how do I know that this time you really will have nothing more to do with that family of yours?'

'Because they will have nothing to do with me. My cousin already told you that, when you visited them in the Angel Towers.'

'So you know about my visit?' he asked in surprise.

'How could I not?'

'And you weren't moved to get in touch with me?'

'Being moved to do things is not in my nature Justin. I can make decisions. Or I can receive orders. At the moment I am waiting for orders.'

'In that case, can you wait a little longer, until after our meeting with the accountant, when I have had time to think?'

'I am meeting Yunus at twelve. So you have till then, three hours by my watch.'

She smiled, a firm, hard smile that gave nothing away. Then she kissed him tenderly on both cheeks and sat down across from him at the desk. He was still in a state of confusion, both elated and apprehensive, when his secretary arrived, looked through the door, greeted Muhibbah with a gasp of astonishment, and then withdrew again.

Muhibbah begged him to be understanding about the accounts. She had not meant to damage the business, had kept meticulous records of which transactions belonged to the Shahin account and which to Copley Solutions. It could all be disentangled and rewritten. The loss of the computer wasn't important:

she had copied her work, and told her brother that the copy was lost. She took a CD from the little carpet bag she carried and placed it on his desk, with an earnest look as though to imply that this was a sufficient exculpation. When Laura arrived a moment later Justin rapidly withdrew his hand from Muhibbah's, which she had reached towards him across the desk. Muhibbah's hand, however, remained where it was. And it was on the long fingers of that outstretched hand that Laura's eyes rested, as she paused in the door.

As they worked together on the accounts, checking the print-out from Muhibbah's CD with the transactions contained in the file, and collating both with the company account book, Justin became yet more convinced that Laura was not quite right in the head. He could understand Muhibbah's confused and shame-faced reaction, understand why she refused to say what the Sha-hin business involved, or why the sums were so large. He could understand why Muhibbah sat for long moments with her elbows on the desk and her face buried in her hands. But he could not fathom why Laura, who managed everything with brisk and cold instructions, kept looking Muhibbah up and down, her eyes often wide with astonishment as though trying to match that face with another in the archive of her memory. She spoke to the girl as though addressing a ghost. And once or twice Laura trembled involuntarily.

It was evident from her way of proceeding that Laura was efficient and clear-headed. It was evident too that she would dissociate herself from any attempt to cover up illegalities, and that her recommendations would be entirely transparent. But it was also clear that she was working under considerable emotional strain, as though fighting a depression that threatened constantly to get the better of her. At the same time there was a gentleness and concern in her attitude to Justin that contrasted vividly with her cold, even vindictive, approach to Muhibbah.

At a certain point Laura asked to look in the archive. While she was out of the room Muhibbah took Justin aside and whispered to him.

'My brother will be here soon.'

'You mean he is coming *here*?'

'Yes, I asked him to. He wants to meet you. After all, you know too much about him.'

'I cannot imagine what we have to say to each other.'

'Can't you? I have asked you a question. The answer is yes or no. And whichever it is, you should say it in front of him.'

She swept the hair from her forehead to reveal blazing and defiant eyes. Her lips lay together without pressure, soft, sand-coloured, sphinx-like. He shuddered at the thought of what she asked for – not love only, but an absolute unity of being.

'Good God, Muhibbah, you are not going to tell me that the decision is really his?'

'No. It is really yours.'

She turned away. When, a second later, the door opened and the familiar young man with Muhibbah's regular features stood beneath the lintel, Justin's heart sank. It was immediately clear that what Muhibbah had asked of him was impossible. To be brother-in-law to this confused delinquent, who could hardly look him in the eye and who, on being introduced, collapsed at once into a chair as though suffering from some congenital weakness – this was simply off the agenda. Even if the boy should be lost somewhere in the Yemeni desert among Salafi fanatics – even then there could be no alliance between them. He made up his mind to say this, to say it directly to Muhibba, ignoring

215

whatever presumptuous rights over her the boy might claim. He stepped forward, holding up his hand.

'There is something I want to say to Muhibbah, which in my view concerns her alone.'

The boy looked up at him with a nervous smile. Then the smile suddenly gave way to a look of shocked recognition and he rose from his chair.

'Fucking Hell! Catherine!' he cried.

Justin swung round to see Laura, her face tense, silent and full of resolve, standing in the door of the archive.

Chapter 25

You are going to be in shock for a long time. Whatever normality you are able to maintain will be a mask, and occasionally the mask will drop. This you know from those months after Father died. But you also know that there is one person who can help you. That person is Justin Fellowes. You think of him in the taxi, on the way to your 9.30 appointment. He is what a man should be: sympathetic, considerate, but imaginative and ambitious. If you were to tell your story to anyone – to any man at least, and what woman could help you? – it would be to Justin. You can even imagine him stroking your hair, your words overflowing as he wipes your tears away. And he would join you unhesitatingly in the search for revenge.

Crazy to have become attached so quickly to a person you hardly know. But perhaps he too is attached. In the labyrinth into which you both have strayed maybe you are gripping a single string.

The taxi is driving through the older part of the city: Victorian offices, neo-Gothic churches, banks in the style of Renaissance villas, and a town hall of stone with a giant Corinthian portico and a clock tower above. Well-dressed people are hurrying to work, and a modern-looking café has set up tables on the pavement. A few office workers are already sipping cappuccinos and engaging in the conversation of the day. Again normality, a modern English normality that says in genial accents that what happened to you could not have happened.

By the time you enter the office at 9.30 you are able to smile. How nicely Justin greets you, and with what a gentle protective look in his bright blue eyes. Or was the look intended for the Afghan girl, who is already there, and who seems to be reaching across to him on the desk with those long, fine walnut-coloured fingers, the very same fingers that were yesterday wrapped around a knife?

Your shock returns and for a moment you are trembling. She turns to look at you. The same eyes, the same oval face and sandy lips, the same dark olive hair – but neat, clean, self-contained, as though she has mastered her problems and can fend for herself.

The suspicion that she is Yunus's sister is already immovable as you begin to observe her tricks. She is a cheat and a manipulator. Not the untouchable jewel that her brother has placed in the only sanctuary that his broken soul acknowledges, but a canny and scheming fraudster, who has made a set at Justin in order to slip past the barrier of her crimes. She is utterly bewitching of course, and Justin is bewitched. You feel an almost motherly concern for him, a desire gently to prise his fingers loose from this toy before it explodes in his face. For you know, as he does not, the stuff the toy is made of.

She is clever too. She has kept exactly the records required in order to unpick the ravelled accounts. She has foreseen the very event that has been sprung upon her, when she has to come clean without describing her business – the business that no doubt brought the little witch to this country in the first place. How

218

cleverly she and her brothers have used their privileges as immigrants, always linking to operations beyond our national borders, and relying on political correctness to protect them from investigation at home. And why speak of home? This country is not home for them, but a hunting ground, an unbounded lucrative elsewhere. You would like to see them all in gaol.

But Yunus? The confused boy who rescued you, and who begged you to keep quiet? Of course he should be punished. But he appealed to you, and by freeing you he placed his life in your hands. Should you think of him, one of your kidnappers, as a fellow human being, to whom you are bound by moral obligations? And what would this clever manipulative girl say, if she knew that her place in her brother's heart had prevented him from raping you? And then again, do you not owe something to that other girl they mentioned, the one that is going to replace you as a sex slave? Should you not be thinking of her and how to save her? And how can you save her without betraying Yunus? And is it really a betrayal, when the boy has conducted the whole affair, from start to finish, by force? All these questions are spinning in your head as you search for the remaining Lesprom correspondence in the archive. And not one of them has received an answer when, emerging into Justin's office, you see Yunus seated in the chair by the window, looking nervous and defeated, his all too perfect sister gleaming at his side.

'Fucking Hell! Catherine!' he cries, and you are obliged to correct him.

'My name is Laura. Laura Markham.'

'Why did you tell me Catherine?'

He gives you a hurt look, and then glances at his sister, whose face shows every sign of alarm.

'It is not as though you had any right to honest dealings, Yunus. Why should I let you steal my name as well?'

He is blushing now.

'OK, OK,' he mutters, and again looks sheepishly at his sister.

'What's going on?' asks Justin. 'How come you two know each other?'

'Maybe Yunus would like to explain,' you say.

The Afghan girl says something to Yunus in Arabic, and he nods. Clearly she is trying to get him out of the door, since her whole body gravitates in that direction. But Yunus remains slumped in the chair, addressing you with a baffled look.

'This is just great, man, meeting you here, you and my sister in the same place. And you gonna tell her what a shit her brother is.'

He seems to be crumbling visibly before you. You decide to address Justin instead.

'You see, Justin, I spent yesterday with Yunus here. You laughed when you spoke of me being kidnapped. But it was true.'

'It wasn't me did it!' Yunus cries, starting forward from his chair.

'Whoever *did* it,' you reply, 'hardly matters. I was kidnapped, and you were part of the action.'

'Yes, but it was a mistake see, a mistake!'

Yunus is looking at his sister imploringly, and shame is written all over her face. It is not a face made for shame. Its impeccable symmetries are designed to meet the other eye to eye, to outstare fate, and to go toward death in proud defiance. Now it is beginning to soften and collapse. She has raised a hand to her temple, and tears are gathering, ready to mar those perfect cheeks as they burst the banks of eyelids that were never meant to flutter as they are fluttering now.

220

'It was not a mistake on your brother Hassan's part that he tried to rape me.'

'Hassan!' the girl cries, and claps both her hands over her eyes.

'But he dinna do it. You said so yourself.'

Yunus's tone is urgent. It is not that he is trying to exculpate his brother. He is trying to shield his image of *you*. Somehow you have broken into the sacred space where the image of the weeping girl beside him has until now been the sole occupant. You are a woman he could love, and he is helpless before you.

'Listen, Justin,' you say. 'You can see that I fell in with a nasty crowd after I left you, when was it? Only the day before yesterday. But even if Yunus is not entirely innocent, he rescued me in the end.'

Justin has gone white and is staring at you speechless. For a moment there is no sound in the office apart from the girl's stifled weeping. Then she stops and speaks in a whisper.

'We had better go. I'm sorry, Justin. I made such a stupid request this morning. Let's not refer to it again.'

She pulls at her brother's arm and he half rises from his seat.

'Just a minute,' you say. 'There's someone else we need to think about. It was a mistake to kidnap me, because I was the wrong girl. Who was the right girl, and are you going to deliver her to that evil man Bogdan?'

'I can reassure you, Laura.'

It is Muhibbah who speaks, whispering still.

'Yes, but who was she, who is she?'

Yunus is spluttering. There are tears in his eyes as he rises.

'She is Hassan's bitch inna she? Like he decided to punish her, dinn'e, for going with that teacher guy.'

'And is she still going to be punished?'

'Depends if she talks dunnit? Is none of my business, man. Bogdan'll have it in for her though.'

'Tell me how I can get hold of her.'

'She's with that teacher guy, in the place where you live. Must be the flat above or maybe below, otherwise how could Zdenko make such a stupid fucking mistake?'

The girl is pulling at her brother's sleeve.

'I'm sorry,' she whispers. She has got him to the door. With a sudden movement she takes the sleeveless coat that is hanging there and reaches into one of the pockets.

'Justin,' she says, 'I meant to give you this months ago. And this, Yunus, is for you.'

She hands a piece of paper to each of them, one with what looks like a poem in English, the other densely covered in Arabic script. And she runs sobbing from the office. Yunus stands for a moment in the doorway, and then stumbles after her. Your legs are giving way beneath you, but Justin is beside you now, handing you to the chair that Yunus has vacated. The tears flow silently down your cheeks, and he stands beside you, stroking your hair.

'Laura, my God, Laura. What have you been through?'

You lean towards him, and you sense that healing has begun.

Chapter 26

Sharon's body is translucent, lit from within like a lamp of alabaster. On her small breasts the nipples glow blood red, and young life shines from her skin as though surfacing from sleep. Her eyes sparkle and her parted lips speak in silence the lingua franca of desire. Even the little scar beside them plays its part, as though she had bitten herself in her hunger. And the blond hair falling on her shoulders makes a soft cushion for her jewel-like head. Stephen approaches in fear and trembling. Never in his life has a girl made so complete and ingenuous an offering of herself, and he strives to put out of mind all that Sharon has been through in order to lay the gift finally before him. Love, he believes, can heal all wounds, restore all innocence and resurrect all hopes. It is love that he is offering, and a warm stream of tenderness flows to his fingertips. She draws his hand to her breast, slotting the nipple between his fingers, and runs her moist tongue along his upper lip.

'Bin wanting to do that for ages. You taste of knowledge, Stephen.'

Then she presses her mouth to his. Stephen's body is aflame. All barriers have been burned away. He nods towards the bedroom door, turning her in that direction, as footsteps sound on the stairs.

It is the first time the doorbell has ever rung during his residence. There is consternation in Sharon's face, and he steps away from her, holding a finger to his lips. The bell rings again, this time accompanied by a beating on the panels of the door. A loud male voice resounds on the stairwell.

'Open the door please. This is the police.'

Sharon snatches up the bathrobe and flees into Stephen's bedroom. Someone is trying keys in the lock. The wisest thing, Stephen realises, is to open the door before it is forced.

Two uniformed officers are on the threshold; one holds a bunch of keys; the other is a young woman with a tidy face, carrying a small suitcase. Behind them in the half light is a figure in a lime green tunic.

'I am Inspector Vines, and this is Sergeant Pinsent. With us is Iona Ferguson from the Council's department of social work. May we come in please?'

Stephen steps silently aside for them. The inspector sweeps the room with his eyes before resuming his prepared speech.

'Stephen Haycraft? We are investigating reports that a child has been abducted. She is Sharon Williams, a pupil at St Catherine's Academy, where you are a teacher. We have reason to believe that you have knowledge of the child's whereabouts.'

All formalities have become instantly pointless in Stephen's mind. The ground has gone from beneath him and he is falling. Without the letter of resignation, without the open dealings with Iona Ferguson, which he has delayed for no reason that he can now recall, he will fall until he breaks in pieces on the ground. Best to bark out the truth from the void. He stutters a little as he does so.

'Sharon is here. She has been living with me for the last two weeks. Not as a lover I should say, but there is nothing that will convince you of that.'

He notices that the female officer has opened the bathroom door where Sharon's clothes lie scattered on the floor – a cream-coloured skirt and blouse (yesterday's purchase), a cardigan, underclothes, two endearing white socks.

'So where is she, Stephen?'

It is Iona who speaks. Her assumption of familiarity – as though it is he and not Sharon who is the abducted child – arouses him. Now that he is to be stripped of all honour and dignity can he not retain his surname at least?

'She is in the bedroom, Miss Ferguson, where she fled from the bathroom when you lot started bashing the door. You can see for yourself.'

He nods towards the bedroom. Iona glances at the female officer and together they advance to the door and gently knock on it. There is no response, and Stephen's heart goes out to the child who trembles there in silence, her brief hope of happiness now utterly lost.

'Bastards!' he mutters quietly.

The two women open the door, advancing behind a shield of soothing words.

'It's all right, Sharon. We've come to collect you. You'll be OK. We're going to take you somewhere safe. Just let's get you dressed. There's no hurry.'

Suddenly the girl comes running into the living room, clutching the loose bathrobe to her chest.

'No!' she screams. 'This is home. You canna take me away!'

She clings to Stephen, who does his best to hold her at arm's length. After all, he says to himself, they must not get the wrong idea. And he utters a bitter laugh.

'It's OK, Sharon. You had better go with them. There's no future for you here. Or for me either.'

Sharon stares at him wildly.

'I'm no going back there, Stephen, not never. It's them that done this, Mum and Bogdan, innit?'

She turns on Iona.

'Innit?'

Iona greets the question with professional softness, reaching a hand to the girl's arm, and murmuring quietly.

'Exactly where the information came from is a matter for the police, Sharon. Just be assured that we won't be taking you back to Angel Towers. You'll be in a new place, with other girls of your age. You'll be completely safe.'

'No without Stephen I wunna.'

She throws her arms around Stephen and he pats her hair. He is crying now, and Inspector Vines looks away in embarrassment. His colleague has placed the suitcase on the table next to Sharon's books and papers. She opens it and looks shyly in Stephen's direction.

'I need to collect her things, Mr Haycraft. The things that are hers which she'll need.'

'There they are,' he says through his tears, and points to the little pile of books that the girl had built, the altar to knowledge at which she prayed each day.

'And her clothes?'

'She keeps them in the drawer of the sofa, where she sleeps. Don't you, Sharon?'

She is pressing her head into his side, silent, her hands fiercely clinging to his body.

'Don't you, my darling?'

Chapter 27

Often Laura broke down as she recounted her story, and some details she hurried past since they were clearly too painful to recall. But Justin was struck by her way of describing Yunus, who appeared in the character of her rescuer, the one who had fallen into this hell from a better place, where people reach hands of succour across the void. And just as Laura made a protective wall around Yunus, so Justin made a wall around Muhibbah, so that it was tacitly agreed between them that neither Yunus nor Muhibbah would be singled out for punishment.

Meanwhile, Laura insisted, the other girl must be rescued. Justin recalled the case of Sharon Williams, as Iona had described it. Almost certainly it was Sharon Williams whom they had to rescue. Almost certainly Iona would be aware of what must be done, and was probably already doing it. The first move, therefore, would be to get through to Iona and impart what she needed to know of Laura's story. That afternoon he tried several times to ring her, but was told always that she was out on a case and would probably not return to the office until next day. The case clearly required Iona's complete attention, for her mobile phone was also switched to the answer service.

In a few hours, Justin reckoned, Yunus would be out of the country, taking Muhibba with him, not to safety indeed, but to the rock hard discipline of the desert, and a marriage that would protect her honour by killing her love. So it had to be, and she herself had decided it. He looked with the remains of his love at the poem that she had given him: Yeats at his most vapid and sentimental, and Muhibbah likewise. For all those months, the poem said, she had looked at Justin and sighed, and for all those months he had been to her like wine: intoxicating, attractive, but forbidden. Such was the meaning of the poem as he now read it. And yet he lacked the surgical skills to remove her from his heart.

In the few hours of their re-meeting he had come close to loving her, close even to marrying her. He had suffered through her humiliation, had burned inwardly with shame as she was shamed, had sought in every corner of his mind for the excuses that she needed and the ways of healing her wound. And when she had fled – fled because honour required it, and only love could hold her back, a love that he had so veiled in hesitation that she could no longer rely on it – he saw the gesture as wholly admirable. She was saving him from her disgrace, and taking it with her into the void. She would disappear now, and this time finally. And he was never to know, never to enquire, what became of the girl he had so much loved.

Laura was adamant that she could not take her story to the police. There were no witnesses to what she had suffered save Yunus, but what kind of a witness was he, whose side was he on, and where would they find him? Besides, she would have to face up to her own behaviour: self-defence? Attempted murder? Maybe murder by now. She longed to be released into a purer world, where things like this could not happen. To be part of a police investigation, to revisit the foul sewer that she had escaped

228

from – how could she do this now? And what would it mean for her rescuer?

But they should explore the block of flats, Laura said, where she was staying, to see if the other girl were really there. Maybe this story of a mistake was invented for the occasion, by way of scraping together what few morsels of blamelessness might have dropped from between their criminal fingers.

Two police cars were parked in the street outside, a driver sitting in each of them. The first person they encountered on the stairs was Iona. She had her arms around a young girl, whose blanched and tear-stained face Justin had seen once before, on the staircase of the Angel Towers, during his ill-fated visit to Muhibbah's family. Iona looked up in astonishment.

'Justin!' she cried. 'How strange. Busy now, but I will ring you tonight.'

And she turned again to the girl, whom she was coaxing step by step down the stairs, and into one of the parked police cars. A woman in uniform followed them, carrying a small suitcase, which she stowed in a business-like way in the boot of the car. As Justin and Laura turned the key in the door of her flat another police officer passed, leading a young man in a tattered sports-jacket, grey flannel trousers and an unbuttoned shirt. The young man was thin, good-looking, with a crown of dark hair slightly receding at the brows. His brown eyes were bloodshot, as though he had been crying, and there was a nervous tremor around his mouth. He was carrying a plastic holdall in one hand, and a book in the other, and he stumbled slightly as he passed them so that the officer reached out to support him, only to be shrugged away.

That evening, as Justin, Iona and Laura sat together in Laura's flat, over a magnum of Justin's favourite Rioja, they each rehearsed their separate pieces of the story. Laura objected violently to the arrest of the teacher, saying that he might be the best thing, the only good thing, that had ever entered the life of that poor girl, and the only obstacle between her and a life of slavery.

'That may be true,' Iona said. 'But when the adoptive mother comes to us with a tale of abduction, saying that the girl has been absent from home for two weeks, we have to act by the rules. Sure Mrs Williams was put up to it by that vile seaman she lives with who, because he couldn't have the girl, decided to punish her instead. But that doesn't alter the case.'

'But she clung to the teacher, wanted nothing but to stay with him!'

'Listen Laura, that's how it always is. The girls in our care are vulnerable, needy, desperate for affection, and easily tricked into giving it. We have tens of abduction cases every year. And usually, when we come to collect the girls, they cling to their seducers and tell us to fuck off and leave them alone.'

'So will he go to jail?'

'That depends on the girl's testimony. Usually they clam up, and say nothing. Wendy – Sergeant Pinsent – has to get her to talk, and it won't be easy. Also it depends on you.'

Iona leaned back in the armchair and sipped from her glass, looking across at Laura in the way she had, when she put her mind on display.

'Why on Laura?' Justin asked.

'If Laura tells her story to the police they will have to investigate Bogdan Krupnik and Hassan Shahin. They will come up with the real tormentors of that poor girl, and why she fled to her teacher. His behaviour will appear in quite another light, and it is unlikely that a jury will convict him.'

Laura shook her head silently, and Justin was glad. Any police response to Laura's story would lead to enquiries about the Shahin business, and therefore about Muhibbah and her role in Copley Solutions. Besides, both of them had invested emotions in the Shahin children that they would rather not openly confess to. And there was something else too. Justin was uncertain what it was, but he saw that Laura was concealing her wounds, and had some reason for not exposing them, even if healing required it.

'Of course,' Iona said with a sympathetic nod, 'there is the matter of sex. Even if she has reached the age of consent he can still be charged with exploiting a relation of trust for sexual purposes.'

'But if she were just staying with him, as he said, sleeping on the sofa?'

Iona laughed.

'Do you believe that? A pretty girl with a crush on her teacher, all ready and willing to be used? Do attractive girls stay overnight with attractive men on the sofa next door? Besides, we found her in his bedroom, dressed in nothing but a bathrobe. Mrs Williams testifies that he had been hanging around the Angel Towers, obviously in wait for her, that he had even come knocking at the door on some excuse, hoping to find her. And of course he had twice come to see me, hoping I would prize her loose from her adoptive family and make it that much easier for him to take her under his wing.'

When Iona had left them Laura turned to Justin with a worried look.

'You know, Justin, I don't want to stay in this place. I shall lie awake shaking as I did last night. If I were to sleep on your sofa, assuming you have a sofa?'

'Do attractive girls stay overnight with attractive men on the sofa next door? Of course, I don't mean to imply that you find me attractive.'

'Oh but I do,' Laura replied. 'However I still want to lie on the sofa, and to sense you sleeping next door.'

Justin's sleep was disturbed by a dream. In the dream Muhibbah was crying, imploring him to help her. A strange hand was on her shoulder and a knife was held at her throat. He explained carefully that the time had come to play by the rules, and that her past behaviour must be taken into account when deciding what it would be permissible for him to do. 'Please, Justin!' she cried, 'I love you, will be good to you, will never leave you!' He consulted the file of correspondence with Lesprom, in which he was sure he could find instructions as to how he should respond to her. But the pages were written in Arabic script and he couldn't read them. There must be some other source that he could consult and he hastily searched his desk for it. Then she reached across to him. In her hand was a piece of paper, on which she had written 'I look in your eyes and I sigh'. He looked in her eyes. And they stared steadily into his as the knife speared her throat.

With a cry Justin awoke. A figure in a white nightdress stood above him, shimmering in the twilight that seeped through the curtains.

'Perhaps Iona was right after all,' Laura said. 'I don't want to do anything. But would you mind just holding me for a while?'

Justin pulled back the bedclothes and guided her in beside him. She was warm, soft, with a clean smell like a freshly bitten apple. She put her head on his shoulder and her arms around his body. And she sobbed herself to sleep.

Chapter 28

Stephen's arrest, which hit both the local and the national
newspapers within a day, coincided with one of the periodic
panics over paedophilia. The letters pages were full of the topic,
and while no accusations could be directly printed since the case
was *sub judice*, the commentators made a point of emphasizing
the risks that children were exposed to from figures in authority,
and especially from priests and schoolteachers.

One argued in mildly exonerating terms that paedophilia
lacks a precise definition and that a girl of sixteen is, after all, no
longer a child in law. One commentator even dared to suggest
that the presumption of innocence should favour the teacher
rather than the pupil. For in our sexualised culture, he wrote, in
which young girls are routinely dressed as whores and larded
with make-up, in which pornography circulates freely in the
classroom, and children as young as twelve are in the habit of
texting provocative photographs of themselves to the boyfriend
or girlfriend of the day, it can hardly be expected that a teacher
should remain unmoved when a sixteen-year-old makes a pass at
him. But the writer of that piece was promptly fired, and things
returned to the norm, which was one of guilt-ridden hysteria,

among people who know that they have lost all influence over the sexual lives of their children and are in deep need of some-one – someone else – to take the blame.

Stephen was refused bail, partly for his own protection. His address was freely circulating among the residents of Angel Tow-ers and stones thrown from the car park soon broke the windows of his flat. Although the school issued a notice to all parents explaining that Stephen Haycraft had been dismissed from his post, this did not prevent a new series of protests, many initiated by the local mosques.

Muslim girls, the imams said, were exposed to a licentious way of life, propagated through schools in which the culture, the cur-riculum and even the teachers themselves conspire against their chastity. St Catherine's Academy was a prime example of this, and they called not only for its closure but for the establishment of an Islamic secondary college that would serve the local com-munity and enjoy exemptions from the National Curriculum as required by the Faith.

Meanwhile Stephen, held on remand in a Midland city, where he was housed in a unit reserved for sexual offenders, was treated to a continuous stream of abuse from the officers who guarded him, and required several stitches in his wrist after being attacked by another prisoner, who screamed 'kid fucker' in his face while swinging a broken bottle against the hand Stephen raised to pro-tect himself.

Conditions for prisoners on remand are little better than those for convicted offenders, and although Stephen had a cell to him-self, and was allowed visits from a solicitor, contact with the out-side world was minimal. Sharon had been placed in secure Council accommodation, and all communication between her and Stephen was strictly forbidden while the case was being prepared. In the two months that led to his trial, therefore, Stephen was isolated, threatened and suicidal.

It was especially difficult at night, when his fellow prisoners, most of them habituated to their status as social outcasts, joined in a chorus of welcome, accompanying themselves by sounding spoons on the heating pipes and mounting a crescendo of obscene abuse that ended only when stopped by threats from the supervising officers. In the silence that ensued, Stephen sat in darkness on the edge of his bunk, his hands fallen between his thighs, knowing that there was nowhere downhill from the place he had got to.

His career was over – so what? It was only because of Sharon that he had taken any joy in it. What did it matter that he would be punished for conduct that was more stupid than criminal? But Sharon! The girl had lost her only protector; she would be dragged back into the sewer from which he had tried to lift her. The one moment of happiness, when her body glowed before him and her face was radiant with joy at his approach, would be the last that she would know. He regretted many things, but most of all that he had never told her that he loved her.

He tried to guess what she was feeling. Guilt at having dragged him down. Fear for him and for herself. Terror at what awaited her, when her tormentors finally got her from the children's home. Despair too, recognizing that the vision of a shared future, in which his knowledge and her poetry would flow together in a single creative stream, was no more than a hallucination.

On the day before his trial Stephen was notified that one of the charges – abusing a position of trust for sexual purposes, as defined by the Sexual Offences Act 2003 – had been dropped. Expert examination of the abducted girl had shown that there had been no sexual relations with the accused. Stephen felt only desolation on hearing this news, for it brought to mind the humiliating tests that Sharon would have been forced to undergo, polluting the body that she had washed in so many tears to make a gift for him. He wished that the trial were over now. Perhaps some other man, less stupid and less besotted than himself, would stumble across this pure soul and strive to rescue her. Let him only be a man with a heart!

All that night Stephen prayed for her in those terms, not knowing to whom, not knowing how, but chasing the thought before him into the future, begging the world to make a place for it. In a brief sleep before dawn he dreamed of her: she came to him, naked as he had seen her in their last moment of joy. She held a lighted candle above her head. She spoke to him as though reading aloud from one of her essays, with only the trace of a Yorkshire accent. 'I am young, Stephen, like Juliet or Iphigenia. I chose you because you are there, like a mountain. Send me soon your letter of acceptance. And please include your knowledge.' She smiled at him, and the scar across her mouth was clearly visible. 'Who did it to you Sharon?' he asked. 'It's a secret, Stephen. I'll tell you though, when we're married.' He reached out to her, and a breath of wind issued from his body, extinguishing the candle. She vanished, and he awoke with the conviction that Sharon would soon be dead.

Chapter 29

Whether you will ever make love to a man again you do not know. Justin is gentle and considerate. As you work together in the office, discovering more of that girl's intrusions, he constantly engages you in conversation, always expressing himself with a kind of nuptial tenderness that you never experienced from Mick. In the evenings you enjoy each other's company over wine and music – though not *his* music, which sounds to you like the croaking of a desiccated frog. He seems to feel no resentment when you describe Spiral Architect as narcissistic and Metallica as pseudo-poetry, and this is amazing since Metal is a part of his life and the thing that he and Iona share. He seems really interested in your taste, and happy to dig up the Beethoven quartets in the Guarneri performance, which he has not listened to for years.

At night, too, when you start awake in terror as the sack on top of you begins to squirm and you climb for comfort into Justin's bed, he is ready at once to put his arms around you, to stroke your hair and soothe you back to sleep. Perhaps it is through pure good nature that he makes no attempt to arouse you, or perhaps he has not recovered from that witch, who has poisoned his manhood.

At times you are almost jealous of the girl, who captured Justin's heart without deserving it. If you were to make love to him, maybe it would be to take revenge on her. But then you think of Yunus. You wonder what has happened to him, and the strange murmur begins again in your heart, the murmur of the voice that says 'forgive'.

After a week or two it is clear that things are not yet getting better for you. Of course, you are bright, efficient, professional. You are good company too, so long as you can keep your mind occupied by normal things. But the work of healing is slow and tortuous. And somehow your case becomes entangled in your thoughts with that of Sharon Williams. Iona is working with Wendy Pinsent on the testimony, and she does not hesitate to pass on the details.

The girl will say nothing about the ordeals from which she fled to her teacher. She refuses to see her adoptive mother, and goes white at the mention of Bogdan Krupnik. Medical tests suggest that there was, after all, no sex between her and the teacher, and the only charge to be brought is one of abduction and false imprisonment.

The Crown Prosecution Service will rely on the girl and Mrs Williams in evidence. But the real crime – and here Iona agrees with you – is the one from which Sharon fled. Superintendent Nicholson refuses to investigate the Shahin family. He has had too much trouble from the anti-racists and besides the Shahins are well connected throughout the Afghan and the Iraqi communities, and connected too with the Mosque. The Superintendent will act only on clear proof of a crime.

You can give that proof – or you thought you could. But now the nightmare has taken over. You are no longer certain of what happened. You owe your life to a confused boy who wanted to rape you and couldn't go through with it. You attacked the one who almost succeeded where his brother failed. But all this occurred because you were not the person you should have been.

You dream of that person, dream that you *are* her after all. You are the abused girl they sought to punish. You had fled to your teacher, the one who would provide culture, knowledge, language, ease of manner – all those things that guaranteed, in the world of Laura Markham, a life in the open, and which rendered kidnap, abduction, rape and slavery inconceivable.

You recall the teacher's looks as he stumbled past you on the stairs – spectral, other-worldly, seeming to consult some distant vision that made him blind to his immediate surroundings. You imagine his loneliness and his defiance of the world. You are his sole raison d'etre, the pure soul that he will rescue from corruption. How could you not love him, and what purer longing could there be than yours – the longing to bring peace and hope to the person who brought peace and hope to you?

At night you imagine him as he prepares himself for sleep. You rehearse the goodnight kisses, which are all that the two of you allow, since the restoration of purity is more precious than the transports of desire. You settle on the pillow and a tranquil breeze of affection wafts about you. Gradually your nightmares recede, and the image of the teacher comes in place of them.

You are sometimes in London now, searching the flat in Camden town for your former self, but meeting always someone else in the bathroom mirror. And each time you return with relief to Justin, as an adolescent returns to the parental home. By the time of the trial you rarely need to take up your allotted place in Justin's bed, and he, being the decent person you have come so much to like and respect, is pleased by this, imagining that you are at last on the mend. In fact you have acquired another person's peace by acquiring her fears.

Thus it is that, on the day of the trial, you are alongside Justin in the public gallery, amid a crowd of vindictive morons who are hissing beneath their breath at the teacher who sits with bowed head on the bench below them, like Orestes before the Furies. You are shaking with fear, not for him only, but for yourself. There, summoned by Counsel for the prosecution, is Mrs Williams, a wan housewife in a flowery cotton dress, who looks shiftily from side to side as she responds to Counsel's promptings. There is no doubt that you, Sharon, have become a thorn in her flesh since Krupnik came on the scene. You are acutely aware that for Krupnik you are Hassan's bitch, and therefore should have been part of the deal. That is one reason, but not the only reason, for your punishment.

According to your adoptive mother Mr Haycraft would often hang around the Angel Towers. It made Mrs Williams very uncomfortable, she could certainly say. The teacher even came knocking on the door with a feeble excuse, but suddenly ran away when he caught sight of you fleeing in the distance. Yes, it was clear that Sharon was stressed, was under pressure, was trying to escape from something. Mrs Williams couldn't rightly say that Sharon was fleeing from Mr Haycraft's pestering, but it is more than likely.

Counsel for the Defence makes short shrift of Mrs Williams, who leaves the witness box shame-faced and shaking, no longer the adoptive mother of Sharon but the manipulated mistress of a criminal seadog, who had his own reasons for shopping the girl to the police. Called by the Prosecution, Iona Ferguson gives her even-handed version, emphasizing your vulnerability, and the

240

many attempts that the social workers have made to ascertain whether you are the target of abuse.

You were attracted to the teacher, Iona concludes, because he offered so much that is lacking in your adoptive home. This tempted him to overstep the mark, inviting you to his flat, and then deciding to keep you there. Whether this amounts to abduction she leaves it to the court to decide. But in Iona's view you were certainly under emotional pressure to stay in the place to which he had enticed you.

You listen with a measure of surprise to Iona's account of things. Why does she not mention the abuse from which you were fleeing? Is Iona protecting someone? You cannot tell, but when she leaves the witness box, her reputation as a wise and impartial helper undented by the opposing Counsel's few respectful questions, you accept that her testimony, offered on behalf of the Prosecution, is also a kind of defence.

You watch from the gallery as your alter ego is handed by Iona into the box. Once before you had glimpsed the girl, as she was coaxed as though unconscious down the stairs of your block. You too had been carried unconscious down those stairs, to the fate that was hers in intention, but yours in fact. Now you can study her more completely.

Her hair is blond like yours but disordered, falling over her forehead and into her eyes. Her dress – white blouse and cream skirt, white socks and Mary Jane shoes – is the dress of a child. Across the edge of her mouth is a slight scar, the only blemish on an angel face worthy of a Sienese fresco. Her expression is solemn, as though she has stepped into the witness box from a place where truth has already been established, and no discussion remains. As she walks forward to take the oath she looks resolutely across at her teacher. It is him and not the court that she addresses. Prosecuting Counsel asks her to confirm that it was true that she left home on the fourth of April, to live with her teacher.

'No, sir,' she says. 'I dinna leave home then. I come home then.'

The barrister rephrases the question.

'There be two o' me, sir, one in prison, t'other free. The free one, sir, answering your question, she belongs with Stephen, Mr Haycraft there. T'other one dunna answer no questions never.'

This response baffles the barrister, but you understand it at once. 'Yes,' you say beneath your breath, 'that's how it is, how it must be.' You start forward in your seat, Justin restraining you with an anxious hand on your arm. You speak the girl's words, and think the thoughts that she does not speak. Again you are she, as she spells out the ordeal that you have undergone.

You have been divided in two by what has happened. You have been trapped, beaten, cajoled and threatened into becoming someone else – some *thing* else, an object to be played with, a toy made of flesh. How do you respond to this? There is only one way: to leave behind the thing that has been battered and bartered, to remake yourself as a gift. But a gift for whom? All your efforts have been devoted to that question, and at last they were rewarded, when knowledge, poetry and grace appeared before you in the person of a kind young teacher, with whose predicament you alone could sympathize.

All this you understand through the girl's quirky idiom. But Defence Counsel wants more. He wants to force that other thing to speak. He wants to impress on the jury that you had no choice but to seek help from your teacher and that he had no choice but to offer it.

'T'other thing,' you say at last, 'is Hassan's bitch.'

'And who, Sharon, is Hassan?'

'Canna tell you, sir.'

Yes, but you must. You must begin your revenge, our revenge. Prosecution objects that the question is irrelevant. But the judge allows it nevertheless. Counsel for the Defence resumes.

'Listen, Sharon. The future of my client depends on your testimony. I need to know why you went to live with him. There are before us two answers to that question. One is that my client, in order to satisfy his sexual desires, enticed you into his home and kept you there. The other is that you had been targeted by people who abused you, and begged my client to take you in. Which answer is the true one?'

'The second one, sir.'

'So now you must tell me something about those who abused you. If you do not, how can I persuade the jury that my client took you in because he had no moral alternative?'

The girl allows her eyes to wander from those of her teacher. She is trembling. You are trembling. The assembled morons are leaning forward with intent and greedy faces, and there is a hush in the courtroom. Suddenly you burst out with a sob:

'They done it, sir, Hassan and his brother down on the eighth floor. It was them done it to me like they done it to Moira Callaghan.'

No exoneration for Yunus: you clench your fists against him. The teacher sits with his face in his hands. He too is weeping. Only one thing in the ensuing story surprises you. While the sister was at home the boys behaved correctly. 'She was Yunus's idol, like you dinna touch her or use bad language in front of her or speak about those dirty things.' She was holy; even Hassan was different around her, like he was secretly wanting her to bless him. But the sister ran away. Then, bit by bit though you fought against it with every weapon you had, you became two people: Hassan's bitch, and Sharon. Sharon was pure as Muhibbah: she was going to be someone's wife, the wife of a poet. You had your girlish dreams, just as Catherine had.

By the time they take the girl away you are sobbing uncontrollably. Justin wants to leave but you shake your head. Sympathy has veered towards the teacher. But the judge instructs the jury to convict him of abduction if they believe he has made improper use of his position in order to entice the girl from her home. Following the guilty verdict the judge accepts Defence Counsel's Plea in Mitigation, agreeing that there had been no sexual exploitation of the child, and also that the teacher had been under a clear moral obligation to protect her from the abuse that she suffered. But Stephen's failure to alert the police casts a dim light upon his actions, and the judge therefore has no alternative but to sentence him to a year's imprisonment, with a recommendation that the Prison Service consider, for his own safety, a secure unit for sexual offenders.

You watch as the teacher is led away, face white, eyes staring, a policeman at either elbow. You turn to Justin. He too has been weeping.

'So, Justin, if you'll come with me, it's time for me to go to the police.'

He takes your hand and squeezes it.

Chapter 30

After a week or so Justin had begun to be much in awe of Laura. Her courage, her ability to confine her terrors to the night, her uncomplicated appeal to him for affection and comfort, her honesty in all that concerned her – those virtues commanded so much admiration that he did not dare to move things forward for fear of looking cheap. But nor were they just good friends. They were joined by something huge, subliminal and dangerous and they were side by side in knowing this.

Dealing with the effects of Muhibbah's trickery was not always easy. He tried to excuse the girl; Laura tried not to accuse her. And often they had to move around each other carefully, like boxers feinting in the ring. But difficult though the day might be, they were entirely at one in the evening, Justin cooking, Laura listening to music or reading his books.

He was surprised how much he could appreciate classical music, which filled the space that Laura made for it. He felt no need to pluck the strings of his guitar; he was happy to forget the iPod and only rarely, when she was asleep or out, did he listen to his favourite Metal songs. Metal expressed, it is true, a cherished ideal of manliness, and he still played his Thursday gig at the Crustafarian. But he left his manhood there, as a costume to be donned for the crowd. On other evenings he was a kind of housewife, appreciating Laura's beauty from his place at the stove.

Once he caught himself singing 'The Disappeared'. But when he got to the H on *Habibah* he stopped. 'Don't go there,' he said aloud. And he went back to Laura's supper, which involved h's of a less blood-stirring kind: hake, halibut and haddock, in a sauce of egg yolks and cream.

He understood her reluctance to go to the police. Reliving the event would be difficult. Explaining her assault on Hassan could open her to criminal charges. But there could be no healing until she had seen her abuser punished and his criminal network exposed. Gently he urged her to lay a complaint. Iona likewise wanted this, though she too was reluctant to press Laura too hard. And so things continued for two months, during which time Laura would often go to London, as though to recapture a life of which he was not a part. But always she came back to him, with the look of one returning home, quietly to resume her place on the couch.

One Thursday, after his gig at the Crustafarian, Justin went with Iona for a drink. It was the day after the trial of Sharon Williams's teacher, and he was curious to know why Iona's evidence had been so reticent, and why she had veered away from the crucial fact of Sharon's persecution.

Iona became pensive, and her face assumed a puffy appearance, as she half closed her eyes. She pushed her gin and tonic to one side and leaned forward on the table, her chin in her hands.

'It's like this, Justin,' she said. 'Everything in that world is governed by a code of honour. Girls who have sex have lost their honour, and are therefore the property of the man who mastered

246

them, even if he did so by force. I have been through this, and I know. And honour codes are not enforced as our codes are enforced, by legal sanctions. Defence Counsel thought he was doing his client a favour, by trapping that poor girl into naming her abusers. Now of course it will be all over the papers and the police will have to step in.'

'So? Isn't that what we want?'

'Eventually yes. But only when that girl is safe. I don't have much time for Jesus, though when it comes to the treatment of women I give him a bit more credit than Muhammad. However, he did say one true thing, which is "Greater love hath no man than this, that he lay down his life for his friend." That, I fear, is what Sharon Williams has done. There is a whole network of criminals out there who depend on her silence: one reason for packing her off to Russia. A lot, you see, has become clear to me over the last couple of weeks. When that teacher first came to see me I have to admit that he got up my nose, talking to me as though I hadn't had to deal with case after case of this kind of thing. So I dithered until you told me about Muhibbah, and the pieces began to fit together in my mind. I realised we are dealing with a full-scale business of people trafficking. Of course there is not a lot we can do now, but it would help if Laura went to the police, so that Sharon's evidence isn't the only evidence they have.'

'It's exactly what Laura decided, when she saw what the girl was going through.'

'Then she must act quickly. And that means now, before that girl is killed.'

It clearly did not please Superintendent Nicholson that Justin, who had been placed in the mental file for problems solved, was once again sitting on the other side of his desk, this time with a lovely woman beside him. The Superintendent was already agitated on account of the Haycraft trial, which had been all over the newspapers and the local radio. The suggestion was being widely made that political correctness had caused his force to turn a blind eye to cases of sexual abuse. But as Laura's story unfolded, she meanwhile gripping Justin's hand and dabbing away tears with a crumpled handkerchief, the Superintendent's expression changed from bewildered resentment at this new intrusion to grim recognition that the day of judgment had come. At a certain point he raised his hand to interrupt the story.

'You can pass over all the details Miss Markham. If they are relevant you can tell them to Sergeant Wendy Pinsent. All I need from you now is a specific complaint against specific persons.'

But when the names turned out to be those blurted out by Sharon Williams in the Haycraft trial, brothers of the girl whose disappearance he had refused to investigate when Justin had requested it, the Superintendent's face registered his disturbance. He dropped his eyes, which had until that moment been outlining Laura as though to store her in digital format, and focused instead on the photographs of his wife and children. By the time Laura reached the end of her story he had covered two sheets of paper with notes, and was on the telephone to colleagues in Hull, asking them to take a statement from a patient admitted to hospital two months earlier with a life-threatening head injury. The message came back that the patient had left the day before, without waiting to be discharged. An officer sent to Angel Towers reported that Block A flat 8/1 was now unoccupied, the family having moved out a week ago, in response to an order from the Council.

'I know where you might find him,' Justin said, and he recounted the events that led from Laura's disappearance to the discovery of Muhibbah. The Superintendent criticised Justin for not reporting Laura's disappearance immediately to the police, but he let the matter drop when Justin reminded him that he had reported a missing person once before, only to be brushed aside by the Superintendent.

The decision was taken to leave Laura with Wendy Pinsent, while Justin accompanied the Superintendent and another officer to the village of Buckton.

It was late morning when they reached Falkin's Yard, under grey skies and a faint but persistent drizzle. The rubbish had not been removed from Muhibbah's holiday home. The curtains were drawn, there was no car parked outside, and the place had an abandoned air. Justin assumed that she and Yunus had left for Yemen and that Hassan would soon be following them if he could escape whatever net the police were laying. He was surprised, therefore, that the door was swinging on its hinges.

'Bad sign', said the Superintendent. 'Better get the gloves. And you, Mr Fellowes, had better wait outside.'

Justin protested, but to no avail. The two officers, wearing latex gloves, examined the lock of the door before they entered. After a minute Justin donned a pair of gloves that they had left on the driver's seat and followed them. It was dark inside, the grey daylight barely making it through the curtains to lie like a dirty crust on the cluttered furniture. A faint odour lingered in the sitting room, like the smell of a wild animal's lair, an odour of dead and dismembered things. All the curtains were drawn, and all the windows closed.

The officers turned on the wall lamps in the adjoining room, and a band of yellow light shot across the dirty white carpet from wall to wall. Cushions were heaped up in one corner and this, he saw, was Muhibbah's corner, with a neat pile of books, one on top of the other, including all the novels of Jane Austen and George Eliot, as well as poems in Arabic. There was a notebook too, in which she had written remarks in English and Arabic: he put it quickly back on the pile, respectful of her fiercely defended privacy. In the opposite corner was a television, the floor around it littered with DVDs. The walls were bare except for a framed text in ornamental Arabic script, picked out in green and gold.

The silence was strange, as though it had been stored there, and he wondered why there was no noise from the adjoining room. An oppressive grief descended on him, long shadow of his love. In this secret place she had been alone except for her brother's visits, trapped by the futile imperatives of a culture that she could have escaped at any time if she had reached a gentle hand to him. Loneliness lingered there, the loneliness of Muhibbah and her pride. He remembered her kisses, three of them, each more needful than the last. And he wondered whether she would ever kiss again, when she had been bartered away in the Yemeni desert. A stream of regretful love sped from his heart towards that distant place, and he sadly whispered her name.

His thoughts were interrupted by the Superintendent, who stepped in from the adjoining room.

'Ah, I didn't intend you to come in. Hope you haven't touched anything. You are wearing gloves I see, which is good. If you could just come in here a moment. Tell me if you recognize this woman.'

She was wearing a pale blue nightdress and lying on the floor beside the unmade bed. Her eyes were wide and staring, and dark blood from a wound in her neck had soaked the carpet.

'Muhibbah!' he cried, and dropped to his knees beside her.

'Don't touch!' the Superintendent ordered.

'Muhibbah! Darling! Why?'

The officer took him beneath the armpits and lifted him away from the body.

'Is she dead?'

'Stone dead,' the Superintendent replied. 'For several days already, if you ask me.'

'Muhibbah!'

'I'm sorry, Mr Fellowes. I realise she meant a lot to you. But it's what we expect in the people-trafficking business. The rewards are great, and the punishments likewise. We can leave Sergeant Meredith here to wait for the pathologist. I'll drive you back to town.'

Chapter 31

Nothing in the trial of his teacher surprised Farid Kassab. And if it were true, as the tweets and blogs repeated, that the Shahin brothers were the culprits, this too he had half foreseen. Why had their sister fled, if not to escape their pollution? He knew in his heart that Mr Haycraft was good, knew that he had diverged from the path of illumination and righteousness only because a weak human being had appealed to him for help, hoping to recover her purity through his need for it.

Of course, Farid didn't put it quite in that way, but that is how the puzzle came together in his mind, and he resolved to write words of comfort to his teacher. His father also wished for this, and had already begun a letter headed with the *fatiha*, and beginning 'Esteemed Mr Haycraft'. Through the Prison Service they were given an address and a prisoner's number, and Farid spent several evenings at the living room table, writing, tearing up, and writing again. When at last he felt able to sign the letter it was much shorter than he had hoped. But his father approved, and the sheet that they put in the envelope read as follows:

Dear Mr Haycraft,

You are always in my thoughts and in my father's thoughts too, and we dearly hope that this letter reaches you. I want to say how sad I am that you have been sent to prison for helping Sharon Williams. It was because you are a good person that you did it, and my father agrees. Also you were the best teacher I had last year and I am going into the sixth form now without you to teach me, which is such a shame for me. Perhaps one day you will come back to St Catherine's, and maybe we can go on reading together. I have been writing more poetry and taking your advice seriously, you will be pleased to learn. I hope you will come to visit, and my father hopes so too. When you come I would like to show you my poems and you can correct them.

Yours sincerely, Farid.

Mr Kassab put his letter too in the envelope. It said merely 'I hope you are well, and that you will let us know if there is anything we can do for you.' To which Abdul added a verse from Rumi: *Something opens our wings. Something makes boredom and hurt disappear. Someone fills the cup in front of us. We taste only sacredness.*

Farid felt better after writing his letter. The downfall of his teacher, first in his affections, and then in the eyes of the world, had been blows as great as the disappearance of Muhibbah Shahin. But by seizing the chance for kindness he had set himself on an upward path. Maybe in a year or two it would be as though nothing very bad had happened.

But then came another blow. It was from the small print in the local newspaper that they learned that a woman, a refugee from Afghanistan, had been found dead in one of the villages, that her name was Muhibbah Shahin, and that the police suspected suicide.

Farid kept to his room for several days, refusing food and staring gloomily through the window at the drab green panels and dirty lace curtains of Block A. There were rumours that Muhibbah Shahin had been involved in some shady business with her brothers. But nothing was proven. And no such information interested Farid. When, at last, he was able to accept her death, it was because, after days of prayer and fasting, he had been granted a vision.

Muhibbah appeared one night, dressed in a long robe of green silk and gold braid, like the angels in the Persian book of hours that was Abdul's proudest possession, and which had no doubt been burned with the rest of his belongings on the day of their flight. She was looking down on him from a place above his bed. She did not smile, but in her eyes he saw that she was withholding nothing from him. She thanked him graciously for his love, and said 'I died for my purity, Farid. This they could never take from me.' And then she vanished.

A week later there was a notice, placed in the local newspaper by someone called Justin Fellowes, who invited friends and relatives to attend the cremation of Muhibbah Shahin. Farid wondered greatly at this. Why no Islamic burial? Why the week's delay? And why was an Englishman in charge? He prayed for guidance, but the cloud that descended in his feelings would not be dispelled. There was one thing however that he could do for her. Farid began to rehearse, as he did each year for his mother, the Surah Ya Sin.

Chapter 32

You wanted revenge on Muhibbah, but not this kind of revenge. Now it is Justin who lies awake at night, sometimes crying out in distress, sometimes weeping like a child. It has not helped that the police found no fingerprints on the knife except her own. There was no sign of a struggle other than the forced lock on the door, and that could be explained in many ways. Justin is convinced that she killed herself, and that he himself is to blame.

They have caught Hassan Shahin, but not his brother, who is presumed to be in Yemen. They have investigated your claim of kidnap and attempted rape, but Shahin denies everything, arguing that he had no knowledge of your presence on that ship or how you got there, and that he was engaged in his legitimate business of advising asylum seekers from Afghanistan who wish to move from the Russian Federation to the United Kingdom. According to his story his injury resulted from a fight with his brother.

As for the ship itself, it has disappeared, taking Captain Krupnik and all his crew. It might indeed have been a painted ship upon a painted ocean, for all the credence that it will be accorded in a court of law. Only one person's testimony can help to nail Shahin and that is Sharon's. But Sharon has vanished from the children's home where Iona placed her and nobody knows where she is. In the hope of finding her, Superintendent Nicholson has charged Shahin on two counts of rape and attempted rape, and is holding him in custody awaiting trial. His force's reputation has been damaged by the girl's testimony in court, and by subsequent cases that have come to light in which the police turned a blind eye to sexual abuse for fear of the 'racist' label. The Superintendent has therefore put all his resources into the search for Sharon.

Perhaps, in these circumstances, it is not surprising that things between you and Justin are less than perfect. You are stronger now, but with a residue of anger, and sometimes you take it out on him. Soon, when your report is finished, you will move back definitively to Camden Town. They are wanting you at the office, with two new cases that they hope to place on your desk. If ever Hassan Shahin is brought to trial you can make the journey north to serve as a witness, and maybe you can get together with Justin then, when your anger has abated.

Or is it so simple? Are you still the person who made clear decisions and changed course when things went wrong? Often, in the evenings, as you sit side by side with Justin on the sofa that will shortly be your bed, holding hands in silence, listening to music, or just letting the minutes slide by, you feel that you belong to him. And when, for no other reason than to be alone with yourself, you make the journey to London, you gravitate instantly back to him, returning within days. A single leviathan swims in both your seas, a monster that has taken peace and love from both of you. No one else will understand this – unless it is that girl, your alter ego, who is the latest one to disappear.

One evening you confront him.

'Look, Justin, we have both been through hell, we both need to move on. What are we doing about it?'

'It takes time, Laura. Maybe, when they bring that bastard to trial, some kind of closure will come.'

You don't like the word 'closure'. Everything lies open for you, the past as much as the future. Only in music is there closure, and then only in the music you like. And how can there be a real transition for any of you, until your alter ego is found, arising cleansed from the pool of her tears, which are your tears too?

Always she is there in your thoughts. You imagine her conversations with her teacher, their words imbued with a tenderness that you do not know from real life, but which you guess from the music of Schubert. Sometimes, in Justin's presence, you feel hopelessly retro. You don't like pop music, and the more advanced it is the less you like it. You don't like films and – apart from *The Wind in the Willows* – you like only serious literature. You are funny about sex – not screwed up, but waiting for a self-confidence that has been crushed within you and which must grow again.

'I am sorry, Justin,' you reply. 'I am not what you need right now.'

'Nor am I what you need right now, Laura. But right now is unimportant. There is the future. Our future.'

'Maybe,' you say. And 'maybe' is how you proceed from day to day.

When the time for parting comes Justin drives you to the station in silence. There is pain in his face. You too are tense and unhappy. At the station you embrace. You promise to return as soon as you are able. Next time, you say, we will have sorted ourselves out. He kisses your lips and for the first time you feel desire for him. You turn away before it can express itself.

257

Through friends at the criminal bar you easily trace the whereabouts of Stephen Haycraft. To gain the right to visit him is not so easy. You must ask him to put you on his list, and he must apply to the prison governor for a visitor's order. You take the direct approach.

Dear Stephen, you write, *please forgive my use of your Christian name. I can think of you in no other way. I attended your trial, lived through what you felt, and saw that you were technically guilty but in reality innocent. I would like permission to visit you. Can you arrange it? Yours, Laura Markham.*

The reply comes back within a week.

Dear Miss Markham, I will arrange for a Visitor's Order number. Thank you for thinking me to be innocent. I wish I could agree with you. Yours, Stephen Haycraft.

The man who is conducted into the visitor's centre is a wasted remnant of the one whom you saw on the stairs of your block and later, bowed in defeat, in the courtroom. He approaches with stooping gait. His hair has receded further, his eyes have sunk into pools of shadow, and his mouth is pressed tight between dark wrinkles at its edge. He is thin, and his hands emerge from the sleeves of a prison jacket like the hands of a Guy Fawkes dummy, sewn onto the cloth.

You have used your charm on the staff, and the allotted officer stands at a respectful distance, as though you were lovers. It is clear that few of the prisoners are visited: most are being protected from a form of justice in which their own relatives would be happy to join. You shake Stephen's hand: it is limp and cold.

He does not smile but merely nods at you, brushing your eyes with a sad, questioning glance, as though noticing someone else who is flitting beyond the place where you stand. He is reminding you that you belong to a world of illusions that he can no longer share.

'I want to talk about Sharon,' you say.

'That makes one of you.'

'I want to find her.'

'You mean that she is lost?'

'Did they not tell you?'

'Of course I knew she had been taken away. She was my life, Miss Markham, and I did not protect her. How could she not be lost?'

'I mean that she has disappeared from the children's home where they placed her.'

A blank look comes across Stephen's features. He seems like some senile patient striving to recall the name of the person visiting him, who happens to be his wife.

'I cannot see why you have come to visit me, unless it is to torment me.'

'I think I can find her, and I want to know whether you will meet her, when all this is over.'

He is sitting now on one of the chairs provided, his hands in his lap, his head sunk on his chest.

'In this place, Miss Markham, you learn what happens to those accused of paedophilia. They have no future in society. They have no chance to make amends. They are hounded from place to place, forced to live alone, ostracised and shamed. For Sharon to be with such a person would be the end of all her hopes. She had one chance of rescue, and I spoiled it.'

'But you love her, Stephen. You love her properly, and not just as the child she was.'

This causes him to raise his head and look at you intently.

'That is true,' he says, after a pause. 'But it's also why I should leave her alone.'

'Others won't leave her alone, Stephen. Think of that.'

'I think of nothing else,' he says. 'Of all the torments I suffer in this place, that is by far the greatest.'

He drops his head into his hands with a moan of pain. For a moment you are overcome by pity, and reach across to him. The invigilating officer steps forward, however, and you withdraw your hand.

'Listen, Stephen. With remission for good behaviour you will be out of here in a few months. Suppose I have found Sharon by then, provided her with what she needs. Will you at least meet her?'

'Why are you doing this for me, Miss Markham?'

'I am not doing it for you. I am doing it for her; and also for me. One day I will explain.'

'You must forgive me. I am shut away here with monsters. I have to share my cell with a man whose only topic of conversation is the kind of sex that landed him in gaol for fifteen years. I will carry the pollution of this place around with me wherever I go. How can I face that pure soul again?'

'As you are facing me.'

He returns your look, not quite grasping your sincerity, not quite understanding that you know from the inside what it is that Sharon will feel, or that you have found a way of healing yourself through her. After a moment Stephen's face softens.

'When Sharon came to me,' he says, 'it was as an angel, who had fallen into a nasty place but was drying her wings. She was always proud, seeking respect, never cheap. I think you are the same, Laura. By what miracle you picked on me I don't know. But you are the first good thing that has entered my life since they took her away.'

When, ten minutes later, you leave Stephen, his demeanour has changed. He stands upright, looks at you directly, not smiling but nevertheless with a kind of openness that suggests he is striving to recover his dignity. He nods goodbye, still looking into your eyes, and you nod in turn.

You had never intended to make use of the number that Yunus gave you. But your instinct to arm yourself against the future has led you to retain the piece of paper on which he wrote it down. You key in the number with a hunch that you are reluctant to make explicit to yourself. The ringing stops and there is silence.

'Is Yunus there?'

The silence continues.

'Yunus, this is Laura, Catherine to you. There is something we have to talk about.'

'Catherine.'

The whisperer is Yunus.

'I will meet you wherever you are.'

'London,' he replies, and then 'Catherine,' with a stifled sob.

'I know, Yunus, I know. It's one reason we should meet. I will be careful; no one need know. I am in London too.'

'Your office, then, five o'clock. I looked it up when Muhibbah – when she told me everything.'

He chokes and rings off.

You are sitting on a stone seat in the Inner Temple, your favourite resting place in a recess at the bottom of King's Bench Walk, where no one ever comes. It is a pleasant late summer evening, with the shadows sloping across the lawn behind you and the plane trees scattering flecks of yellow sunlight on the Queen Anne facades. You are sitting with your rapist, a young man with a beautiful haunted face. He has told you he is shit-scared and now totally destroyed by his sister's murder – and yes it was murder, he has proof of it.

He cannot look at you for shame, but stumbles to speak in short phrases full of habitual obscenities. He wants you to know how everything changed for him when he came across you in the place where Muhibbah once worked and when, some time later, he read the letter that his sister thrust at him as she fled through the door. Here he breaks down and, without meaning to, you lay a hand on his arm. There is a kind of trust in the expression with which he then looks up at you and you allow your fingers to rest for a moment on his wrist before withdrawing them.

'That was the letter she never fucking give me before.'

'When before?'

'Before I fucking took her away because I couldna do fuck all without her. Back at school in Yemen see I was clever like she was – but it never worked out here. I couldna write English, and I spoke only shit language, *lourat al-mzrab*, she called it. You dunna know what she meant to me. She wasna just clever, like she wrote the most beautiful fucking Arabic ever, she was always climbing up see, learning, speaking nice, being a modern woman, and when she run away I was on her side, only I was scared too, scared I'd be shit without her, because she was everything good, see.'

He broke down again.

'Those Polish fuckers think I canna mess with 'em. But Krupnik is gonna die, see. And Zdenko too. I got proof they done it.'

You listen to this for as long as seems polite. Sure, the best use of your pet rapist's energies would be in killing those who kidnapped you. But this is beside the point. The boy is visibly crumbling before you. He clings to you, as though you are the one hope remaining in his shattered life, just as he, at a certain moment, was the one hope in yours. You too want vengeance for Muhibbah, having once wanted vengeance against her. Your destinies have become mixed in ways that only sympathy can untangle – the delicate lifting of a hungry arm, so as to place it elsewhere.

'So tell me about Muhibbah's letter.'

'You dunna wanna know.'

You can now look into his eyes without fear or contempt. You are equals, and he knows it.

'You made her important to me.'

Yunus's eyes waver under the impact of yours. He breaks down again, and you wait, listening to a robin as he begins his late summer evensong from the rooftop. For three years now you have been visiting this place. Its discreet display of long-standing privilege extends an understated welcome. It tells you that it is good to be ambitious, good to be successful, and that power can be sweet, gentle and amusing too. At least, that was what it used to tell you, before your life was punctured, and your confidence flowed away.

Yunus recovers enough to resume his story. Constantly he appeals to you for sympathy, repeating your borrowed name again and again, as though you had assumed his sister's place, as the only respected woman in his life. Muhibbah's letter said she hoped to marry her boss, and that she would stay in touch with Yunus only if he had nothing to do with Hassan. She was ashamed of him, she wrote, and could not accept his proposal that they live together.

But that is what he wanted. To be side by side with her, to clean up their business, to become respectable, to fight for each other against the world, as they had fought for each other in Yemen, watching those Turkish soaps on the telly and crying out, yes, yes, we will be modern people, just like them! He weeps as he elaborates on his childish dream, how he insisted on it, took her away from the life she had planned, worked on her as he had always worked on her to get what he wanted, and then led her down into the hell from which she had tried to raise him. She was all goodness and courage, he just a worm.

'A fucking worm, Catherine.'

'So how come you left her alone in that place? And how come you didn't go with her to Yemen?'

'Hassan was in hospital wannhe? He was shit-scared of that Polish gang. So was I. And she just sat there in the dark, saying nowt. And then other things happened. It was like this see. When I didna come back with Hassan's bitch they grassed on her, saying she'd been kidnapped. After that I couldn't grab her cause she was kept secure to be a witness in the trial of that teacher bloke. And then she come out with it, dinna she? naming names in the court and Hassan says she's gotta be fixed for good. I got her then, from the place where they keep bad kids. But I couldna do the job. It was you stopped me. I'm not a killer Catherine. That girl, OK Hassan and me, we'd done bad by her. But you made me see things different. And when I got her from that place and she just looked at me, white and quiet like someone made up her mind to die, I freaked out. I couldna touch her.'

'So where is she now?'

'I let her go, see.'

'Let her go where?'

'Fucking Hell, it's not her I wanna talk about. She's toast anyway. So I let her go on the moor at Buckton, and when I get back, the door is swinging wide open and there she is, my sister, lying dead on the carpet. Muhibbah *mayetah*! Her life all gone, gone. Muhibbah!'

All that he says is irrelevant now. That he recognized Zdenko's way of forcing a lock without making a sound, his habit of creeping up on his victims unawares so that there is never the sign of a struggle, his peculiar smell like the smell of a chicken hut that was still lingering so that Yunus knew Zdenko was there in the house; that Yunus ran away then to some Afghan relatives in London, and dithered over how to get to Yemen, dithered until Hassan was arrested and he was on his own, that he was a fucking useless worm without the only person who had ever shone a light in his life except you, Catherine – all this information, which you absorb from his sobbing form and answer with silence, is unimportant beside the knowledge that your other half was abandoned three weeks ago and left to wander on the moors.

It is dark when Yunus leaves you. You give him your phone number, in case he can tell you something more about the girl. You leave him at the bottom of Chancery Lane, and as you climb into the taxi that will take you to Camden town he leans towards you. He is pale, distraught, shaking.

'I dinna say, Catherine, Laura, I dinna say I loves you.'

You look at him, and shake your head.

'Nor did I say I have forgiven you,' you reply. He nods sadly.

'But I have,' you say to yourself. And he watches motionless as you drive away.

Chapter 33

Justin was sitting with Iona when Laura's phone call came. Somehow, after Laura's departure, the habit of cooking supper had stuck with him. He often cooked for Iona, who had the knack of distracting him from his worries with worries of her own. And her worries were great. Following the Haycraft affair an official enquiry had been set up into the abuse of girls in Council care, and the disappearance of Sharon Williams from the Council home had turned a spotlight on Iona's department. Suspended on full pay for the duration of the enquiry, her first concern had been that Sharon should be found, and found in a condition to testify against the charge of negligence. Now, after nearly three weeks with no news, Iona was convinced that Sharon was dead.

It was ten o'clock. They had opened a second bottle of Rioja. They were not gloomy, but the conversation, which veered always around to the Shahin family, pressed on their several wounds. The coroner's open verdict on the death of Muhibbah, the disappearance of the younger brother, the arrest of the older brother as he attempted to flee to Amsterdam, the fact that the father, two wives and cousin had decamped as suddenly as they came, leaving no trace other than verses of the Koran painted in Kufic script all over the doors of their flat – these facts went around in their minds, reminding them that they had been allotted minor parts in a complex drama, and that in so far as there was a role for either of them it was to be horribly damaged by events that they could neither influence nor predict.

It was exactly at such moments that Justin most regretted Laura's departure, and her phone call caused him to sing out her name. She had important news, she said, and was coming on the first train next day so that they could act on it. Her voice was not happy but radiated what she most represented in Justin's mind, which was the determination to put things right. Maybe the process of healing had advanced, and he would once again meet the beautiful self-confident woman who was to put the image of Muhibbah in the shade.

As he drove her from the station, however, Justin listened with astonishment to Laura's story. He concluded that she was imaginative, clever, intrepid, but after all slightly crazy. He took her to Iona's office, where the narrative, neatly summarised under Iona's poster, with the ginger beard of James Hetfield melting into Laura's hair, sounded like a quiz test for social workers – what would you do if? That, in any case, was how Iona took it. You would shop Yunus to the police, give up on Sharon and find Stephen a safe job as caretaker in an old people's home: such was her answer.

'I mean,' she said, 'you can't honestly say that we go out and look for that kid on the moors, on the off chance that Yunus Shahin didn't kill her? Since when has he disobeyed his brother's orders? Anyway, the police have combed the moors from North to South and East to West, including all the spots where bodies tend to accumulate. They are as keen to find that kid as I am. I reckon it's too late to bother now.'

267

Worry had not been kind to Iona's face, and the worse her face became the more she berated it with make-up, expensive make-up that reinforced the contrast between what she was and what she could not be. Justin remembered the other Iona, whose lively, confident features had a speaking charm of their own. But that Iona had retreated behind a mask, and the mask spoke words of defeat. Iona was telling them that they were all out of their depth, and all refusing, each for a personal reason, to move on. Laura especially, who had morphed into Sharon Williams.

One good thing about Sharon, Iona noted, was that she took seriously the collective view that she was a mistake and should never have existed. But Laura was intent on doing all the existing for her, making Sharon stay alive long past her sell-by date, which was the point when, as Iona had put it, she had seen the opportunity to lay down her life for her friend.

'But you are not seeing it with her eyes, Iona,' Laura said, and her face lit up with passion. 'Just imagine: she is lifted from that home by one of her abusers, gagged, taken on to the moors, sure in her heart that this is the end. She has one thought, which is that she will never again set eyes on the person she loves. Even if this love is only calf-love, a pupil's crush, it is still the only love she has known. And then as she is taken from the car to stare speechless at the man who is about to murder her, he turns away and drives off. What then does she do? Just think. She has only known one home and that is her teacher's home. Let's suppose he gave her the key by way of a pledge. It would be the only thing of his that she has, so she would keep it close about her, always pressed against her body. So of course, she goes to his flat.'

'Don't be daft, Laura. The police would have searched the place just as soon as she disappeared.'

'Sure. But not three days later, which is the time it would take to get there on foot from Buckton.'

'So what do we do?' Justin asked. 'Are we going to take your story to the police?'

'And reveal that I have had a secret meeting with someone they are trying to arrest?'

'So what do we do?' Iona echoed. 'Go ringing at the intercom and shout "we know you are there"?'

'Justin took a six month lease on the flat beneath Stephen's, of which a few weeks remain. I still have the key to the building. I shall knock on the door of Stephen's flat. It's worth a try.'

As they pulled in to the car park behind the block, and looked up at the smashed windows of the teacher's flat, Justin reflected on the consequences of his decision to rent accommodation for Laura rather than place her in a local hotel. He made a mental list of them: Laura's kidnap and the ordeal that had destroyed her happiness; the rediscovery of Muhibbah and the fatal rebirth of his feelings for her; the revenge on Sharon; the arrest and ruin of her teacher; Muhibbah's death. It was as though *he* were the true kidnapper, the one who had set this whole stream of disasters in motion. And for what? In order to seduce a girl who would have come to him in any case, and come as the healthy, confident, therapeutic person he had picked from the website of her firm, and not as this half-crazy obsessive who had somehow mingled her identity with that of an abused and abandoned child.

And he too was half crazy; his mourning for Muhibbah was formless, random, like the lowing of a herd of cattle. Anger, remorse, grief, resentment all fought in him and nothing resolved. As he climbed the stairs with Laura he began to be alarmed by himself: he was the sheepish conscript of a fruitless obsession, an

269

obsession that he did not even share. What was this ruined child doing in his life, and why was it she, and not he, who had brought Laura back to Whinmoore?

They were outside the teacher's flat. Someone had managed to get into the block and spray the door with graffiti: 'Perv's Paradise' was the kindest of them; others made Justin feel sick. It looked as though someone had tried to force the door. The Yale lock was bulging from its socket, and there was a crack in the wood beside one of the hinges. He stepped forward to administer a push. Laura put out a hand to restrain him and held a finger to her lips.

She knocked and listened. There was no sound save the gentle gurgling of a dove that was trapped on the stairwell beneath the roof. Laura knocked again.

'Are you there, Sharon?'

There was a faint scraping within.

'I've come from Stephen,' Laura said. 'He was hoping you'd be here.'

Silence.

'I'm Laura, by the way, a friend of his.'

The scraping resumed: a mouse maybe. Justin shrugged his shoulders at Laura, who shook her head.

'Sharon, please let me in. It's about Stephen, something you can do to help him.'

There was a faint gasp, and then again silence.

'Let me in, Sharon. There will be more trouble for Stephen otherwise. Believe me, I want to help.'

Another silence. And then a voice spoke faintly, like the voice of someone dying.

'I canna.'

'You mean you won't open the door?'

'I canna,' came the reply, yet more faintly. Justin understood. She did not have the strength. He pushed against the door and it moved a fraction, showing that the lock had been forced. But it was held fast by a piece of furniture wedged under the handle. It was ten minutes before the three of them, pushing together, were able to open a gap wide enough for Laura to squeeze through and pull the teacher's desk from the door.

The girl was lying on the sofa, emaciated, pale, bloodless. There was a clinging acetone smell in the room, the smell of starvation. She turned her eyes to them, looked startled at Iona and then accusingly at Laura.

'I inna going back there,' she whispered.

Laura went across to her, propped her against the sofa, and took one pale wasted hand between both of hers.

'Of course you're not going back there. Stephen sent me to look after you. These are my friends.'

Justin beckoned to Iona to come away. She was in a state of shock, and for a while just walked beside him silently in the car park. Justin had his mobile phone in his hand and was ringing for the ambulance when Iona began to speak.

'Laura's right,' she said. 'This thing we've been living through. It's not about people trafficking, immigration, community relations; it's not about racism, multiculturalism, and all the things I am supposed to put at the top of my agenda as a social worker; it's not even about forced marriage, honour killing or the enslavement of women. It is about that girl and how to give her back her life.'

Justin had never before seen tears in Iona's eyes. Pity was not her line: she didn't think anyone more worthy of pity than herself, had forbidden self-pity, and *ergo* pitied no one. But Sharon had touched something in her, and Justin guessed what it was.

There was, in that broken fugitive on her teacher's sofa, the vestige of a hard-won dignity. Time and again she had been dumped in shit, kicked into a corner, run up against a wall, and yet her default position was pride, like a baited lion always turning to its tormentors.

And then, as they watched the girl lifted on to a stretcher and taken to the ambulance, Laura still holding one of her hands in both of hers, something else became clear to Justin. It was through Sharon that Laura was being healed. This girl, who had suffered the extreme of degradation, had also safeguarded what was most precious to her. She was proof that you could be raped, humiliated, treated as a thing, and still able to give yourself freely. If Sharon could do it, so could Laura. And thinking that maybe this was what Laura intended, he felt something stir in himself.

Chapter 34

Looking back on that summer nothing embarrasses you so much as your failure to prevent Justin from being fired. True, Muhibbah was his responsibility, and he had turned a blind eye to what she was doing. True, he had lost interest in the project for carbon-neutral houses, allowing the materials that Muhibbah had purchased and stored to rot away unused. Nevertheless your report was carefully phrased to protect him, and there were signs that he could take a renewed interest in working for the firm. For a man like Justin to lose his job, after devoting ten years to becoming the best at it, is not easy. For a while you could not console him; not that he reproached you, of course, though he was aware – how could he not be? – that it was you, your expertise and your honesty that had caused his downfall.

But there was a good side to it too. Going to that office each day, staring at the desk that Muhibbah had vacated, tinkering with the plans that she had drawn, and remembering the endless enquiries with which her eager young mind had filled his days, he was tempted to dwell on his loss. Things were particularly bad at the time of her cremation. None of her family had come forward to take charge of the obsequies: all had disappeared apart from the brother who was being held on remand and who would merely weep when her name was mentioned.

The mosque would have nothing to do with her. There had been angry teenage displays of contempt towards the imam and the faith. And there had been the notorious tantrum over the marriage, to which the imam had devoted much time and energy, only to discover that the girl had disappeared, leaving nothing behind her save her curses. The elders did not consider it appropriate to stage a funeral for such a person, who had in any case killed herself as such a person should, and therefore lost her right to a religious burial.

When, after the inconclusive investigation, the police released her body from the morgue it fell to Justin to dispose of it, and there was no quick way save cremation. This was not the way of her people. But 'I do things *my* way', she had said to him. She had described herself as an atheist, a free thinker and a modern woman, and Justin believed that those lonely and fruitless ambitions should be honoured in death, even if she had never achieved them in life. He therefore chose cremation, and stood silent and grieving as the coffin was placed on the chute. You and Iona were the only other mourners apart from a young Arab boy who appeared unannounced, recited some verses of the Koran as the coffin slid through the curtains, and then fled in tears.

After that Justin was subdued for a while. Once or twice he played a gig at the Crustafarian. But it was only the shock of his dismissal that awoke him to what he was becoming – a limp puppet who had bequeathed his manhood to a bass guitar and his heart to a fiction. But you had stuck it out, making the journey to Yorkshire on every free weekend. When he decided it was time to move on you were there, and he moved on to you. Crazy, of course, to have fallen in love with a dreamer, an idealist and a

Heavy Metal fan. But you had shared something big, and that thing gradually sank to the depths in both of you, so that a kind of troubled calm came over the surface of your lives, and they began to flow together. It helped of course that he was invited to apply for the lectureship in environmental planning at the North London University. And it helped – you could not deny it – that he had you, the reborn, renewed and reprogrammed you, who were going forward because there was nowhere else to go.

And you, in your turn, had Sharon. It took only a few visits to the hospital to win her trust. Once it was clear she would not be returning to the Council home, she allowed her body to mend. Within a week she was eating solid food, and you were bringing her books, discussing what had happened and making plans for the future. She worried at first about living with Iona. But you assured her that it would be temporary. You were working with Iona on a plan to transfer her to a sixth form college in London, where she would live with you in Camden Town.

Of course, negotiations with the Council were complicated. After all, this 'girl who cannot be named for legal reasons' was at the centre of the scandal, the arch victim who had saved herself from one kind of abuse only to be caught up in another, and as such known to everyone through Facebook, Twitter, Internet searches and websites set up by her admirers and by the enemies of the teacher who had abducted her. She had revealed a can of worms, and the worms were visibly squirming.

All of them, that is, apart from Iona, who had kept calm throughout the enquiry and was reinstated at the end of it. Iona was happy for Sharon to convalesce in her attic flat, where they both could hide from the world.

It helped Iona's standing to be known as the girl's protector, who was taking every step to ensure that Sharon should not be abused again. But she left it to you to raise the topic of Stephen, and this was, during that summer, the most beautiful part of your life. You encountered the precocious, proud and independent girl whom Stephen loved. You followed her into the place you both knew, the place of withholding, where what you have forbidden to happen is happening nonetheless, and you are no longer a woman but a tattered toy. You shared your ordeals together, and by the end of the summer you were no longer afraid either of the past or of the future. She came to live with you in September, and by that time you were both ready to testify in the forthcoming trial of Hassan Shahin.

At first the girl hardly referred to Stephen, except as some remote and untouchable person, whose life she had through her clumsiness destroyed. But gradually he entered her conversation more frequently and more freely. You explained that she could meet him again, in other circumstances, without the weight of guilt. You even promised to arrange it, suggesting that she might write to him, a letter that could be placed in his hand when he emerges from prison into the barrage of adverse publicity that is sure to greet him.

She responded enigmatically, saying that those letters, they belonged to another time. And she gave that peculiar look of hers – half wistful, half astonished – with which she reminds you that she is still a child. You wrote to him yourself, informing him that Sharon will be living with you. And you suggested a day in the New Year, when he might come to meet you on the stone seat in the recess at the bottom of King's Bench Walk, at 4 o'clock in the afternoon.

Chapter 35

Stephen enters Middle Temple lane with short embarrassed shuffles. He is wearing a ravelled overcoat of brown wool, pulled close around the collar. It is a raw January day, and he has eaten nothing since breakfast at the St Martin's Trust Hostel. He has been out for three weeks now. He has not yet visited his mother, whose frantic communications to him in prison he has only once or twice been able to answer, nor has he contacted old friends. He carries Farid Kassab's letter always in his inside pocket against his heart. But still he has not answered it. The Trust provides temporary accommodation for ex-convicts, and specializes in helping those who have, for whatever reason, attracted the hostility of the public. Their hostel seemed to be the only place to go while he made – or postponed – his future plans.

He has a little money. He has a scheme to write a critical study of Nabokov's *Lolita*, a study that will be, in some way that he has yet to make precise, a kind of revenge. And he has another scheme to teach in an English-language school in Turkey. His decision to respond to Laura Markham's request for a meeting was made two months before, when he imagined he would have the strength to confront Sharon Williams and beg forgiveness for the wrong he had inflicted on her. Now he doubts everything. He casts a sideways glance as he enters the lane, expecting to be questioned by a porter and turned away. But no one notices him, and the figures in smart city clothes or legal dress stride past on confident missions that could not possibly take note of a person like him.

He wonders why Laura asked to meet him in this place, symbol of the English law, and of the ease and comfort that comes to those who practise it. The collegiate buildings remind him of Oxford and of all that he has lost since his student days, when he was filled with the love of literature, and hoped for his own place in it. Around him he sees the symbols and pageantry of the law by which he was condemned. The round church of the Templars flags the English law's ancient foundations, and the neo-Georgian buildings, erected after German bombs had smashed the precinct, are symbols of its will to endure. Huddled under grey clouds on a bleak January day, walking across spaces that are ostentatiously private and as though expressly designed to exclude him, Stephen feels again the burden of his social ostracism. The trees are leafless skeletons and the gardens have a cheerless withdrawn appearance, as though they too are avoiding human company. Everything reminds him of the great mistake he once made, which ruined not his own life only, but the life of the one he loved.

And does he still love her? Have his feelings for Sharon survived the humiliations to which he has been subjected on their account, and the daily confrontation with their perceived inappropriateness? Can he honestly say that his last words to her – 'my darling' – convey the enduring stuff of his emotion, and that they were not called from him by the stress of the moment and the desire that entered his heart then and has remained there ever since, to be utterly and eternally unnoticed and alone?

He focuses those questions on the elegant facades of King's Bench Walk; he raises enquiring eyes to the windows behind which the rows of leather-bound law reports keep steady vigil over bowed heads and twined fingers; he lowers his eyes again when a man in barristers' tabs and gown appears in one of the windows and looks down at him curiously. And his questions remain unanswered, slowly settling within him to join the ever-growing pool of self-doubt that is the centre of his being.

There is only one stone seat in the recess at the bottom of the walk and a young woman is already sitting there. She is elegantly dressed in a full-length woollen coat of powder blue, and with a coral coloured scarf around her neck. Her blond hair is pulled back in a ponytail, and her face, turned down to the book that she holds in her lap, is invisible.

He is struck again by the remarkable character of this woman, who appeared out of nowhere to bring him a message of hope, whose poised and self-confident manner led him to trust her as he had trusted no one since Sharon was taken away from him, and whose elegance and beauty ought to have set her far above the dismal world into which he had fallen, but into which she nevertheless stooped to offer rescue. Perhaps it was another weakness in him, that he saw women in this way, as angels of mercy, and so overlooked their true and self-centred motives. But what selfish motive could there be to offer rescue to someone who had fallen as low as he had?

He approaches her slowly, shaking off the convict's slouch and walking with even and upright posture. With every step his self-doubt increases. Laura belongs to the confident world all around. She is at home with the law, as she is at home with every profession and every success. And if she is sitting here now, picturesquely reading a book in the last light of a January afternoon, it is only to show that professional competence and poetic imagination are wrapped together in her life like a double helix, inseparable strands of her unique and original DNA. And then, of a sudden, she closes the book and looks up in his direction.

'Sharon!' he says softly.

'Stephen!'

She smiles and gets to her feet.

'I was expecting to meet Laura Markham.'

'She sent me instead, dinna she?'

Still the same Yorkshire accent; but what a different person this is, who takes both his hands and kisses both his cheeks. How smart and tidy she looks, and how direct and confident is her gaze.

'I was going to write you a letter,' she says, 'like I used to. But then I thought that's silly, when I could see you.'

'Sharon!'

She sits him down beside her, no longer the schoolgirl waiting his permission.

'Laura says you're going to start apologizing for all I've been through and that I'm to stop you because what you did for me was wonderful and you suffered for it horribly because the world is cruel and you're not in no way never to blame.'

She looks at him from the corner of her eye, ascertaining the effect of her words. He says nothing.

'Been a long time since they took me away from you, Stephen, but I havena changed – towards you, I mean. Well, that inna true totally. I dinna have no crush on you no more. I loves you though.'

Is this a step up or a step down from his point of view? And what *is* his point of view? Teacher? Lover? Penitent? She has taken his hand and is cheerfully talking about her new life with Laura. She is studying A-level English, French, History and Maths in a private sixth-form college, and hopes to go to Oxford in the autumn. Stephen listens with mixed emotions: the mind that he had treasured is beginning to flower, but the light that shines on it and that causes its sweet petals to unfurl is no longer his. His months in prison have cut him off from the most beautiful thing he has known. He nods, says little or nothing, and allows her to control the conversation. It is not long before she raises the difficult topic.

'It wasna you behaved wrong, Stephen. I wouldna talk about the thing. I was that scared after what they done to me. I had shut off part of myself, and I couldna face you with it. Laura helped me. She has issues too: you wouldna believe, but it happened to her.'

She repeats what she knows of Laura's ordeal at the hands of the Shahin brothers. He listens in astonishment as she tells him of the way in which Laura faced down those who tried to violate her, and how she has since faced down the effects of their attempt.

'She showed me how to be honest about it. Said I should be honest with you which I couldna be before, because I was so scared and ashamed and because I was only half real. I come back, see, to the home we had, when one of them was going to kill me but let me go. I come back, and the place was broke into and all smashed up. I tidied up as best I could and shut myself in. There was a bit of food around though nothing like we had in the time we were together. And I thought I would wait there till you came or till I died. It was like I was nothing. Like they'd just wiped out everything except the bit I'd kept for you and which was now lost, because I was supposed not to be in touch with you never again. Then Laura found me and everything changed see. She said that what'd happened had happened to *me*, and I was to be truthful about it, and face up to it.'

She turns to him, and her eyes shine with an unprecedented candour. He knows he must accept what she says as the sign of renewal. She owes him nothing, neither loyalty nor love. And if she can remake herself only by ceasing to desire him, that too he must accept. She mentions her Facebook page, which Laura set up for her, and laughs at the silliness of it. But she has been friended by people who have learned of her ordeal, and who offer their support. She is trying to live honestly with her past and hopes that Stephen can accept it for they will be together again one day in one way or another, she is certain of it. She reminds him that she is to be eighteen years old at her next birthday, and if she goes to Oxford she hopes he will visit her there and show her his old college and his favourite haunts.

And then she moves the conversation on again. She relates Yunus's escape, the death of Muhibbah, the disappearance of the Shahin family and of the Polish gang who were in partnership with them. And she comes at last to the trial of Hassan, put down for the first week of February. This time she will say the whole truth in the witness box, and so will Laura, who is so proud of her that Sharon can now do what she must do, what she should have done when it happened over a year ago, and seek justice, not revenge. But she will need Stephen's support, begs him to come to stay up North for the length of the trial. He can stay in the cottage that Laura and Justin now rent, and which they are hoping to buy in the spring when they are getting married.

'Will you come, Stephen? Say you will!'

Roger Scruton is a writer and philosopher, author of over forty books including several works of fiction. He has taught in London and Boston universities, and been visiting professor elsewhere in Britain and America, but now lives as a freelance writer in Malmesbury, Wiltshire. His recent books include *Notes from Underground* (a novel) and *The Soul of the World*. Roger Scruton is a Fellow of the British Academy and a Fellow of the Royal Society of Literature.